semiDETACHED

Also by Cynthia Holz

Home Again
Onlyville
The Other Side

semiDETACHED

Cynthia Holz

PATRICK CREAN EDITIONS

An Imprint of

KEY PORTER BOOKS

Canadian Cataloguing in Publication Data

Holz, Cynthia, 1950-
    Semi-detached

ISBN 1-894433-00-9

Title.

PS8565.0649S45 1999   C813'.54   C99-931313-4
PR9199.3H64S45 1999

The publisher gratefully acknowledges the support of the Canada Council for the Arts and the Ontario Arts Council for its publishing program.

Canadä

We acknowledge the financial support of the Government of Canada through the Book Publishing Industry Development Program (BPIDP) for our publishing activities.

Key Porter Books Limited
70 The Esplanade
Toronto, Ontario
Canada M5E 1R2

www.keyporter.com

Electronic formatting: Heidi Palfrey
Design: Patricia Cavazzini

Printed and bound in Canada

99 00 01 02 03 6 5 4 3 2 1

ACKNOWLEDGEMENTS

For their wisdom and good advice, many thanks to Sheila Ayearst, Eliza Clark and Jane Finlayson. Thanks as well to Zsuzsa Monostory, who bravely let me loose in her pottery studio. And here's to my keen and diligent editor, Patrick Crean, who truly loves the written word.

I am grateful for the assistance of the Ontario Arts Council and the Toronto Arts Council.

FOR BILL WITH LOVE

1

Dividing the House

The way they divided the house was this: Barbara got the ground floor and semi-finished basement and Elliot got the upper stories. It's true that his view of the street and yard was superior and that his apartment was sunnier, but Barbara got the original kitchen and, of course, the basement, a large, uncluttered space for her wheel and kiln. A low-ceilinged room barely five foot ten in some places, the basement never would've suited Elliot anyway, who was still nearly six feet despite having lost an inch or so over the past years, and who never went down there anyhow except to check the furnace and the hot-water heater or to get tools.

Elliot was handy with a hammer and nails. He put up a door at the end of the hall for Barbara's apartment and one at the top of the stairs for his (doors with locks, at her request). After that they moved sheets and towels from one floor to the next, as well as personal items. Then they divided kitchenware. Elliot had never shown the least interest in cooking before, but now that he was on his own and had to prepare meals for himself he thought he'd take a course in the basics, then go on to something advanced, and wanted his kitchen well equipped. So he got measuring spoons and she got the timer; he got the bread knife and she got the cleaver. To Barbara went the salad spinner, food mill and spatulas; saucepans, casseroles, baking tins and mixer. Elliot chose the can opener, wooden spoons, fish poacher, cast-iron skillets and a bean pot. Dishes, cups and cutlery were split in half: each took service for four. Nevertheless, in the end they both felt short-changed and hurried out to buy replacements for what they'd lost.

Mostly it was perfectly clear who should get what. Because she did the gardening, Barbara kept the gardening tools. Elliot took the household tools, which she had no interest in, and both felt satisfied. Books, tapes and pictures were distributed according to taste, and their preferences were different enough to rule out any problems. Barbara liked novels, whereas Elliot read nonfiction—history and politics and books on investing. Barbara listened to folk music, while he enjoyed classical. In art she was partial to drawings and watercolors; he went in for bold acrylics, abstract and oversized. They agreed that the TV and VCR would go to her, the tape deck, CD player and speakers to him. This, too, more or less paralleled their habits, since Barbara would rather watch a movie than hear music to unwind, and Elliot's pattern was the reverse. Plants remained in whatever rooms they happened to be growing in, and even the furniture was easily divisible, Elliot choosing modern pieces and Barbara taking antiques. The goldfish went to her (they were simple pets to care for) and he adopted Hammer, their ginger-colored tabby with a big head and long body, and so too a medley of chores he'd never had to do before: buying cat food, clipping claws, checking for fleas, changing litter and brushing ginger-colored hairs off the sofa and his clothes. But of course he'd learn to care for Hammer, just as he would learn to cook, sew buttons and pay bills.

And wasn't that the point of dividing their lives in the first place—to learn to do new things and make independent decisions; to set personal schedules, follow their own whims and become at last, in middle age, mature individuals? Barbara thought so, at any rate. It was she who introduced the idea of amicable separation as far back as last spring, a year after her husband retired, financially set and fed up with dentistry. No, not divorce, she'd said, but a slightly different living arrangement for personal growth. Elliot never liked her phrasing; he thought he was grown enough and didn't need to experiment with an alternative lifestyle. There was nothing wrong with the life they were living as far as he could determine. Now that Barb was also retired, they'd have to adjust to being together day in, day out, but that was just a small knot that would practically unravel itself. All they had to do was wait. After thirty-two years of married life, a successful career, two kids, a starter home and now this one, mortgage-free, he was looking forward to spending his retirement comfortably with his wife. After all this time he was still happy. Wasn't she?

Well, she was and she wasn't. Little things rankled: an accumulation of minor grievances over the years. The way he hated parties, for one—hated going to other people's and hated when they threw one themselves. (He'd say, "Who enjoys sitting around making small talk with people you hardly know?") She was bothered as well because he didn't want to travel. He refused to leave Canada—especially to go to the States, an imperialist country with an adverse exchange rate—and had to have a damn good reason to leave Ontario. In fact, since he liked Toronto, why leave the city? Why leave their neighborhood, where shopkeepers knew their names and they could walk to the bank or the library in minutes flat? But Barbara liked traveling, she liked the change of scenery and not having to cook meals. And yet, besides occasional vacations in the country and an ill-fated trip to Manhattan after his retirement, they never went anywhere special. Sometimes she visited friends in Ottawa and Montreal, but that wasn't the same thing: they never went anywhere special *together*. They could never discuss medieval churches, mountain peaks or frescoes. They would never abandon the ordinary for the sublime.

He didn't like restaurants, either. Waiters made him uncomfortable and the portions were never big enough. He wouldn't eat food he could barely identify and hated being served on enormous, Frisbee-like plates decorated with darkly colored swirls of puréed whatnot and sprinkled with minced parsley. More than anything else in the world, Elliot hated parsley. Then there was the exorbitant cost. Why pay an outrageous amount for small bits of strange food when Barb could fix as nice a meal to be eaten in their own home? He didn't understand that his wife might appreciate someone cooking dinner for her. She might enjoy a glass of wine or the chance to put on a good dress and have an interesting chat with her spouse. Although, whenever they ate out, Elliot mostly talked about the service, price and portions.

My God, she could go on and on! The sulking and bickering, the halfhearted settlements: telling herself to give in, it wasn't so important; telling herself she was too mature to fight about ridiculous things—but losing bits of herself along the way, it seemed to Barbara, as if she'd been leaving trails of vital cells behind her.

"Well," she had answered when he asked if she was happy, "I am and I'm not."

They were sitting in the ground-floor kitchen having dinner, at a time when they shared everything and still had service for eight. Barbara had stuffed and roasted a chicken, which Elliot had carved and served and already covered with gravy when the meal suddenly stalled and she put her elbows on the table. "It's all the little things . . . ," she said. "I think I need more space. Do you understand what I'm saying?"

His blood congealed to hear that. More space? What did she mean? They had the whole house to themselves! He didn't know what was troubling her, but Elliot was certain it involved him. All of her indefinite feelings of dissatisfaction had something to do with him. As if in working most of his life to support a wife and family he had overlooked something more essential to her happiness than food, clothing, a house and car or summers in the country; and now she was going to tell him what that something was.

What it was, as it turned out, was the need to get away from him before they got on each other's nerves in a big way. Picking at her chicken she'd said, "I'm just too aware of you lying around with nothing to do, waiting for instructions or something: set the table, mop the floor. And all the stupid things you do that really annoy me . . . like wearing that baggy sweatshirt and those track pants with holes in the knees."

"You don't have to worry about me," he protested. "I've got hundreds of books to read. And if you want me to dress up or do more around the house, just say so."

"You'll get tired of reading. And there's not enough to do around here to keep us both busy. Besides, you'd only get in the way. You don't even know how to make a bed or where things go in the kitchen."

"Would you like me to take a class or something? Learn to play an instrument? Do volunteer work? Is that what this is all about?"

"This is about you and me—doing what we want to do without the other's say-so. I don't think that's possible with all this togetherness."

He figured she was in one of her moods. Sometimes she got restless and wanted to turn her life around, but never knew how to proceed. He decided to let her talk herself out and fixed his eyes on the ceiling light burning like a lantern on a foggy night.

"I feel squeezed," she went on, "and I'm not saying it's your fault. It's just that we're in the habit of playing certain roles and there's no need for that anymore. The kids are grown, we're retired. . . . We don't have to go on and on in the same way for the rest of our lives."

He blinked at the light. "What way is that?"

"You know what way—the way we *are*. I don't know where you stop and I begin."

Elliot lowered his eyes then. He'd heard enough about feminism from his daughter Susan to get the gist of what she was saying. But Barb and Susan weren't alike: Barb was more sensible and loved her creature comforts. She would never embark on a dubious journey of self-discovery at her age if it meant having to teach again or living in a two-room flat. Indeed, she didn't want to move out, she wanted to move downstairs.

It wasn't a conversation they had once or twice but many times, and after several months of thought he began to see advantages in living alone on two floors. Four whole rooms to himself (one of which was large enough to hold a small aircraft) to decorate as he saw fit, to roam around in as he pleased with his hair uncombed, hands unwashed, shirt stained and pants torn. He could smoke his pipe without seeing her wrinkle her nose and stomp off; he could read books, take naps, or, if he felt like it, lie on the couch for hours on end—for days, if he cared to—playing Bach and Beethoven again and again.

And wouldn't have to speak to anyone if he didn't want to. Wouldn't have to listen, either. Wouldn't have to see a soul—especially Dora, Barb's mom, sharp-tongued and interfering, who phoned and visited often. He could eat pizza every night and leave the boxes piled up behind his apartment door. He could make some new friends, buy a microwave and ask them to dinner, assuring them it was perfectly fine to walk in with their shoes on. He was thinking of male friends, of course, men like his pal Ivan who drank beer straight from the bottle and didn't meet with Barb's approval. The question of whether or not he'd invite women home too hadn't even occurred to him yet.

Privacy was on his mind; that's what he was thinking about. The intoxication of solitude. Married since he was nineteen, he was going to get the chance to be single at last. On his own. He'd lived with his parents, then with Barb (eighteen and pregnant); then he lived with Barb and the kids and finally just his wife again, but never—not in his whole life—completely alone. And so the idea grew on him.

"It might be a good thing," he said, "this business of living alone. Moving to your own rhythms, filling rooms with your own sound." He imagined the stereo turned up, playing full blast while he sang along to *Easy Favorites* first thing in the morning—something he'd never dare with his wife in the house.

"Exactly!" said Barbara, who was actually thinking of silence: waking up and making coffee, sitting alone in the hushed kitchen; no clatter of frying pans, cutlery and dishes or the creak and thump of the fridge door; no one reading aloud to her from the *Globe and Mail*. Eventually, from the backyard, the soft trill of a small bird.

But somehow, in all their talks, certain subjects were never broached. Instead, embarrassing matters seemed to come up in public, among friends. This was during the time when they were still invited to dinner parties and various celebrations, after his retirement and then after Barbara's, but before they divided the house. B.D. they called those months: Before Division.

They told their friends about their plans to live together and apart, insisting it would be a happy experiment for both of them. Most people wished them well, although they added caveats like "This is a big risk you're taking" and "Things could go either way." But some were openly doubtful. Ida Murray-Meyers (more an acquaintance than a friend) asked them over cocktails at a middle-sized party, in the company of her husband Jake and Sam and Mindy Kapinsky, "Do you really think this is going to work? Have you thought about all the problems? Sex, for instance. What about sex? Will you still sleep together or are you looking for new partners?"

Jake spun the ice cubes in his glass, which made a grating sound, and the Kapinskys simply walked off. But Ida wouldn't let up. "Surely you've considered it. Or maybe you don't do that sort of thing anymore, is that it?"

Elliot gazed down at his shoes, which he'd shined for the occasion, and his startled reflection stared back. He was going to say that actually they hadn't really discussed it yet, that sex was one of the subjects they still had to talk about, when Barb spoke up. "Of course we'll keep having sex. Maybe we'll meet for dinner first, or make more deliberate plans, and if we're both agreeable, we'll go to Elliot's place or mine."

"Like when we were teenagers," Ida said, "and snuck our lovers up to our rooms when our parents were out for the evening?"

"No, not like that at all." Barb's tone was righteous, but still Elliot wouldn't look up. What they were doing did sound awfully silly, put like that.

"There are several couples here tonight"—Barbara

scanned the vast, crowded living room of the Murray-Meyers—"who sleep alone in separate rooms for comfort and convenience—not because they don't get along. I know who they are and so do you. Have you ever asked *them* if they still have a sex life? Elliot and I are simply taking things a step further: separate kitchens and living rooms too."

Jake was a little drunk. "When I was in college," he said, "we snuck girls back to our dorm. You shoulda seen the pretty birds flying in and out of our room. Nonstop daily flights, except for Christmas and March break—but then we flew to Lauderdale and humped our way across the beach."

Elliot finally looked up. "That's not what this is all about," he said in a voice he thought appropriately forceful.

Now it was Barbara's turn to study her shoes. She'd worn a dress, sheer stockings and pointy-toed high heels, which she only did tonight to appear more conventional, and could feel blisters rising on her baby toes. Nevertheless, she felt as if her feet were bare. As if she were standing barefoot and shivering, her toes curled, on Jake and Ida's kilim rug. Why hadn't she and Elliot brought this up earlier? How could they be so unprepared? They talked more than ever now about all sorts of things. But sex? Not about sex.

"If it isn't sex," Ida said, "it must be you're sick of each other. You want to live separately but also economically, so what can you do but carve up the house?" She elbowed Jake in the side and the ice cubes in his glass jumped. "I know what it's like when a man retires. How long has it been?" She winked at Elliot. "One year? Nearly two?" She looked down her nose at Barbara. "He's always underfoot, right? You can't even sweep the floor without having to sweep your husband out of the way first."

Barbara wiggled her toes in her shoes and felt hot bullets of pain. Not sick of each other yet; more . . . those little things. Smoking was another one. He'd started smoking his pipe again and she hated the smell of tobacco in her hair, on her clothes, on Elliot's breath—not to mention what his nasty habit was doing to their health. And this: in the winter, when she turned up the thermostat, Elliot would turn it down because he was "roasting." In the hot, humid summer months he'd turn off the air-conditioning because he preferred "real air" and throw open the windows wide.

But noise bothered her most of all, an aura of noise that circled him and radiated to fill the house. There was no getting away from his tuneless humming and yodeled yawns, the squeal of the sofa as he shifted from hip to hip. Or his fondness for the Hoover, which he ran several times a week with all its silly attachments (a nozzle for upholstery and one for hard-to-reach spots), though the growl of the motor stiffened her hair and set her teeth chattering. Often he would follow close behind her from room to room, reading aloud from magazines (What was it last time—totem poles of the Haida?), whether she wanted to hear him or not. But no, she wasn't *sick* of him. That was going too far.

She signaled Elliot with a look and they crossed the room to where hors d'oeuvres were spread on a long mahogany table. Barbara was eating sushi and Elliot nibbling melon balls when Mindy Kapinsky cornered him at one end of the table. She flashed a white, toothy grin and asked what he thought of her new crowns. Elliot nodded and looked away. Then she patted his shoulder—"You know, there's something I have to say"—and he turned to her politely. "When someone spends her life with you, the mother of your children, you don't just throw her out when you get a little tired of her. What are people going to say?"

"I'm not tired of my wife," he said. "None of this was my idea." Then he strode the length of the table to where Barb was cutting bread, grabbed her by the elbow and whispered, "Let's get out of here."

They drove home without speaking, Elliot grumbling under his breath, and walked directly into the kitchen. The cat curled around her legs and Barbara fed it a can of something runny and brown. Then she made a pot of coffee and served up slices of pie. Elliot relaxed as he chewed, his legs stretching under the table until his feet touched hers. He said he might study baking at some point, you never know, although he wouldn't expect to make anything as wonderful as Barb's strawberry-rhubarb pies. His very favorite dessert, he said, rubbing his foot across hers.

And Barbara wondered if Elliot expected her to carry fresh pies to his apartment after he moved out. Did he still envision her, even in retirement, with flour on her hands and clothes, red-cheeked and ready to serve? When was it her turn to curl up with a paperback and delight in sweet smells from the kitchen? When would someone bake for her?

She was feeling old and worn out (her feet burned, her calves ached, and her face seemed to be drooping) and even sugar and caffeine couldn't perk her up much. But Elliot didn't notice. He was gazing at her with hooded eyes—a shy, naked, knowing look—and she guessed he would take her hand as soon as he finished eating pie and suggest that they make love. He wasn't in the mood for sex very often these days, and she knew she ought to jump at the chance, but just wasn't up to it. She couldn't be a lover tonight. Aunt Jemima, maybe, or the Pillsbury Doughboy.

Weariness made her daring. "Look," she blurted, "tell me something, tell me what you really think. What you told Jake—when you said this isn't about sex—does that mean what I think it does? What did you mean exactly?"

Elliot dripped strawberry-rhubarb filling on the front of his shirt, just above his abdomen. He rubbed it with a napkin, which only made the stain worse. Barbara said, "Cold water and Ivory soap. Or else use a stain remover before you do your laundry."

He stared at the red blot as if it were a drawing on a Rorschach test. It resembled a pair of breasts. "I haven't thought this through yet," he said vaguely, stalling for time. "I know we haven't been doing it much . . . getting older and all that. . . ."

"Remember when we were newlyweds and went at it twice a day?"

"But that doesn't mean. . . . What I told Jake. . . . I don't want to sleep with anyone else."

Barbara leaned across the table and squeezed his hand. "Just wait till we separate. It'll sharpen our appetites."

He drew in a hoarse breath. "You mean you're not sick of me? We'll really keep making love?"

"You know and I know this isn't about money or sex or incompatibility, even if no one believes us."

And no one did. Not anyone. Not just Barb's friends or friends they had in common, but Elliot's buddy Ivan, too, a man he'd known since grade school and who'd known Barb right from the start, when she was just a teenager sneaking in and out of Elliot's bedroom in his parents' home.

Ivan was never married himself. He'd lived alone his whole life, although there was always a woman he was seeing at any given time. Who better to talk to about the solitary life? So what if Barb questioned Ivan's sexual orientation and thought him a bad influence? Over the years she'd never liked any of Elliot's friends much, but now that didn't matter: soon she wouldn't know how he was spending his time or who with.

He met Ivan for a beer and explained that after all these years he and Barb were going to carve the house up, two floors each, and live apart. Ivan offered to throw an ex-girlfriend Elliot's way, but Elliot shook his head and laughed. "It's not about sex," he said.

"You want to get away from her but can't afford your own place?"

"I *can* afford my own place if I wanted to get away from her, but I don't . . . not entirely. I'd like to try living alone but don't want to lose her."

Ivan thought in absolutes. "Either you live alone or you don't. You can't have it both ways."

Elliot couldn't see why not. "We'll see each other when we like. We'll do our own housekeeping, make our own daily plans, meet our own friends and enjoy ourselves the way we choose, together or not."

"Why can't you live together and do that anyway?"

Elliot hadn't thought of that and didn't know what to answer. And so he said lamely, "I was hoping you'd understand."

At home again he finally cornered Barb in the basement. She was trying to find the best spot for a new tensided kiln with an interior diameter of twenty-four inches. "The window or near the sink?" she said, speaking to herself.

"Can I talk to you a minute?"

Before he could breathe Ivan's name, she said, "My mother was here today and I told her what we were up to. She said we're being selfish and she doesn't think it'll work out. She said, 'Look what happened to your hippie friends from the sixties: burned out has-beens or neoconservatives. Too much freedom is a terrible thing.'"

Barbara dropped her measuring tape and sat down

abruptly on the cement floor. Elliot sat down too, crossing his legs and feeling cold and damp, as if he'd landed in mud. Their eyes met and he said quietly, "So, do you think she's right?"

"I think we'd be risking more by not doing anything. How long before we started hating each other? Tell me that."

"But why can't we stay together and just learn to be a little more independent? Do our own laundry and things, go about our own business?"

"You don't get it, do you?" She slapped her knee. "As long as I'm here where you can see me you'll just start talking, whether I want to listen or not. If I take down a basket of laundry"—pointing to the washing machine stern and white across the room—"you'll ask me to do yours too. Just a few things, you'll say. Isn't it more cost-efficient to do one big load instead of two little ones?

"And if I'm going out at night, you'll want to know where and when I'll be back, and I'll go ahead and tell you so you won't have to worry. If I'm going to be late I'll call or maybe even change my plans so you won't be sitting home alone with nothing to do. And if I'm back early enough, I'll whip up a nice dinner"—her voice getting high-pitched—"since you don't know how to do that. And as long as I keep cooking you'll never have a reason to learn, will you? *Will you?*"

And Elliot would have to take the garbage out, as usual, track their investments, shovel snow, change the furnace filters and apologize for Ivan. The way they've always done things . . . without even thinking whether they want to do those things or not.

She bent over and hugged her knees, trying to calculate how many dinners she'd cooked for Elliot over the years: six a week (on average) times fifty weeks (on average) times thirty-two. Nearly ten thousand! The numbers leapfrogged in her brain, bumping into images of baked potatoes, pot roasts and rows of strawberry-rhubarb pies. Then her thoughts veered to the day she retired last June. There'd been a lively party in the staff room after school, and many people brought gifts. Someone gave her a black beret; others gave her modeling tools and bags of red and white clay because she'd told everyone she wanted to be a potter. She came home in a birthday mood. (She'd never have to face a class of bored adolescents again!) Came home to find a trail of mud balls, like mouse turds, leading from the hall to the kitchen, where Ivan and Elliot sat drinking, an empty pizza box on the floor. Ivan lifted a bottle of beer in her direction when she approached, then swung his work boots off a chair to make room. Barbara stood over her husband with her hands fisted on her hips. "I thought we were eating out tonight," she said in a wired voice. "You told me we were going out." There were grease stains on Elliot's shirt and a blot of tomato sauce on his chin. His eyes wheeled when he looked at her: he wasn't going anywhere.

The night of her retirement was a disappointment, certainly, but no worse than other dreary evenings she'd known as his wife. The problem was that over time those little letdowns added up, and she was cursed to remember them all.

Barbara straightened up on the basement floor. "Everyone ought to live alone at some point, don't you think? But you and I never did. We went from being children to man and wife. And now we're so used to pleasing everybody else that we've lost track of our own needs. I'm getting old, Elliot. I don't want to die a stranger to my own self."

In that suspended moment, in a way that bypassed his brain, he understood his wife completely: as if she hadn't said the words but breathed them directly into his soul.

And once more he resolved to live with her separately and lovingly under the same roof.

This was two weeks before they began to sever their household. Later that night the phone rang and he picked up the receiver. "Hello?" he said, and his daughter answered, "Tell me this is a bad joke. I just got off the phone with Gran, who told me what you're up to—that you and Mom are going to give up half of all you own and live like antiquated hippies."

"That's not the plan. She got it wrong."

Barbara whispered, "Who's that?" and Elliot covered the mouthpiece. "Susan. I think she's upset. She spoke to your mother earlier. . . ."

"Tell her to come for supper tomorrow. Tell her to bring Mattie and we'll talk this over quietly."

Susan agreed to come at six. "But don't think you'll change my mind. Don't think you can talk me into liking what you want to do."

"You don't even know for sure what it is. At least get the story straight before you turn your nose up."

Susan humphed and the line went dead. When he hung up the phone Barb said, "Call Dennis and say we're meeting tomorrow to discuss—well, say what you like. I'd rather he heard it from us first. Tell him to bring Natalie and the kids. I hope Natalie's free."

When Elliot spoke to Dennis he said, "We're meeting to discuss renovations to the house which will change the course of the future, your mother's and mine." Dennis said, "Excuse me?" and asked him to repeat himself. "Six o'clock," Elliot said. "We'll talk more about it then."

The mantel clock was chiming and the wall oven had just turned off automatically when the bell rang the next night. Elliot went to open the door and there was Susan on the step, holding her daughter by the wrist. Mattie snapped her hand free, tripped into the foyer and tied her arms around his waist. He kissed the center part of her hair and tugged her brown ponytail, half undone. Susan hurried past him.

Mattie hopped onto his feet and he goose-stepped her into the kitchen. "Pot roast," Barb said, and Mattie slid away from him to peer through the oven glass.

Susan was leaning against the counter, her arms folded under her breasts. She was still in her work clothes, a gray jacket with padded shoulders, white blouse and slim skirt. Her cheeks were flushed with makeup and her lipstick nearly rubbed off; her eyes were sooty, as if smudged. Barbara stood beside her daughter, a hand on her shoulder. They were talking about Susan's job. Susan was the art director for a midsized magazine, work which seemed to require constant outbursts of energy that left her limp and panting at the end of the day. As a child she'd been underweight, as pale and skinny as a stick of unpainted furniture, so that you'd often overlook her in a room. At twenty-eight she was angular, with sharp features, elbows and knees. There was a time she'd resembled her mother, but the years had softened Barbara's lines and made her more rounded, so that now they were dissimilar.

"It's so exhausting," Susan said. "They expect me to do my job and everybody else's too."

Barbara brushed a stray hair from Susan's eye. She was thinking about her daughter young: late afternoons they'd sit in the kitchen, the table striped with long shadows as sunlight died in the windowpanes; Susan's hair veiling her face as she bent over a drawing pad and Barbara talked about color and line. Who knew how much the girl absorbed as she scratched the paper furiously. Probably little, or nothing at all, because when she was older she confessed to having always hated her mother's stern teacher-voice; the way she'd talk to her like she was just another student. It was all Susan could do to keep from sticking her fingers in her ears.

Now she spoke even louder. "You ask them to do the simplest thing—a little something extra—and they think you're nuts. They have this damn *attitude*." And Barbara's scalp tightened at the shrillness of her daughter's voice.

Then Mattie said, "When do we eat?" and Susan snapped, "Just wait!" Before her mother could shout again, the girl got up and left the room. The ginger cat followed her. She sat on the floor in Grandma's bedroom, a dark room at the front of the house that used to be the parlor, turned on the TV and pulled Hammer into her lap. She'd brought along a book she was supposed to finish up for school but didn't feel like reading. When her mother found out she hadn't read it she'd get even madder. Her face would turn cranberry-color and then she'd start screaming that she couldn't keep up with everything, especially Mattie's homework, which was her responsibility and no one else's, blah-blah. Mattie switched to "Sesame Street." At ten she was too old to be watching a kiddie show, but stared at it anyway and stroked the cat.

In the kitchen Susan and Elliot sat down. Barbara kept her back to them, stirring something on the stove. Her long wooden spoon beat rhythmically against the pot. Wouldn't they be surprised to know how tired of cooking she'd become? Didn't like it any more than her mom did. Dora hated household chores, and yet she'd bought her daughter wooden spoons before she could hold them; she had Barbara fixing meals while other girls her age curled their hair and swapped lipsticks. So that she grew up serious, without friends.

Elliot stared down at his hands folded on the table. "Your mother and I," he began, but Susan interrupted with "What's going on here?"

Barbara said, "It's simple. We want to live separately."

"You want to live *separately*? A trial separation? What're you saying? What do you mean? You love each other, don't you? Dan and I split up, okay, and look where it got us. Look where I am today—running, running, running and I can't keep up."

Barbara turned to face them, her wooden spoon batting the air. "This isn't the same thing at all. Your father and I have been together almost thirty-three years—"

"While Dan was on his way out in thirty-three months, right?"

Why does it always come back to *her*? Barbara thought sharply. Susan's marriage and divorce, Susan's daughter, Susan's work. Wasn't it someone else's turn? Wasn't it time she listened to her own mother for a change? "Why are we talking about Dan? This is about your father and me."

"Because you're going to ruin something," Susan cried, "like he did!" She flattened her hands on the table and blinked hard.

"Don't be upset," Elliot said. "It's just a small change we're making, not a big deal at all. Why is everyone so upset?"

From across the house the noise of the TV grew louder and Susan shouted, "Turn that down!" Then the doorbell rang again.

"I'll get it," Elliot said.

"I will," and Barb rushed past him with a slap of air.

Susan swung around in her chair, her knees showing bony and white underneath her stockings. Elliot gazed at his daughter's knees. So many things he ought to say, but his mind was stitched to what he saw: her knees like a pair of long faces, bony and protruding, blotchy in places where she'd picked scabs and picked them again. His little girl who clawed her skin, who scratched and bled through childhood. Who watched her parents with drilling eyes and somehow disapproved of them. As far back as he could recall she wanted something more of them—more attention, more love? She never said just what. He might have tried even harder, so that she'd stop picking scabs, but knew whatever he did wouldn't be enough.

Natalie came into the kitchen carrying the baby, wailing and thrashing in her arms. Susan jumped in her chair and Elliot covered his ears. Barbara rushed around the table to pull out the highchair, an old wooden thing that she used to put Dennis in, and after him, Susan. Something she'd kept all these years as a talisman for grandchildren—although at the moment she was hard put to remember why she'd wanted them so badly. Grandchildren made noise; they whined and bickered, broke things and cried more loudly and piercingly than grownups. They expected your attention. They expected you to be as plump and sweet-tempered as Mrs. Claus.

Natalie put the baby in the seat and he banged on the tray. He twisted his body and tried to stand, but Natalie shoved him down again. Barbara gave him measuring spoons to play with and he banged harder. Next year Raymond would be old enough for a booster seat, and then they wouldn't have to lug the heavy highchair upstairs if he ate supper in Elliot's kitchen instead of hers. Next year he'd be old enough to understand if she yelled at him to stop making a racket.

Dennis and Stevie walked into the room next, hand in hand. Susan waved at them and Elliot forced a smile. Barbara kissed her son's cheek and patted Stevie on the head. The boy dropped his father's hand and ran off to find his cousin. He'd learned a new elephant joke and wanted to make Mattie laugh. *How do you know if there's an elephant hiding under your bed at night? Because your nose bumps the ceiling!* He'd been practicing all day and wouldn't make mistakes this time. Still, it was hard to make her laugh. Sometimes she was mean and told him to go away and pushed him, but he never stopped trying.

Natalie had been standing all day and her feet were killing her, so Barbara pulled an extra chair to the table and made her sit. She told her to take her shoes off and brought her a pair of Elliot's slippers. Natalie was a doctor. Dennis had a desk job as a policy adviser at the Ministry of Municipal Affairs and Housing (though no one knew for sure what he did) and didn't want to sit down. He pushed his glasses up his nose, leaned against the fridge and smiled an undemanding smile aimed at everyone and no one. Barbara stroked his arm lightly, as she was in the habit of doing, and his muscle softened under her touch. He'd always been her favorite, though a mother hates to admit preferring one child over another; though everyone expected she'd be closer to her daughter, as mothers are. Maybe it was his silence she loved, the wordless affection that passed between them, light as a tickle. Or maybe just that he didn't sulk.

Natalie tied a bib around the baby's neck and addressed Susan, sitting next to the highchair: "So what's this I hear about renovations and the future? Dennis didn't understand what Elliot said to him on the phone. I hope it's nothing serious."

"Only if you happen to think that Mom and Dad splitting up is no big deal."

"Now, Susan," Barbara said, "you're not being fair to us. We're not splitting," she told Natalie, "just going to live apart." Then, for the hundredth time, she went on to explain their plans—two floors for Elliot and two for herself. You'd think they were dividing a nation the way Natalie's eyes popped.

When Barbara was finished, Natalie said to Elliot, "And you agree? You want your own apartment? You think that's a good idea?" Elliot's thoughts were jumbled and he didn't even try to speak. He looked at his wife and nodded. Raymond started chewing his bib and Natalie tugged it out of his mouth. He flung the measuring spoons on the floor and resumed kicking the highchair. Barbara pressed two fingers against her left temple.

Natalie picked the spoons up and dropped them back on the baby's tray. "After all these years," she said, "you finally get the chance to live quietly and have fun. You could travel, see the world, go to museums and matinées. Time enough for everything—what Dennis and I wouldn't give for that." She glanced at her husband, who was beaming one of his dazed smiles somewhere to the right of her ear.

"Like our trip to New York?" Barbara said. Their long-awaited holiday, almost two years ago: a week of museums and restaurants and half-price theater tickets to celebrate his retirement. A small hotel in midtown. Uptown to the Guggenheim, Whitney and Frick. Westbound to Lincoln Center, the Museum of Natural History and Hayden Planetarium. A subway ride to SoHo, then north to the Cloisters.

But Elliot was overwhelmed. He wanted to do one bookstore, one record shop a day. A quiet lunch, a short nap; a jazz club in the evening, yes, but back to their hotel by ten. He tired out so quickly. While Barbara wanted to *gogogo*—to eat in crowded cafés and weave in and out of throngs and stalled, honking traffic. The rude, impersonal noise of the city, unlike that of her family, was light on her ears.

She wanted to ferry to Ellis Island and then the Statue of Liberty; to see the Empire State Building, Wall Street, Bloomingdale's, Rockefeller Center and a dozen Greenwich Village bars. But in the end she did hardly anything, because of him—because he wouldn't come along—and the notion of exploring strange places on her own made her unaccountably nervous.

Then one night after dinner, walking back to their hotel (the last grains of light in the sky quickly disappearing), a young man came up to them on the sidewalk and yanked her purse. A boy really, a teenager, shaggy-haired and stocky, with a sparse mustache. They'd been walking on a treed street of narrow, solemn brownstones and no one happened to be around. She was carrying a shoulder bag and at that first, surprising pull the strap cut deeply into her flesh, through the thin sheath of her blouse, and her arm twitched in a bolt of pain. Instinctively she grabbed her purse with both hands and hung on tight. The teenager should've run. Instead, he tugged her purse again but couldn't wrench it away from her. Back and forth, back and forth, the shiny black bag shifted from him to her, her to him.

"Give it to him!" Elliot screamed, and she glared at her husband open-mouthed.

"I will not. He has no right!"

The young man grunted and pulled, and Barbara did the same in turn. Back and forth, back and forth, the bag lurched between them.

"Help me, Elliot. Help me!"

Her husband stepped forward then and gave the boy a big shove. The boy pushed him back, hard. "Fuck off!" he said, reaching into a pocket. "I got a gun."

Elliot was panting. "You hear that—he's got a gun. Give him the damn bag!"

"Do something else!" she cried. "Don't just stand there and tell me to let go."

The teenager sneered at them. Elliot saw that his teeth were crooked, but square and white. A little orthodontia, he thought, and his smile would've been perfect. The boy was wearing a sleeveless shirt and his muscular arms

31

glinted in the buttery glow of a streetlight. "What else can I do?" Elliot winced, and Barbara howled "Sonofabitch!" at him or the mugger or both of them, she wasn't sure.

The boy gave a final jerk and twisted her bag free. He loped away with it under his arm, not even hurrying, and paused at the end of the block to give them the finger.

She stormed back to the hotel and marched up six flights of stairs to their room. Elliot took the elevator and got there first. As she opened the door he said calmly, "He told us he had a gun. Tourists get killed the world over trying to hang on to their wallets. Really, was it worth your life? A few dollars and credit cards?"

She stood in the doorway, quaking with rage, which Elliot mistook for fear. "There, there"—he opened his arms—"everything's all right now."

"Everything is *not* all right," she said through her teeth. "We're going home tomorrow morning, first thing."

And so they ended their trip early and flew back to Toronto. "That was enough vacation for me," Elliot announced on the plane. "We're not going anywhere again for a long time."

Natalie jiggled the measuring spoons, which snapped Barbara back to the kitchen and her children. "Not a trip like that," said Natalie. "Not another trip to New York— something more relaxing. You don't even have to leave town, there's lots to do in Toronto. Or just putter around the house."

"The point is togetherness," Susan said. "Appreciate your free time and one another's company. I can't believe you really want to live alone."

Everyone looked at Barbara. For her part, she was looking down at a covered dish she held tightly, as if the meaning of all this were bubbling and thickening under the lid. No matter what she said to them, they just wouldn't get it. Not Susan, abandoned by Dan and frantically raising a daughter alone; who'd like nothing better than a man to come home to at the end of the day. And not Dennis and Natalie, bound in a web of schedules and chores, passing children back and forth and breathlessly tripping from day to day, chasing a slippery dream of family togetherness. How could they appreciate Barbara's situation? What would they know about filling time, of finding meaning and focus? Of privacy and silence and the need for adventure?

The dish slipped through Barbara's hands and crashed with a bang and slurp. A mound of puréed peas flattened, oozing at the edges, and a gush of steam rose up: she vanished for a moment in a wet cloud. Everybody dipped forward, as if suddenly pulled by gravity into a black hole. Then Barbara reappeared and everybody leaned back. She used a plate and spatula to scoop up the mess on the floor, wiping the last of it with a sponge. "Everything else is ready," she said. "Why don't we just eat first and talk later."

Stevie and Mattie were called to the table. The boy trailed behind his cousin. "It is *too* funny," he said, "but you don't laugh at anything."

"Is not," Mattie answered and sat as far away from him as she possibly could.

"It is too!"

Barbara pinched the bridge of her nose, walked up to Stevie's chair and put her mouth against his ear. "Stop whining." Then, relenting a little, "If you promise not to tell jokes, I'll ask Mattie to sit with you." He scratched his head and nodded. Next she stepped behind Mattie, undid her ponytail and twisted her hair into a braid, pulling the strands so hard the poor girl writhed in her seat. "Sit with him," she ordered, "or I won't let you feed the cat." Mattie stood up and changed seats.

Then Barbara set the table and passed around a platter of meat and heavy bowls of vegetables. Elliot offered to help but she waved him still. Susan filled her plate but only picked at her food. Stevie wouldn't eat his carrots and Natalie said monotonously, "Eat them, they're good for you. They help your eyes to see at night." Stevie said he didn't care, he kept his eyes closed at night—which Elliot declared was a very clever thing to say, then laughed too heartily.

Mattie skipped the baked potatoes, which made her think of eyeballs now that everyone was talking eyes. The baby ate a little of this, a little of that, drank milk and spat up on the kitchen floor. Natalie rushed to clean up the slop with paper towels and sponges, and by the time she finished she had totally lost her appetite and bunched her napkin on her plate. Barbara ate sparingly. She thought the roast was overdone, the carrots and turnips undercooked, but no one complained. No one ever complained, it seemed: as if they couldn't really taste what was in front of them because they expected it to be the same as always, and expectation has a way of blurring reality.

Barbara pushed her plate aside. Elliot hurried through the meal and Dennis had seconds of everything. "Mom is still Mom," he said rather obliquely.

Elliot washed, Dennis dried, and Barbara put the dishes away because, after all these years, her husband still didn't know exactly where things went. That would never happen in his own apartment, she was sure.

Natalie wet a blue cloth and scrubbed Raymond's dirty face while Susan wiped the table. "All right," Susan said, straightening her padded shoulders, "let's get back to what we were saying."

"What about coffee?" Barbara said, as if that would settle everyone's nerves. "And I made a couple of fruit pies."

Dennis, who loved his mother's pies, thought that was a good idea. "Apple?" he said (his favorite), but she wouldn't let on. He snuck up behind her and locked her in a bear hug. "Don't disappoint me," he said.

Barbara slipped out of his hold and sat down in the extra chair at the head of the table. She *would* disappoint him, of course, by being unpredictable and just a little daring. Children want you to match whatever image of "mother" they hold inside, no matter how impossible. But more than anything else, they want you to stay the same. Mom isn't Mom anymore, Dennis will grieve when they split the house, and he'll be more or less right.

She rubbed her hands over her face and pressed her fingers against the tender, nervous flesh of her eyelids. "The pie can wait a few minutes. There's something I have to say first." She dropped her hands and turned to glance at Dennis standing by the sink, no longer smiling. "I know we're confusing you. You don't know why we're doing this." She fixed her eyes on the window. "But we're going to do it anyway."

When she looked at her son again his brow was creased, his jaw tight, his eyeglasses opaque. She swung her head around slowly to gaze at Susan and Natalie, Stevie and Mattie and the baby in his highchair. No one dared breathe out. They stared ahead, seeing nothing, their lips thin, pressed together. Barbara wanted to shake them. *For godsake,* she wanted to cry, *stop being children! Let go of us—just let go!—so we can lead our own lives.*

Instead, she got up from the table and uncovered a pair of apple pies on the counter. She cut them into neat wedges, served pie, cups of coffee and glasses of milk for the little ones. No one had seconds of anything. No one said more than was necessary: "yes, please," "thank you" and "pass the sugar." Minutes after they finished dessert they all went home.

Then Barbara looked at Elliot and he had nothing to say either. He pulled at his fingers. No one understood them, he was thinking, and no one approved. It was like he and Barb were on an island in a rough sea . . . except she didn't want him there. She didn't want to see him, though he didn't know exactly why. And soon it would be just him, alone on a bare rock. When he glanced up at Barbara his eyes were hot and stinging.

They didn't talk about it again. A few nights later they started the work of dividing the house, two floors for Elliot and two floors for Barbara. It took a lot of energy, all that packing and unpacking and stamping up and down stairs. And so, for several days at least, they were far too busy to think about anything else. But when everything was finally in place and they closed their respective apartment doors to lie down in separate beds, the enormity of what they had done rose from the sheets like the smell of sweat.

It was late, but their rooms were unlit. Their eyes were sore and stretched wide, staring helplessly back in time. Elliot was remembering the day they swam at Murphy's Point, Susan and Dennis, he and Barb: sitting on a boulder while a stranger took their photograph, kids in front, parents behind, their damp shoulders stuck together. How shivers of serenity passed swiftly between them.

Barbara was reliving the night in July, 1963, when they made love in a blueberry patch on the island of St. Pierre: the surf crooning in the fog; his skin tasting salty and his thrusting slow and lazy at first, in time with the breakers. In the morning he was still in her arms. Later she would find a rash of blueberry stains on her underpants. Alone in her bed now, Barbara pulled her nightgown off, cupped her breasts in her hands and cried.

On the nightstand beside his bed, an alarm clock ticked off the dismal seconds going by and Elliot covered his ears with his hands. The sound grew sharp and louder still—like hammering behind his eyes—and he squeezed his ears until they hurt. Finally he grabbed the clock and hurled it across the room. But even when it struck a wall and fell in pieces to the floor, he felt no relief.

Barbara stopped crying when she heard the noise from upstairs. She called to Elliot in the dark, her voice low and tentative, then listened to the silence of the stunned house.

2

JAR and Lid

The wheel spun. She wrapped her hands around the clay and it fell, rose, fell again. Pressing her thumbs into the clay, she made a hole and widened it to form the shape of a vessel.

The wheel slowed and Barbara raised the sides of the pot. Her fingers were coated, slimy, slick, like when she was little and played in mud and her mother slapped her afterwards for dirtying her good clothes. Like when she was hit in the face with a ball and blood ran from her nose into her cupped hands. Like the glutinous, primeval feel of semen in her navel those times they didn't have protection but neither of them could bear to wait, so Elliot promised to pull out and they agreed to take a chance; which worked well enough until the one time it didn't and their young lives were changed forever.

She rounded the pot and collared the rim: a gradual ballooning like the outward curve of pregnancy.

Dennis was difficult, Susan was not. With Susan she could feel her head pressing against the seat of the cab on the way to the hospital. The baby was out so fast Elliot couldn't get there in time and missed the birth. He was sadder about this than Barbara would've imagined and seemed to feel from the very start that he owed something to Susan.

But Dennis . . . that was another thing entirely. Twisted around the wrong way, heavy on the small of her back, then finally turned properly, but his head wouldn't drop down. Waiting and waiting, long past her due date. Sleepless with the weight of him, the pressure on her legs and bladder, the aches and cramps and swelling, then the heartburn and hemorrhoids. And finally her water broke, pooling on the kitchen floor, but still no labor. She was ordered to the hospital, where she lay in bed and kept waiting. Elliot, restless and overheated, went to a room at the end of the hall to watch the news on TV. And then, after midnight, a twinge, a spasm, a strong cramp— another and another. But she wasn't dilated nearly enough and the baby's head hadn't engaged, so they hooked her up to a fetal monitor, black cords running from the back of a screen into the distant depth of her body. And she saw as plain as fear the white curve of her contractions on the black screen, saw them climb slowly and peak, a little curve, a medium one, a screamingly awful giant wave. Five minutes apart, three. Two minutes apart. Constant. Line upon line, wave after wave, a graph of pain to watch and anticipate. So that she would start hurting before the white squiggle even climbed; so that she would moan and cry out the moment the screen lit up. The anesthetist, that sonofabitch, wouldn't answer his pager, and there was no one else to give her drugs so she thrashed and cried and cursed them all. Hold still, they told her. *Hold still. Hold still. You'll disconnect the monitor.* Elliot

was at her side, shushing her and wiping her brow—
remember to breathe, remember your breathing—and she
swung her hand and grabbed him, digging her fingers
into his flesh, trying to tear his arm from its socket. What
did he know about pain that stopped the very breath in
your nostrils? What did he know about anything?

Barbara cut the pot from the wheel and set it aside to
dry. She stretched, doubling over, then paced a nervous
circle from window to washing machine, kiln, sink and
window again. It was hard to keep her mind on clay. Hard
to spend hours alone in the damp gloom of the basement,
hearing only the turning wheel, the furnace clicking on
and off, her own thoughts. She ought to get a radio.

She ordered herself to sit down.

She threw another ball of clay onto the wheel head
and made a lid with a straight flange to sit on the rim of
the jar. Then she set the lid down beside the pot.
Tomorrow they'd be ready to trim, but tonight they were
newborn, too wet and fragile to touch.

The joke, of course, was that Susan grew to be col-
icky and then a fretful little girl, while Dennis was (has
always been) even-tempered, placid. As if he had decided
not to cause his mother further pain. *Just sit on the couch,*
she'd say, *while Mommy goes downstairs to put the clothes in the
dryer,* and when she returned she'd find him exactly as
she'd left him, his legs dangling over the side and his
hands fisted in his lap. *Such a good boy,* she'd say, but something about his frozen posture made her want to cry, too.
What if she were training him to be subservient? Raising
a child from parenting books, you were bound to make
certain mistakes. Would Dennis pay a terrible price for
her lack of experience?

Her mother proved to be useless, a reluctant source
of dated advice: "Feed him every four hours and not a
morsel in between"; "Let him cry till he turns blue, it's

good for his character"; "You were trained at eighteen months and not a day later." But mostly Dora couldn't remember the business of raising a child. Her own mother had looked after Barbara as a baby so Dora could return to work, and the old dear had been dead for years.

Even after Barbara eased up on her firstborn and let him take the lead in deciding what he wanted to do, he seemed to want nothing but to follow at her heels like a pull-toy on wheels tied with string to her ankle. He would play on the floor at her feet, toddle behind when she moved, grab her by her pants leg and gaze up benignly. She concluded it was his nature to be passive and obedient—or at least that she wasn't entirely to blame.

Susan preferred solitude. She would stamp into an empty room and slam the door behind her. Through the door you could hear her barking at her Raggedy Ann, instructing her to sit up straight, use the potty, clean her plate, and always the doll refused. Then she would whack Raggedy Ann and start whining and sniveling, playing both parent and child. Behaving not like Barbara but like Dora, her granny, who used to smack her little girl. How could that happen? Was it possible that ornery genes skipped a generation, or that Susan had picked up a signal, however submerged, from Barbara and given it play?

Now she washed the wheel head and emptied the pan. She sorted bits of clay into buckets and vacuumed the floor. Her mother was coming for dinner at five and, at Dora's request, Elliot would be joining them later for tea and dessert. Her mother was fond of Elliot (though he had never warmed to her), and on more than one occasion Barbara had been jealous of the attention she paid him. Because he was male, no doubt. Because her mother, nearly seventy-five but never married, changed when a man entered the room: her voice rose, her back straightened, her eyes glimmered like doubloons. Is that what comes from never having actually lived with a man? From never having picked up a man's pajamas, scrubbed his shirts, smelled his stale morning breath or heard him whimper in a dream?

Barbara washed her hands and picked clay from under her fingernails. She took off her coverall, happy for an excuse to stop potting and go upstairs. Of course her intention was to spend most of her time at the wheel, but she'd have to work up to that.

Her mother wasn't fussy, so she'd make something easy and quick, pasta salad and feta cheese, served with that half a loaf left in the bread box and a pie she baked this morning. Long accustomed to eating out, Dora enjoyed home cooking, however plain. Long accustomed to lunch hours, she'd be on time.

And she was. The bell rang curtly, half a ding, as if no more were needed to announce Dora's arrival. Barbara made the short trip from living room to front door via her new apartment door and the corridor that ran beside the stairway to the second floor. (She'd agreed to sweep the hall if Elliot kept the steps clean.) Then she opened the front door, kissed her mother and took her coat. Dora strode along the hall, looking like a black crane in her turtleneck sweater and slim pants. Softly Barbara closed the apartment door behind them.

In the kitchen her mother stopped, arms out-stretched, and Barbara leaned against her. Dora hugged her for a moment, cupping the back of Barbara's head, and she sank into her mother's arms. When was the last time anyone had held her? It had been months since she and Elliot . . . since they'd been intimate.

Then her mother straightened up and turned toward the counter. "I see you've been baking," she said.

"Strawberry-rhubarb pie."

"Isn't that Elliot's favorite?"

"I like it too, you know. And so do you."

Dora stiffened. She crossed the room, spread her hands on the kitchen table and sat down. She could shake her daughter, she really could, because she'd been such a fool, telling her husband to live upstairs. Just because he lay around, talked too much and smoked a pipe: what kind of reasons were those? It was Barbie's idea all along, playing a game of independence—but won't she be surprised when he brings home another woman and recreates his old life with someone new. Because he will. Sure it's fun for him right now, coming and going as he pleases, no one to answer to, but how long before the silent afternoons get to him, before he tires of ironing, canned spaghetti and dirty sheets? Men don't like living alone, they want to be part of a family. Sure they fool around sometimes, looking for adventure, but you'll never get them to leave their wives.

Barbara bent over the counter and dressed the salad. It was going to be the sort of night where her mother asked embarrassing questions and Barbara avoided answering. *Aren't you lonely?* she'll want to know. *Isn't it cold in the basement? How can making cups and plates compare with the pleasure of being at your husband's side?*

"I'm not hungry," Dora said, "so don't go to any trouble. We play bridge on Fridays now and I've been nibbling all afternoon. You know what a hostess Margaret is, sandwiches and little cakes. Though I don't imagine I'd say no to a piece of pie later on."

Barbara put the salad bowl and slices of bread on the table. She pulled back a chair and sat down. "Well, *I'm* hungry," she announced. Her mother raised her eyebrows as if she simply couldn't believe her daughter had an appetite. After all that had happened. Living apart from her husband after—what? . . . close to thirty-three years.

"You're not offended, are you? You know how much I

like your cooking. I should've said no to Margaret, but she's always so insistent. Oh, never mind all that. Tell me about your day."

"I worked on the wheel this afternoon, part of an enormous vase and a couple of smaller pieces. I was thinking about your birthday too. Your birthday's coming round again. Would you like a new teaset?"

"The one you gave me years ago is still going strong, thanks, but I'm sure you'll think of something. Just please, Barbie, don't fuss. At my age, there's not very much left to celebrate."

Barbara buttered a slice of bread and picked at the crust. Was there ever much for Dora to celebrate? she wondered. A raise, a promotion? Meetings with her lover behind locked doors? The birth of her misbegotten child? At least Barbara's father had another, bigger life beyond his secret life with Dora: a wife, kids, a mortgage. A normal life; a real one. A life that went on in spite of Dora and her baby.

Barbara probably wouldn't have liked him one bit if she knew him, that two-faced philanderer. But not knowing him was worse. "Tell me," she asked her mother, "how old would my father have been?"

"If he was alive today?" Why did they always wind up talking about that man? Why did she miss what she never had? Dora didn't miss things, certainly not marriage or men. "Ninety," she said. "April fifth."

"It would've been nice to give him a present on his birthday. I think he would've liked that."

"You were a baby when he died. How can you know what he would've liked?"

Barbara chewed her buttered bread, her jaw working fiercely. Somehow she knew—her body knew. His rough hand on her soft face: her body remembered something. Did he brush against his baby girl, even accidentally, and the imprint of his flesh remain in the distant memory of her cells? A question she would never ask. She couldn't bear to hear her mother say, *Well no, dear. He never came as close as that. He kept a certain distance.* "And let's not forget that he had a family of his own. Do you think you could've walked in, pushed everyone aside and blown out his candles?"

Barbara dropped a large scoop of pasta salad on her plate and offered her mother some as well, but Dora only waved her off. "Oh, I'm sorry, I shouldn't refuse. Now you'll be eating leftovers all week." And Barbara replied that she liked leftovers just fine.

"I know you don't want me to say anything, but really, Barbie, *leftovers?* Haven't you made your point already? Six weeks on your own—isn't that long enough? Don't tell me you don't miss Elliot and want him back. I know you like the back of my hand: you have to be part of a family. Even when you were little and you played with your stuffed toys . . . one a mommy, one a daddy, and all the rest were children. So how can you throw out a perfectly decent man without a second thought?"

"Not without a thought—and I didn't exactly toss him away. We agreed to remain husband and wife but live separately, that's all."

"You're talking to someone who's lived without a man all her life, so I know what I'm saying." She reached for her daughter's hand and rubbed her cold fingers. "The single life is difficult, it's not for everyone. Someone like you, who isn't strong—I worry about you all the time. You'll wilt like a head of lettuce left out overnight."

Barbara pulled her hand free, shoveled pasta onto her fork and swallowed the pieces whole. Strong! Not strong enough! What would Dora know about the strength it takes to work all day, come home and meet the endless needs of a family, then find the will and energy to meet your own? Dora always came first, while Barbara and her grandmother made do.

She emptied her plate and stood up. "Why don't we go downstairs and I'll show you what I'm working on."

Dora followed her from the kitchen down the steps to the basement, sniffing at the sudden gloom. Her daughter was living the life of a mole! She bumped her right hip against the corner of a worktable. "My goodness, Barbie. If you had to divide the house, why choose the bottom?"

Barbara showed her mother two halves of a large vessel, a fruit bowl, casserole and several mugs with decorative handles, all drying on stacked shelves. She didn't show the jar and lid, set aside in a dark corner, as if they would melt into puddles under Dora's gaze.

"Lovely, lovely"—her mother's eyes flitted over rows of shelves—"but I worry about you sitting here day in, day out, hunched over a muddy wheel and turning out utensils."

"I like it." A half-truth. But she would grow to like it more in time, she suspected. Or find something else to do.

Her mother sighed. She circled an old kitchen chair sprinkled with fine white dust, wiped the vinyl seat with a tissue and sat down. "Oh Barbie, dear Barbie. I liked my work too, writing letters, making appointments, keeping files and all that. The seams of my stockings always straight, my blouses whiter than china. . . . They gossiped about me behind my back, but I didn't care. Those empty-headed secretaries weren't going anywhere, while I—" Dora stopped short. "I was executive assistant to Mr. Wilkes."

"But he died. And they let you go."

"*He* didn't let me go. He never would've done that."

Her mother turned her face aside and Barbara patted her shoulder. "All that was long ago."

"Work isn't enough, you see."

"It doesn't matter anymore."

But Dora remembered everything, everything about him, and it did matter. Mattered still. The way he looked, moved and spoke; the way he buttoned his jacket and adjusted his tie. Stolen minutes in locked rooms; the gifts she'd find in her desk drawer (a bracelet, a cameo). Barbara didn't understand, she knew nothing of the man. Nothing essential. The feel of his skin, the cast of his eye, the huff and hum of his breathing.

"Come upstairs," her daughter said. "I'll make tea."

Someone knocking at the door as they climbed up the wooden stairs: that would be Elliot. Barbara crossed the living room, smoothed back her hair and let him in. He stood there a moment, looking past her, pulling his earlobe, scratching his neck. He would've liked to be smoking his pipe but knew his wife would never allow it in her own apartment. When he saw Dora he nodded at her and she waved back with all the exuberance of a passenger on a ship pulling away from shore. She was never that thrilled to see him when he lived with Barb.

The old woman opened her arms and Elliot stumbled, drew back, glanced at Barbara, at his feet, then walked into Dora's embrace. She hugged him stiffly and quickly, then moved back and examined him at arm's length. "My goodness, you never looked better. Doesn't he look terrific, Barbie?"

"Yes," she said, "he looks fine."

"Have you lost weight? A new haircut?"

"Nothing like that," Elliot grinned. "I'm learning new things, that's all. Tai Chi and cooking, and I've even started playing the sax."

"Three floors down I still hear him," Barbara said.

Dora hooked Elliot's arm and led him into the kitchen. "Well, I think it's wonderful. Good for you! All this new activity certainly agrees with you, you're positively glowing. While poor Barbie sits in the dark, up to her elbows in wet clay. You should take her out for a walk. She never sees the sun anymore."

Barbara filled the kettle with water, banged it sharply down on the stove and turned on a burner. She dropped tea bags into a pot (one of her recent efforts with a hairline crack below the spout), folded her arms and stared out the window at the backyard, crusted with gray patches of ice. The long, bare branches of shrubs were white-coated and glossy, as if they were fingers in surgical gloves. A cold stillness in the yard, like a held breath. Her breath. Why couldn't her mother ever mind her own business?

Behind her they were stuttering and whispering like schoolgirls: "Do it, do it—let's see!" "I only know part of it." "Do it anyway, do what you know." "You're sure about this?" Elliot said. "You won't be bored? You're certain?"— as if he were coaxing a young lover. When Barbara spun around, he had already raised his hands and was launched into the opening moves of Tai Chi Chuan.

Barbara saw him do this before, two or three weeks ago, the evening he invited her up to his third-floor bedroom-study, a big, bright, gabled room (formerly the master bedroom); a room she regretted losing. He was wearing a baggy T-shirt and those track pants torn at the knees, but he looked terrific doing the movements, fluid and muscular, and afterward, without a word, as they hadn't done in too long, they lay down on the double bed. But it barely went further than that. At the first kiss they stopped, embarrassed, too much feeling behind their lips. They hadn't bargained on that. The situation called for something more laid-back. How quickly their resolve might fail in a gasp of passion, and they could wind up more entwined than ever before.

Still too soon, they decided as they hopped off the bed; just a few short weeks since they'd started living separately. It would take time to find a new way to be comfortable and close with each other.

Now Barbara watched as he leaned and bent and turned in the kitchen. "That's as much as I know," he said, dropping his arms and straightening, but Dora urged him to do it again.

"What about tea?" said Barbara.

"Oh, let him," Dora said. "It's so graceful, like ballet. But manly, too, isn't it?"

Elliot started moving again and Barbara had to admit that, yes, he certainly looked attractive. Solid, agile, focused. Better than she'd seen him in years, which was what she was forced to admit that night in his bedroom. Better than when they lived together, awkward in retirement, and he spent a disproportionate amount of time on the sofa with his feet up and eyes closed.

The kettle boiled dry and she had to fill it up again. And how did she look to him now? she couldn't help thinking. Heavy and lumpy, as appealing as a sack of grain? Aging and imperfect in ways he never used to see when he gazed at her up close and her overly familiar form bled into the background?

Over dessert she wondered if she shouldn't be thinking about her weight.

Elliot had a second piece of strawberry-rhubarb pie, a red dab of filling in the corner of his lower lip. There was a time Barbara would have reached out to clean it. Now she only stared at his mouth as he wiped it with the back of his hand. "Wonderful," he said, and Dora smiled at her daughter and winked.

"Barbie's a remarkable cook. How can you resist coming down for supper every night?"

"I'm not so bad myself now," Elliot laughed, then

launched into a monologue about the merits of stock-pots, copper-bottomed or stainless steel, and the kinds of lids that fit best. Which led to a recitation of his recipe for chicken soup. The secret to a great soup, Elliot announced, was to boil the chicken's feet too.

How revolting, Dora thought. But his blue eyes were fixed on hers, glinting with conviction as he chattered on and on, and for a moment she remembered *his* eyes, also blue, shining in lamplight as she lay under him, very still, like a deer frozen on the road in the sudden glare of headlights. Memorizing his face and hands, his weight and smell and movements: knowing this would not go on forever, he would end it.

Elliot continued with a recipe for meat loaf, a recipe for blackened fish, then glanced at his watch and turned in his chair. "Got to run."

"What?" said Dora. "So soon?"

"Where are you going?" Barbara asked in a neutral, composed voice.

"A cooking class, as a matter of fact."

Dora grabbed his cup and filled it. "Have some more tea first. I'm sure it won't matter if you miss a few minutes."

"Sorry, but I can't stay." He thanked Barbara for dessert, said goodbye to Dora and hurried off with an eager step. Light and warmth—the air itself—seemed to follow him out the door.

Dora said to her daughter, "I just hope it's not too late."

"Too late for what?"

"To win him back."

"Win him back? I haven't lost him. Anyway, I wish you wouldn't interfere."

"But I want you to be happy. You have children of your own, you know what it's like when they make a mistake—how much you want to fix it."

Barbara cleared the table and stacked dishes next to the sink. What was life anyway but a series of small mistakes made in the hope of avoiding really big ones? Maybe it was wrong to have married in the first place; maybe it was wrong to leave. But wouldn't it have been a more significant mistake to stay?

"I saw the way he looked at you when he thought we weren't watching. He still cares about you, I'm sure, but of course you hurt him very much. Maybe if you gave him a sign. Maybe if you told him. . . ."

Barbara started washing cups in hot, hissing water, her back turned solidly against her mother's nagging. When she finished and turned again, her eyes were wet.

"I hope I didn't upset you. I only want your happiness." Dora stood up. "But I should be going." She found her coat in the closet and pulled it around her back. "Don't stop what you're doing," she said. "I can see myself out."

The door to her apartment shut, then the front door of the house. Barbara went to the living room and lay down on the sofa, the one from her marriage, familiar with stains and the smell of tobacco. Her head seemed to be full of steam, her thoughts hidden in thick clouds. Moisture seeping into her bones; her limbs heavy and saturated, like fat, soppy sponges. She dozed and dreamt about being submerged. She wanted to swim to the surface but her feet were tangled in slimy vines. On the sofa she gasped and wriggled, fighting for air.

She woke up to darkness and the distant sound of rattling. Coming from the kitchen, she thought. A more violent noise than that—knocking, banging or thrashing—but a small sound for all its fury. She wiped the corners of her eyes, sticky with emotion, shuffled across the living room and turned on the kitchen light.

The noise seemed to be coming from the deep drawer under the stove. She pulled it open carefully and slowly lifted the edges of her roasting pan and broiler, assorted racks and pot lids. Nothing unusual. Then she heard the sound again, moved to the counter and opened the lower cupboard door. Two stacks of cooking pans, one fitted into the next like Russian dolls. She slid forward one stack, then the other, and looked inside.

The noise was coming from her left, from the narrow slot between the stove and end of the counter, a space running back to the wall. She pulled a flashlight from a drawer, got onto her hands and knees and shone the yellow light into the finger-wide opening. A stunned mouse filled the beam; a mouse stuck to a glue trap and struggling to break free.

A leftover sticky trap from another season, no doubt, when mice were a problem and her husband was flinging plastic pads here, there and everywhere as if he were dealing cards. She never paid attention then. She didn't know if he caught any mice or what he did with them after. It was his problem, not hers: one of their tacit agreements.

But this was now. She jerked back, her throat squeezed. *Afraid of a mouse, a little mouse!* Elliot would have laughed at her. *He's more afraid of you,* he would've told her, scornful, *you and your flashlight—a Cyclops with a yellow eye!* Nonetheless, she was afraid.

Still, she couldn't leave it there to hurl against the counter and stove: that would be cruel. Besides, she couldn't bear to hear its death rattle all night. So she got up, reached for the phone and dialed Elliot's number. Three rings, four rings, then his machine clicked on, "Sorry, but we can't come to the phone right now. . . ."She hung up. *We.* Why did he say "we"? Did he still think of them as a couple even though they lived apart? Would he be willing to rescue her from a sticky situation because, after all, they were man and wife?

But what did it matter anyway? He wasn't in. Still out.

In a bar, maybe, having a drink with someone from his cooking class. Or anywhere, with anyone. Enjoying his independence, as she should be enjoying hers.

She'd have to deal with the mouse on her own.

She got a wire coat hanger and unwound it almost straight. Then she stooped down by the stove, shone the flashlight into the gap and hooked the trap with the hanger. Slowly she dragged it toward her, the mouse a still, round shape like a barrel on a wagon. She crawled backward as she pulled, the end of the wire stuck to the pad. She dragged the gray mouse into the glare of the kitchen light.

The creature was stuck by its hind legs, its tail jerking like a baton. Smaller than she expected and helpless as an infant, yet a hot wave enveloped her and she dropped the hanger and slid back. Part of her wanted to cut it free, though she knew the pad was sticky and the mouse would have to run around with squares glued to its paws if she actually succeeded. Part of her wanted to drop it in the toilet bowl, trap and all, and flush it away. But what if it wouldn't go down and spun around forever at the bottom of her toilet?

She'd have to take it outside. Maybe she could use the wire and something else to tear it free, or maybe it could manage to wriggle off itself.

But the mouse's tail whipped around and slapped down suddenly across the sticky glue pad. Now there was no question of the creature escaping its trap. She lifted up the hanger, and with it the mouse and trap stuck to its far end, and backed across the living room, opening first the apartment door and then the one to outside.

The garbage can was next to the porch, lower than the railing. She took off the lid and dangled the rodent over a full can of trash. With a rap of the hanger against the can, mouse and pad dropped from the wire and landed on top of a plastic bag. The mouse blinked up at her, skinny, tiny, solidly stuck and no longer moving.

She stabbed the hanger into the can, ran inside and scrubbed her hands in the bathroom. She got into bed (a new one with a posturpedic mattress) and stared up at the ceiling. It was like she was underwater again, caught again in her gurgling dream, trying to shake off sticky plants. Sleep was impossible.

She imagined the mouse pulling free—maybe leaving his tail behind and jumping over the side of the can to race back home to his nest. A wounded creature squealing tales of the terrible land of the Cyclops.

But what she actually heard was the pounce and wail of a cat and the rattle of the garbage can behind her bedroom window. Surely the mouse was gone by now or had dropped to the bottom of the can, under heavy bags of trash, where a cat could never find him. Otherwise, at that moment, the mouse was in the cat's mouth and the cat's fur and whiskers were stuck to the gluey pad. Tomorrow or the next day she'd see a neighbor's tabby wearing a white square like a surgeon's mask across its face.

Outside, the yowling stopped and night continued soundlessly. But still Barbara couldn't sleep. Shades of darkness deepened at first, then lightened with the first milky streaks of dawn. A key turned in the front door, and then she heard Elliot tiptoeing upstairs. She slithered down the mattress and lumped the covers over her head.

Finally she swung out of bed, pulled on a bathrobe and a pair of furry slippers. She walked to the basement stairs and hurried down. In the dim light of the cavernous room she picked up the jar and lid, drying on a corner shelf. They were leather-hard, cool to the touch, dark gray and smooth as skulls. She fit the lid into the jar and held the container in her cupped hand. It felt as round and whole as an egg.

She fidgeted with the domed lid, taking it off, putting it on, like when she was little and liked to play with shoe boxes, matchboxes, canning jars and milk bottles, opening and closing. Sometimes she would put her ear against a container and hear the sea; sometimes she would look inside and glimpse dreamy pictures of strange things.

Now she put the lid aside and raised the jar close to her ear. From the belly of the pot came a small, feathery rustling, no more than a breath. When she looked down into it she saw a hat rolling away and saw herself, mouse-size, wheeling in the bowl of the hat.

She saw Elliot at the stove, humming as he stirred something round and round in a stockpot: a pair of feet.

She slammed on the lid—no more of that!—but still she heard him singing. The notes of his cheery song slipped through the walls of the jar and filled the dreary basement.

And in that fearful moment she wanted more than anything to be with him in the jar. To live trapped inside a jar, cramped and swollen, with dead feet, in Elliot's consoling arms.

But Barbara left the lid in place: that wasn't what she wanted at all.

She put the jar on the table and switched on an overhead lamp. The shape of the pot was promising, the lip and curved sides forming one continuous fluid line. The lid was a good fit. Fire it, glaze it, fire it again, and dry clay could transform into something elegant; something vivid and lasting, exuding light. Something you could grow to love.

3

Basic Cooking

A waitress brought more coffee and Elliot waited for it to cool. The restaurant was emptying out, people hurrying back to work, and he half rose at his small table, half-inclined to join them. Not that he actually wanted to put on his dentist's smock and return to work. Not that he wanted to spend his days straining his back as he hunched over the worn enamel and puffy gums of various mouths. It was simply the idea of having to be somewhere at a certain time that seemed so appealing. The freedom of retirement, of not having to do a job or (as in his case) of not checking in with your wife, was more than he'd expected to confront in his fifties.

He stirred his coffee till it was cold, remembering how Barb disapproved of his habits. Maybe she'd meet someone new who drank coffee very hot. Maybe this same gentleman would dress well around the house, never smoke or drink beer with friends she didn't care for; a quiet man with good taste. A man unlike Elliot.

The restaurant was empty now except for a man sitting alone, wearing a gray cardigan buttoned all the way up, just like Elliot's: a mirror image of glumness. Elliot looked away at once, gulped down his coffee and left. He took the long way home, through the park. The day was cool and overcast, but underfoot there were signs of spring: a few bright blades of grass and the jagged leaves of dandelion. Squirrels were frantically digging holes, urgent and witless, and he envied them their busyness. Maybe, despite a bad back and occasional tremor in his hands, he should be drilling teeth and fitting dentures after all, gazing into the shallow caves of people's mouths.

Maybe he should run home, bang on Barb's apartment door and rush in on her, shouting: *This is ridiculous! What are we doing? I love you and you love me, so why are we living separately?*

You want to know why? You want to know why? her voice would echo in the room. *Here's a reason, here's one—you don't respect my privacy! This is my apartment, this is my place, my space. You can't just barge in when you like!* And she would wave him down the hall and lock the door behind him.

Then he would climb to his own rooms, his feet heavy on the stairs, carrying the weight of a wronged man. He *does* respect her privacy. He doesn't press his ear to the floor or track her comings and goings. He doesn't phone her every night to ask nosy questions. Only last week, when he saw her talking outside to a skinny man with a ponytail, a man wearing a raincoat that looked like it had been slept in—did he stand by the window and stare? Did he quiz her later? Lose any sleep? No, no, and just a bit.

But surely no one could hold him accountable for sleeplessness, for dreams that woke him, cold with sweat, at two and four in the morning. He'd try at once to forget them but knew by his thrashing and the awful tension in his groin that he was dreaming about sex. Most times, the

57

woman was Barb. Most times the man was a stranger, humped between his wife's legs while Elliot looked on with a pulsing, helpless hard-on.

But how could a man like that, a hungry-looking stranger with a ponytail and ruined coat, be any good in bed? Barb needed someone strong, sensitive and caring: no one knew better than he did. He knew the message of her hips, that uncontrollable circling, and the deep growling in her throat; he knew what every sound meant. More of this, more of that, gentler, harder, faster, slow. . . . It's true they haven't actually made love in several months now, and the last time, as he recalls, was too quick and matter-of-fact, like scratching an itch. But after so many years together, what'd she expect? A tour de force every time? The fire and zip of a wiry stranger half his age?

No, he wouldn't go home yet. He wouldn't think about his wife.

He turned onto a dirt path and headed toward the playground and the cry of children's voices. At this time of day only preschoolers and day-care workers circled the swings and dug like squirrels in the sandbox. The children called and shouted, announcing themselves in the general din. He sat down on an empty bench on a tramped-on muddy hill overlooking the playground and imagined he was part of this, the whistle-blowing uproar, the howling and bleating hullabaloo, the shoving, running and tumbling that overpowered all thoughts, and felt suddenly lighter.

Before she entered his line of vision, Elliot was aware of a woman standing behind him, a presence he experienced as tingling in his upper thighs. He jerked his head around and she was right there, over his shoulder, her red hair bolder than a stop sign. Mary. Ellen. Whelan. The name came to him slowly, as if drawn from hidden files.

"What are you doing here?" he said, and she answered

with a blinding grin. Maryellen Whelan had a perfect set of chompers, square and white and evenly spaced, which could leave a man of his profession—a man of his former profession—breathless and embarrassed and, well, yes . . . tingling.

"I took the afternoon off." She sat down next to him, opened a paper bag on her lap and jabbed her hand inside. "Chicken salad or tuna?" she asked. "I brought two." As if this meeting had been planned. As if she'd expected to find him here on a cloudy weekday afternoon, watching children in the park.

"Thanks, but I've had lunch."

"Oh well. What a shame." She peeled off plastic wrap and ate a corner of chicken or tuna on whole wheat. "I hope you're not disappointed that I'm not eating salmon mousse or caviar or something like that. My students expect me to have exotic tastes"—she showed her teeth again—"but really I'm a meat-and-potatoes girl at heart. Low-fat meat loaf with pimento and fresh herbs and garlic mashed potatoes, that is."

Both of which they made during the course of "Basic Cooking for Men" in Maryellen's big kitchen, as well as other tasty delights: beef stew, ratatouille, omelets and chicken soup. Elliot had thought of himself as her best and favorite pupil. She liked his wrist action when he whipped cream or beat an egg as much as she admired the way he diced onions and minced herbs, and twice a week she praised him for his pressed shirts and polished shoes. Indeed, he dressed well for class, though at home he wore his usual baggy track pants torn at the knees that Barb had always hated. The other men in cooking class— two single, two divorced and one a recent widower— wore dirty sneakers and wrinkled shirts with buttons missing and yellow stains. He didn't want to look like them, shabby in their solitude.

Her thigh was close to his on the bench but not touching, certainly not, and yet his leg felt hot. When she rummaged in her bag again, retrieving a juice box, he slid an inch or two away.

She sipped juice through a tiny straw and her lips puckered and darkened in color, purple-red. In class he had been transfixed, not by her voice or by what she was saying ("Hold the egg in one hand and rap it sharply against the rim"), but by her lips and gleaming teeth: the amazing symmetry of her mouth. Now his eyes were throbbing and he turned away from Maryellen to stare down at the playground. Sorted into a long line, the children rolled out of the field one behind the other, like beads pulled along on a string.

"So how did you like the course?" she asked. "You never said."

"I liked it a lot. I was sorry when it ended."

"What have you been cooking lately?"

"Fresh tomato and basil sauce, chicken with lemon and tarragon, sautéed beef and ginger—"

"All for you?"

"Well, yes. You remember about my wife. . . ." By way of introduction he'd told the class that first night that he and Barb divided their home and lived in two apartments, he above and she below. Then their instructor let it be known that she and her husband called it quits four years earlier and, sad to tell, she's been cooking solo ever since.

"Of course I remember about your wife. I was just wondering." Her face flushed slightly, which made her freckles stand out.

Wondering what? Elliot thought. Were he and Barb together again or had they finally split for good? Was there someone else in the picture?

"Anyway, I'm glad to hear you're making such delightful things. People shouldn't deny themselves the pleasure of good food just because they're cooking for one."

Maryellen dropped the empty juice box back in her bag and pulled out the other sandwich. She unwrapped it slowly and closed her wonderful lips and teeth over the dark bread. "I have an enormous appetite," she said while chewing, "which is probably why I got interested in cooking in the first place." Her smooth, pink neck jumped a little when she swallowed. "But I'm always worried about my weight."

Early forties, Elliot had guessed the night of their first class. Forty-two, forty-three. Red-haired and shorter than Barb, but like her, round and soft, big-breasted, fair-skinned, curious and friendly. A younger, rosy, freckled version of his wife. So why would she be interested in a fifty-two-year-old retired dentist on a park bench? Wasn't she just killing time? What could be more natural than to shoot the breeze with an ex-student?

"I know what you mean," Elliot said. "Every time I think about dessert, I put on another pound."

"I don't believe it—look at you! Straight and solid as a tree."

"I exercise regularly."

"You must be a jogger."

"Tai Chi."

"Tai Chi! I should've known. You must be very good at it."

"I've only just started."

"Why don't you show me something? Maybe I can follow along. I've always wanted to learn Tai Chi, it's so beautiful."

"Right here?"

"Down there." She pointed to where the hill flattened alongside the playground.

"I don't like practicing outside. I don't want people

staring at me." In fact, the playground was empty now, covered by a ceiling of clouds. The air was heavy, gray and still. He could do some of the form in the field and no one but Maryellen Whelan would see his movements.

Her answer surprised him. "Then let's go indoors," she said. "It looks like rain anyway."

Her freckles were bold on her pink face; she seemed as sweet and guileless as a milkmaid. His legs stiffened, tingling again. He hesitated, then blurted out, "My apartment, your apartment—whatever. Who cares? It doesn't really matter, does it? Here, there, anywhere."

"Then let's go to your place"—her teeth winking at him again. "I'd love to see your kitchen."

"I'll make some cookies, chocolate chip." He was panting like a schoolboy and willed himself to slow down: talk slowly, think slowly, don't jump to conclusions. Haven't you learned anything in thirty-five years of manhood?

Maryellen Whelan said, "I'm wild about chocolate, though I rarely indulge," her voice breathy but urgent, too, with something he thought he recognized. Under the casual cheeriness. Loneliness? The need to be held?

His limbs were wooden when he stood and he tripped on a leg of the bench. Maryellen touched his arm a moment to steady him; her hand burned through his sweater. "Fine, I'm fine," he laughed shortly, brushing off her fingers. But still he felt the pressure of five hot-spots on his arm.

She dropped her crumpled paper bag in a wastebasket over the hill, then they walked in silence to the park gate. Maybe he'd got this all wrong. Tai Chi, cookies and milk, then she'd wave and run along, never to cross his path again. Maryellen Whelan had the afternoon off, that's all, and wanted a bit of innocent fun. He'd have to be careful not to say or do anything foolish.

For godssake! Barb would say. *Live for the moment, be spontaneous. You're always scheming and worrying. No wonder we never had fun.*

They paused by an island of tulips just outside the park gates. The leaves of the flowers were dark and straight, their green buds hard and full, about to open but still shut. "They're almost ready," Maryellen said in a whisper.

They crossed a two-lane highway that ran like a frame around the park, then turned onto a treed street of three-story houses with interesting architectural points: gables, dormers, turrets, pillars and wraparound porches. Elliot had been here before on solitary evening walks, subdued by the grandeur of these homes, but now he felt excited, as if he'd suddenly found himself on the set of a movie.

Several blocks farther along, his own home was not so grand. Neither as wide nor quite so tall, with a small, simple wooden porch and a balcony flush on top of it, jutting from his living-room window on the second floor. The roof needed reshingling, the front lawn was bare in spots, and the porch rails were rotting where the paint had cracked and chipped off. But Maryellen Whelan said, "Oh, what a charming house."

He slipped his key in the front lock and turned it with a soft click. Slowly he pushed the door open, motioned for her to go inside, then led her into the hall and upstairs to his apartment. He was tiptoeing, holding his breath, and so was she. Elliot was grateful that his guest was wearing sneakers and didn't say a word till they were safely behind his apartment door, acting as if she remembered the fact that Barb lived on the main floor. She seemed to understand that his recently estranged wife didn't need to know he was bringing his instructor home for the afternoon.

She popped into two rooms on either side of the corridor behind his apartment door. Formerly bedrooms, one was his parlor now and one just a storage room crammed with books, boxes of clothes, assorted tools and doodads he'd never unpacked. She narrowed her eyes at the jumble. "What are you going to do with this?" But Elliot hadn't thought that far ahead yet and only shrugged.

The hallway ended at his kitchen, another converted bedroom, but this one was newly equipped with energy-saving appliances and no-wax floor tiles. Maryellen looked around, grinning at the L-shaped counters and Scandinavian cabinets, her teeth flashing approval. She lifted the lid of a pot on the stove and discovered split green peas soaking in water. The gesture made him squirm, as if she had tugged at his waistband and peered down his pants. "Pea soup?" She turned and caught Elliot's eye. "I adore pea soup. It's so nutritious and hearty"—her breath expelled on the last word, a warm gust that blew into his ears, mouth and nostrils. He heard and smelled, could almost taste her: salty, sweet and a bit fishy.

He backed into a cabinet and fumbled for a mixing bowl. "The cookies," he said. "Remember? Turn the oven to three-seventy-five and let's get started. You don't want to eat them too late and ruin your supper." Immediately he hated himself for his false words and prissy tone; for not inviting her to dinner. She'd think he was an idiot. Or worse, she'd think the awful truth: it had been so long since he'd been alone with a strange woman, he didn't know how to act anymore.

But Maryellen only laughed and played with the oven dial, then stuck her head inside his fridge. "Here's the butter, a dozen eggs . . . here's a bag of semi-sweet. You get the sugar and flour. We really shouldn't be doing this, you know, it's so unhealthy. All that sugar and fat—and the calories! I can't resist."

He plucked a wooden spoon from a rack, then neatly arranged measuring cups, bags of sugar and flour and a mixing bowl on the table in the same practical order he'd learned in her course. Maryellen took the spoon and creamed butter and sugar with a few sure, swift strokes. Elliot watched glassy-eyed, his pulse ringing in his ears. In class he'd hardly noticed her hands; they were no more interesting than the ladles, scoops and spatulas she held at various moments. But now they hypnotized him. He imagined her fingers on his skin, the certain and seductive pressure here, there . . . and there, too.

She cracked an egg on the edge of the bowl and it slid down yellow and thick, leaving a gluey, shimmering trail. She beat it into the butter-ball, stirred in a splash of vanilla and whipped the whole mixture smooth. A nod from Maryellen and he threw in a cup of flour, baking soda, pinch of salt. She passed him the wooden spoon, the handle warm and sticky-damp, and his fingers twitched when he grasped it, as if he'd been shocked. He concentrated on stirring, stirring . . . churning dry ingredients into a wet, rubbery mound.

She tossed in chocolate chips casually, one at a time, popping every fifth or sixth one of them into her own mouth. Then she paused, her face florid, and gazed down at her cupped palm: chocolate chips stared back like moist eyes. Slowly she lifted a single chip; slowly, slowly she turned to him and slid it between his lips, her fingers prying open his mouth and slipping over the fence of his teeth. He grabbed hold of the mixing bowl, his ankles melting into his shoes. Semi-sweet chocolate oozed hot and honeyed under his tongue.

She sprinkled the rest of the chocolate chips over the batter and they winked at him like dark stars in a milky sky. He stared to the point of dizziness. Suddenly she took the spoon, whipped the chips out of sight and began dropping blobs of batter onto a cookie sheet. Minutes later the bowl was clean, the cookies lined up in rows and baking in the hot oven.

Maryellen ran her index finger around the bowl, collecting batter on the tip, then held it in front of his eyes; her finger crooked and nodding. The tip of her pink tongue showed between her lips. Ba-boom, ba-boom, his heart urged. *This is the moment! This is it!*

But his feet were soldered to the floor. With a huge tug he pulled free and dove across the kitchen toward a small gadget on a shelf. "The timer," he said. "We almost forgot. We have to set the timer." He twisted the dial to ten minutes and leaned against a cabinet, breathing hard. The timer clicked the seconds off, low and hypnotic.

Across the room, Maryellen Whelan stood humming at the kitchen sink. She was bent over, washing the bowl, the wooden spoon and other things in a pool of soapy water. Finally she wiped her hands on the back of her jeans and turned around, her freckles black as ink spots. "You were going to show me some Tai Chi. Wouldn't this be a good time, while the cookies are baking?"

Yes, do it—Tai Chi! Mesmerizing movements no woman can resist.

He stepped to the center of the room, half closed his staring eyes, lifted and lowered his hands. Maryellen clapped as he bent his knees slightly and extended his left leg, turned his ankle, bowed forward, swung right. "Don't stop," she said as he paused to draw his hands to his chest. "That's it," she called as he moved through Play Guitar. "Yes, yes, yes!" as he curled his fingers and flexed his wrist for Grasp Bird's Tail. She was making him nervous. He spread his arms for Single Whip, but then, as he leaned left and thrust out his right heel, Elliot lost his balance. For one breathless, endless second he hung suspended in the air, neither falling nor upright. Then, like a pyramid of cans hit by a shopping cart, he fell in a noisy heap.

"Oh my God, are you okay?" Maryellen gripped him by the elbow and helped him up. "You went down pretty hard. Did you break anything? Are you bleeding? You didn't hit your head, did you? It happened so fast I couldn't tell."

She looked him over head to toe, then touched his skull here and there, her fingers firm and practiced: the steady, sturdy hands of a nurse, a mother, a skilled chef. "Does this hurt? Am I hurting you? I don't see anything serious," her voice concerned but slightly remote, as if she'd backed away and was speaking from a distance. Any chance of intimacy was gone now, he understood.

"I'm all right, really," he said. "Just a little embarrassed."

The timer pinged and Elliot took the cookies out. He offered to make coffee but she said, "Never touch the stuff," and asked for tea. So he made a pot of Earl Grey and served tea in hand-painted china cups and saucers (four of which were his now, four were Barb's). He scraped cookies off the sheet and put them on a platter in the center of the kitchen table, avoiding Maryellen's eyes.

He broke off a piece of cookie and pushed it through the slot of his mouth. It tasted metallic, like a coin. He washed it down with a gulp of tea, feeling her eyes on his face and hands. Was she seeing him old and clumsy? Did she think him a pathetic fool? His shoulders dropped forward under the weight of her gaze.

She finished her tea and ate a cookie. "Well," said Maryellen Whelan, "time for me to run along. Thanks for the snack." She scraped back her chair and stood up.

Elliot followed her out the kitchen and down the narrow hallway. Now that she was actually going, his back straightened up and his breathing became regular. She opened his apartment door and hurried down the steps with an elephant's galumphing gait. He waited, wincing, at the top of the stairs. How was it possible for a short woman in sneakers to make such a thunderous sound? Already he was wondering what he was going to tell Barb.

Which noise? *That* noise? Oh, right—the pizza man. Parcel post. Computer repairs. Nobody. No one at all.

She called up, "Thanks again! That was fun!" and the front door trembled when she banged it shut behind her. From downstairs he heard the clack of another door closing. He sat down heavily on the top step. Interviewed by a census taker? A short conversation with a woman collecting for Greenpeace? Tea and cookies with what's-her-name, my former cooking instructor? Barb wouldn't believe him whether he lied to her or told the truth.

Nothing happened! he'd insist.

Elliot, what do you take me for?

Suddenly he heard a crash from downstairs. The basement. Crack, thump, ping and rattle: the shattering of pottery. Something thrown and broken; something thrown again. Then he heard her climbing stairs. A door opened and slammed shut. Sound traveled easily in an old house, divided or not.

The TV was playing now, the volume impossibly loud. The walls in the hall shook with canned laughter and jingles. He got up, drew back and closed his apartment door. But still he heard the television buzzing like a chain saw. He retreated to his bedroom-study on the top floor, where street noises dominated all else, and listened to the beeping of trucks, the rumble of streetcars and the drone of a highway. People working, on the go: a distant, energetic world.

Quickly Elliot undressed and lay down on his double bed—*their* bed, their marriage bed, that sagged with years of history. The sheets were wrinkled and smelled stale. When was the last time they were washed? His quilt was hanging over the side, more on the floor than on the bed. Barb would be horrified by his unabashed sloppiness, but what, after all, was the value of a tautly made bed in the scheme of things? Would clean sheets and a smooth blanket make him any happier? They would only remind him of his wife, of domestic serenity and the busyness of daily life; of what he has lost.

He rolled under the rumpled sheets and closed his eyes. What took shape in the darkness was a figure who was not his wife nor Maryellen Whelan, but a wild-haired woman in a flowing, filmy nightgown that a man was lifting over her head. A pulse throbbed between his legs.

He heard an unexpected sound—something moving downstairs. Elliot's eyelids rolled up like jerked-open window shades. He hadn't locked the front door or the one to his apartment. Anyone could've walked in. Someone up to no good.

One flight down the floorboards creaked and something grated—table? chair? Small, clumsy noises growing louder and more distinct: the pattering of quick steps; the squeak of a stair. Someone had entered and crossed his apartment and was standing at the bottom of the steps to the third floor. He sat up, gaping.

Barb emerged from the stairwell and walked to the end of his bed. She was barefoot and bare-legged, wearing only a long-tailed shirt the color of her skin; her hair loose and tangled. Slowly, slowly, she opened her shirt and stepped forward, watching him. He lay back, helpless.

Later he would not remember how she moved from the foot of the bed to kneel over his body. Perhaps she floated, he would think. He would not recall if they kissed first, if he spoke her name, cupped her breasts or stroked her thick, smooth thighs. But he knew she hadn't touched him. She hadn't uttered one word. Her eyes were black seeds as she sat on him, squeezing him, and moved roughly, violently, as she had never moved before.

It was over too soon, in a roaring, furious spasm. She growled and shouted, Elliot groaned. Then she released him and swung off. She swung away from his wet flesh

69

and passed silently over the floor, trailing her shirt behind her. She vanished into the stairwell as abruptly as she'd appeared.

In the end he couldn't be sure whether or not he had dreamed this. Had someone really entered the room and climbed into Elliot's bed? Whose fury had he felt—wave upon wave of deepening rage? Barb's or his own feelings pulled to the surface? Desire, regret, ferocity and sputtering grief.

He kicked the blanket off his bed, then stripped the sheets and threw them aside. He pulled clean sheets from a drawer and spread them over the mattress, tucking them smartly under the edges, making perfectly tight corners. Then he shook his quilt out and lay it smoothly over the sheets. He sat down at the end of his bed and stared at the place on the floor where his wife had stood in her skin-colored shirt, her feet bare.

The spot blackened before his eyes. Stretching like a shadow, it climbed from his toes to his knees and thighs, fingers, wrists and abdomen. It pushed hard on his ribs, leaving dark prints. Finally it entered his chest and stopped there, widening, a hand on his heart. A hand that ticked with its own pulse, beating in time with Elliot's. A life squeezed against his own, hot and shivering, holding fast.

4

STILL LIFE with Candles

Susan happened to mention that his birthday was in seven days, and if she hadn't mentioned it, he never would have brought it up. Why admit that he was getting older and his life was a mess?

Susan asked if Barb was doing anything for his birthday and he said no, probably not, because she would've phoned by now to book a free evening if she was planning to cook dinner and take him to a movie or just have the kids over for presents and cake. That's the way they did things now: they phoned each other in advance and checked their respective date books. This had something to do with not taking each other for granted, Barb had informed him. They'd been living apart nearly a year, time enough for both of them to develop an active social life. Barb didn't expect him to be available whenever she rang, and Elliot knew better than to tell her he was. If she had called to ask if he was free the night of his birthday, he would have taken a long minute to check his empty appointment book and then say reluctantly, "I think that can be arranged." But so far she hadn't called. And now that Susan had mentioned it, he was contemplating the day with dread. Who wanted to be alone on his birthday, of all days?

"Mom should've got us all together, at least," Susan said. "I don't know what's happened to her. You're still married, after all."

The receiver felt hot in his hand and Elliot wanted to hang up. He said, "It's only a birthday. She's got other things on her mind now."

"You're always making excuses for her. You don't have to do that anymore." Susan breathed heavily, her breath sounding like a storm gathering force in the phone wire. "If she won't do it, I will. Come for dinner Saturday. We'll have a cake and candles."

She didn't ask if he was free. Maybe she knew he had nothing important to do for the rest of his life.

Nothing at all was written in his date book for the next six days. If Barb had called, he would've been free Sunday to Friday—but not on his birthday. In the square under "Saturday, February 22," Elliot had printed in caps, DINNER AT SUSAN'S, filling the space top to bottom and side to side with his writing. There was a time when his daily agenda wasn't thin and pocket-sized but as tall and weighty as a coffee-table art book. It lay on his assistant's desk and was filled with dental appointments from early morning to evening. Only the slot for lunch was blank, and not very often. Two or three times a week he met other dentists for lunch, some who worked in the building and some who worked nearby. Like him, a few had since retired, worn out by the business—the spectacle of pleading patients squirming in their paper bibs ("Don't hurt me!" "Please stop!"); the strain in your back and shoulders. One colleague died of a heart attack at forty-nine, another was a suicide. The rest were still practicing and hadn't been in touch with him. Of course he could easily phone them, but never got around to it. What would they talk about nowadays? Mercury poisoning? Implants? He'd stopped reading trade mags and wasn't up on the latest news. Nor could they talk about car loans, mortgages and RSPs: that was all behind him now; he'd outgrown those subjects. Starting over meant more than writing new names in your pocket-sized agenda. It meant finding new words and new things to talk about. A new way of speaking.

On the morning of his birthday Elliot woke early and practiced scales on his saxophone in his third-story bedroom. Vaguely he was aware of the fact that he might be disturbing Barb, who might still be sleeping in her ground-floor bedroom (once a cozy parlor where they all watched TV or the children played board games), but he shook the notion out of his head. Why shouldn't he announce the morning of his birthday with a fanfare of notes? By right, she ought to be up now anyway, wrapping his present and baking a cake.

He played for twenty minutes, blowing as hard as he could. Then he went down to the kitchen, turned on the radio and had his usual breakfast of cold coffee and cereal, staring out the window at the wet-looking branches of the apple tree in the backyard. There was sunlight on the frosted boughs—first sun he'd seen in days—but the sky was clouding over. From the radio a broadcaster promised freezing temperatures and more snow: an all-round dismal day.

The radiator hissed and clicked, but the room was cold. The whole damn apartment was cold. He should check the rads . . . but not today. So okay, now what? He drummed a spoon against the table, tapped out a tune on his bowl, then sang a line out loud: "Oh, what a beautiful morning. . . ." Ha-ha, anything but! He swept the spoon off the table—and almost, but didn't quite, shot the bowl across the room. His eyes burned and he squeezed them shut. A whole day to fill and already he was too wired to bleed the rads, cook lunch, practice Tai Chi or return to his sax. He shouldn't be indoors today, sitting around wasting time—but what then? What should he do?

Go downstairs, that's what. Pound on Barb's door and say, *Look what you did to me, look how I'm spending my birthday! You went and spoiled everything!*

But he didn't knock on his wife's door. He put on his boots and down jacket and warm mittens Barb had knitted two or three winters ago, and went out shopping. It started to snow. The streets were crusty with old snow and slippery with new flakes; store windows were steamy. He pulled up his collar against the wind, hunched his shoulders and ducked his head. "Wear a hat, it's freezing out," Barb used to nag him, but he never paid attention. Now he was missing both the hat and the sharp pleading of her voice.

He bought a plant to take to Susan's, an odd thing with blue flowers and long, thick, ribbed leaves that seemed a better present for his wife than his daughter. Barb had a way with plants, while Susan overwatered them or neglected them entirely until they shriveled and turned black. (With him they merely existed, neither dying nor thriving.) But he was sure his daughter would appreciate his thoughtfulness. Who would expect the birthday boy to bring a gift to his own party?

Then he stopped at the supermarket for English muffins, cream cheese and a can of franks and beans for lunch. If Barb knew she'd scoff at that—*a man who makes polenta and pesto, eating canned beans!*—but Barb would never find out and he could eat whatever he liked, there was no one to tell him otherwise.

He went into a greasy spoon and sat down on a rickety stool, putting his plant on the counter and his bag of groceries at his feet. He'd been here several times before and the waitress knew him well enough to bring him coffee before he asked and two slices of rye toast. Everyone called her Gracie, which wasn't her real name, she claimed, but how you said it in English. A young, recent immigrant, busty and copper-haired, she never revealed her true name, at least not to Elliot. On her breaks she could be seen in the glassed-in foyer, dragging on a cigarette and gazing out the front door. Maybe she was seeing what she'd left behind in her native land.

She knew he liked his toast hot and unbuttered, his coffee cold, and always brought his cup with a spoon in it to draw the heat. Sometimes she would stir the coffee to cool it before putting it down, and the sound of metal tapping the cup and her plump fingers on the spoon would cause a gurgling in his chest. It wouldn't be hard to love a girl who took pains to bring your coffee to a suitable temperature. Today he wanted to talk to her, to tell her it was his birthday—*can you believe it, fifty-three!*—and maybe she'd say he didn't look a day over forty, then grin enthusiastically. He wondered what kind of teeth she had. Strong and even, he imagined. Milk-white.

But the restaurant was crowded this morning. Gracie didn't have time to chat or show her teeth. She served him buttered whole wheat instead of unbuttered rye and he had to stir his coffee himself. He drank the coffee and left the toast, dropped some coins on the counter, scooped up his parcels and rushed out. On his way home he bought a paper and hugged it under his elbow. Wind fluttered the pages and snow licked his bare wrist like a cold tongue. The plant, held close to his chest, pressed against his ribs like a lover's head.

Back in his apartment the red light on his answering machine was blinking on and off and he felt a surge of optimism. Someone wanted to speak to him! He played back the message. It was Dennis calling, Dennis saying, "Hi, Dad. Happy birthday. We got a little something for you. Is it okay if we drop it off tomorrow around noon?"

If only his son were coming now. If only he'd thought to change his plans and bring his dad a present on the right day. Elliot erased the message, pressing down on the buttons as if he were squashing fleas. Dennis had always been closer to Barb. He'd never be this casual about his mother's birthday.

Not much happened after that. A day like any other. Elliot scanned the *Globe and Mail*, reading parts aloud to the cat, listened to Schubert, smoked his pipe, shined his shoes and ironed a shirt. He skimmed another chapter of a fat book on mutual funds, then watched an all-news channel. Nothing much was happening in the world either.

Barb went out after lunch, slamming the front door shut against the wind and bullets of snow. He ran to the window and looked out, catching her as she turned from their house onto the sidewalk. A scarf tied around her neck covered her hair and ears, too, and over that she'd pulled a hat. She was wearing brown boots and the ankle-length coat he admired that widened at the base like a bell. All afternoon he half listened but didn't hear her come in again.

The sun was going down at last and snow was smacking the windowpanes when Elliot finally dressed for dinner. Susan had asked him to come at eight, but what did it matter if he arrived a little early? He'd blame it on the weather and say he wanted to get there before conditions worsened and the roads became impossible. How could she object to that?

Thirty minutes later when he rang Susan's buzzer she was not pleased to hear his voice. "You're early!" she whined through the intercom. "I just got in."

When he reached the eighth floor and she opened her apartment door she was dressed in her work clothes: white shirt, gray pants and a dark green jacket. "Nothing's ready." She let him in. "I had to go to the office today. There's a special project I'm working on—the deadline is Tuesday. Mattie stayed with a friend and I worked all morning and afternoon, so now I'm running a bit late . . . but of course I wasn't expecting you this soon."

"The roads were getting so bad I decided to leave right away, just as a precaution."

She pursed her lips, then glanced at the plant in his arms—"What's that?"—and Elliot said, "A little something I brought you." He read the tag attached to a stem. "It's called streptocarpus."

"Streptococcus?"

"*Carpus.*"

He passed her the plant and she held it away from her body. "I hope I don't catch anything."

"The thought counts, doesn't it?"

"Sure it does. I was joking." She gave him a one-armed hug and put the plant on a low table facing a northern window, where it probably wouldn't get enough light. She took his shoes and hung up his coat. Then he followed her into the kitchen and sat down on a wrought-iron chair that seemed too slight to hold him. Lightly he rested his arms on her glass kitchen table. The walls were covered with floral paper, a bold red-and-green design that made him feel like a lost boy in a field of giant poppies.

There was nothing on the stove, he noticed, and no smells from the oven. Susan made no motion to get dinner underway. The total lack of preparation set his stomach growling, a fierce and audible sound. "You're hungry," she said, and he admitted that yes, he was. Starving.

"Let's have some wine first." She pulled a bottle from a bag under the table, opened it with one of those silly corkscrews with handles and poured them each a glass of Chablis. He was hoping for chips and salsa but none appeared. "Happy birthday"—she lifted her glass. He drank his wine quickly and it splashed loudly in his gut.

"Supper won't be long now." She looked in the fridge and removed something oblong in a foil tray, something green in a sealed bag and a slim white bottle. One went into the microwave, one was emptied into a bowl, and the bottle, shaken and opened, was tipped over the salad. "We can eat in a few minutes, as soon as the lasagna's hot."

His stomach sank and grew still, as if it had been bludgeoned. This is what he'd waited for, looked forward to, all day? A store-bought frozen dinner heated in a microwave? Why did she have to go to work on Saturday, for godssake? Someone else could've done the job. Why didn't she stay home and start in shopping and cooking right after breakfast? Wasn't anyone going to fix him a decent meal on his birthday?

Then Mattie entered the room, wearing a pink party dress and shiny, tiny-heeled shoes, her lips painted purple. "Happy birthday, Grandpa!" She fluttered blackened lashes. He opened his arms, grateful, and she clattered across the kitchen tiles and hopped onto Elliot's lap. "You look so grown-up," he said.

"I *am* grown-up." She dug her face into his shoulder. He stroked her brown ponytail, tied with a red-and-white band striped like a candy cane.

Susan took her jacket off and hung it on the back of her chair. When she sat down the padded seat gave out an exhausted sigh. She rolled up her shirtsleeves and put her left elbow on the edge of the table. Her eyes unfocused as she scratched her thin forearm with the long, bony fingers of her other hand. "Too grown-up for that," she muttered under her breath.

Mattie giggled and Elliot shrugged: neither was sure what Susan meant but each felt embarrassed. He looked past his granddaughter, staring at the blotch of skin above Susan's elbow, and remembered the scab that was once there when she was about Mattie's age, picked at and reformed, until at last it was thin and glossy, yellow-brown, like a dried leaf pressed between the pages of a thick book. His gaze rose to Susan's face, to a smear of lipstick on her mouth, and of course he remembered the blood too, running bright and leisurely from her picked scabs. Susan watching open-mouthed, unblinking and motionless as he dabbed up the lost blood. She was transfixed by the wet, red proof of her existence.

Several annoying beeps. Susan leaped across the room and turned off the microwave. Her thoughts were colliding and her tongue was pressed against her teeth, but she didn't know what she wanted to say. From the corner of her eye she watched her daughter curled in Elliot's lap, like a baby at a mother's breast. She looked so small and peaceful. "Get up, Matilda," Susan said, "and help set the table," her voice sounding wistful and sharp.

Mattie scrambled out of his lap and latched on to her mother's waist, but Susan pushed her back, saying, "Not now. It's time to eat."

The lasagna was cold in the center but he didn't complain. The salad was soggy, overdressed, and later his coffee was too hot. Nevertheless, Elliot kept his eyes wide, his mouth upturned, and had seconds of everything. When Susan asked trying questions, he answered politely: yes, he was finding things to do; no, he wasn't miserable. "Good days and bad days," he said, "just like everyone else."

"How's the apartment?"

"Coming along. Still some unpacking to do, but I hung pictures, bought a rug, and the kitchen's finally done. You should stop by and see for yourself."

Not likely, Susan thought. Maybe it wasn't right, but she didn't like seeing him while Mom was living downstairs. The last time she'd felt strange, neither with him nor her, but squeezed into a corner, alone. Why could she only have her mother or her father when she wanted both at the same time? "Oh, we will, we will," she said, "but not yet, not for a while. When Mattie calms down a bit. She's been so jumpy lately I can't take her anywhere."

Mattie paused as she circled the table, knives and forks bunched in her hands. I am *not* jumpy, she thought. Then she finished setting the table, forks on the left, knives on the right, blades turned toward the plates. "She doesn't look jumpy to me," Grandpa said, and she wanted to climb back on his lap and kiss his old man's cheek.

"Her father's getting married again."

"Dan's getting married again?"

"And he wants her to be in the wedding party but doesn't know what to do with her—too old for a flower girl and too young for a bridesmaid. So one day she's trying on a crinoline and Mary Janes, the next day it's satin and pumps. We'll both feel better when the whole thing is over." Susan's voice crackled like an unreliable radio and the sudden tightness in her head made her eyes water. This then—Dan's marriage—was what she meant to talk about. She scratched her left arm until it showed a graph of red lines, then abruptly rolled down her sleeves.

Why wouldn't he marry again, Elliot was thinking, a young, attractive man with a good job in software? He looked away from his daughter's arms, planted on the table like signposts. What was he supposed to say—*don't worry, don't cry, everything'll work out*? But today he didn't believe that. Not for Susan, not for himself. Because they'd picked the wrong people to spend their married lives with, or maybe because they were wrong themselves in some unexplainable way. He pulled his chair next to Mattie's, cupped a hand on the back of her neck, tipped her head and spoke in her ear. "Come visit me anyway. I don't care if you're jumpy or not."

All of a sudden Susan was cold. She reached for her wool jacket, tugging it off the back of her chair, and draped it over her shoulders. Goose bumps rose on her flesh and she felt too small in her clothes, remembering long ago and the slippery pool of her father's lap, the heat of his enormous arms. Or maybe it was her mother's lap, her mother's breast she fell against; her mother's hands that brushed her away as she spoke the words Susan had said to her own child: *You're too old for that now.* Or was it her father who said that, firmly pushing her off his knee and telling her to be like Dennis, who didn't bother them all the time? Whose lap did she run to next and the next time after that, Barbara's or Elliot's? It seemed she'd spent her whole childhood being passed from arm to arm, swung from one knee to another, picked up or shoved off, no matter what she wanted. Dashing from one to the other parent, clawing for affection, even when their faces told her *not now, go away,* until she hated both of them and would go to her room, slam the door and talk to her Raggedy Ann. They said she enjoyed solitude, but what she enjoyed was certainty: her dolly never pulled away; her dolly loved her without fail.

Elliot glanced at his daughter. "I'm building Mattie a dollhouse, a geodesic dome made of popsicle sticks and paper. Something for her to play with when she comes for a visit." Once he had started a dollhouse for Susan, but didn't have time to get it done. Now he had all the time in the world.

Susan stabbed her arms into the sleeves of her jacket. Nothing better to do with his time than play with glue and popsicle sticks—and he wouldn't even finish it! Like the one he'd been making for her when she was younger than Mattie, carefully nailing strips of wood until he lost interest and it sat on his workbench, a foot high and roofless, like some abandoned bird's nest, and she refused to play with it. Someday soon Mattie will ask when she can see her dollhouse and he'll look down at his unmatched socks and say he doesn't have the time but maybe her mother can finish it. Mattie will flinch and pull back, and Susan will know exactly the sour feeling in her heart.

"She's too old for dollhouses."

"Sometimes children like to be young."

"I'm not too old—I'm just eleven!"

And still wants a dollhouse. Only a year older than that and Susan wanted nothing more than to be on her own, grown-up. To get away from both of them, the parents who could fill her to bursting with a breath of love, then turn their attention elsewhere and make her shrivel and disappear. She wanted to be tough like Gran and wound up being more like her than she could've imagined: a single mom with a young daughter, struggling to make a go of it.

"There's cake," said Susan. "Chocolate mocha. Mattie, get the candles."

The cake was in a fancy box tied with white-and-gold ribbon, which Elliot thought promising. Susan put the cake on a dish and Mattie poked small blue candles into the icing. "We'll keep it simple," Susan said. "Forget the fifty and go with three."

"And one for good luck," said Mattie.

"Absolutely," Elliot said. "Everyone needs a little luck."

"My dad's gonna have a giant cake with green leaves and twelve layers and a plastic bride and groom on top.

There's gonna be so many people there the cake might be too small!"

Susan sighed. "She's very young, this woman Dan's marrying. I didn't think it would bother me—I mean, I'm not even thirty myself—but it does, it's like he's thumbing his nose. And I don't think she's too bright, she's majoring in *cinema*. But who cares if you're smart if you're built like a movie star?"

Susan pulled a lighter from an inside pocket and lit the candles. "You can't blow them out till you make a wish," Mattie said, and Elliot closed his eyes at once. I wish for love, he thought simply. That she, Barb—still my wife—hasn't stopped loving me.

Susan's eyes were shut too. She was picturing Dan's fiancée as Mattie had described her: hair short as a cat's and as orange as a pumpkin; an earring in her nose and another through her eyebrow, several in her earlobes and one in her lip. And where else? Susan wondered. Through her nipples? Through her navel? *Where else, for godssake!* Her eyes cracked open and she stared at the flaming candles: I wish he still loved me.

Mattie watched her mother's face, cranberry-color, and her eyes burning angry-sad. Even with her face red and her eyes like that she was still young and beautiful. The bride-to-be was pretty too and even younger than Mommy, but Mattie would never love *her*. She promised herself, no matter what, she'd only love her real mom— love her as hard as she could—even if her mother didn't love her back the same way. Because if Mattie didn't love her, who would?

Elliot blew out the candles and Mattie clapped. "I bet I know what you wished," she said. "I bet you wished Grandma was here."

"No, no," he forced a laugh. "I wished today was *your* birthday, that you were getting older instead of me."

Susan plucked the candles and leaned over to cut the cake. She felt a moment of dizziness and imagined herself plopping into a fat pillow of mocha, but then regained her balance. "For the record, it wasn't me who wanted Dan to leave," she said. "It was his idea all along." She slipped off her jacket and handed out pieces of cake. Then she pushed up her sleeves again and started rubbing both arms, her fingers sliding forward and back, making the slight, intimate sound of flesh moving over flesh.

"It wasn't your idea either. It was Mom's doing, wasn't it?" She looked down at the severed cake. "I want you to know I understand. I know what you're going through."

This was no time to discuss marital breakups. Not in front of his granddaughter and not on his birthday. Elliot narrowed his eyes at Susan, but she was never one to read signals correctly. "I'm fine," he said. "Really."

"I never believed for one minute that you enjoy living alone, or even that Mom does. I think you're two stubborn people involved in I-don't-know-what—some kind of experiment—that's not doing either one of you any good." Then Susan got out of her chair and walked up behind him. She looped her arms around his neck, dug her chin into his scalp and pressed against his hunched back.

What did she want from him—*what now*—with her choking and poking? He would not break down, if that's what she thought. Wouldn't pull her into his arms. If there was something she needed to hear, he'd try his best to say it, but how could he guess from her stranglehold just what she had in mind? How could he find the right words, the ones that would make a difference?

Elliot stiffened in his chair, rolling his head to one side, and Susan let go at once. "Must be getting late," he said. The wrong words, he knew that, but the only words his tongue could form.

"Wait a minute—your present!" Mattie ran to another room and came back with a roll of tape, a small box and paper. She spread the paper on the floor, centered the box on top and flipped it over and over till it was shapeless in its cover. She taped the ends half-closed and handed the package to Elliot.

"Shouldn't I open the card first?"

Mattie looked at her mother and wailed, "Oh no, we forgot a card!"

"Doesn't matter," Elliot said, tearing at the wrapping. A birthday present with no card! A day ruined by thoughtlessness. The dots on the wrapping paper ran together before his eyes, then broke apart quivering. He opened the spongy box: a leather-bound appointment book with cheerful quotations on every page. "Just what I wanted," he said.

Susan's mouth flattened and she watched him intently. Like when she was five or six and Dennis would've been turning eight, and Barb dropped them off at his office one particular afternoon. . . . Dennis sat patiently in the waiting room and read a book while Susan followed at his heels from one examining room to the next, arranging bottles according to size, handing him tools he didn't need or hopping into an empty chair and opening her mouth wide. He had to have his assistant, Miss Begleiter, drag her away, and when he came out of the room himself he found her at his assistant's desk, sitting on his assistant's lap, doodling in the margins of his daily agenda while Miss Begleiter braided Susan's hair into pigtails. His daughter looked up at him standing in the doorway and her eyes were knowing and angry, as if to say, *You see this? Any stranger can make me feel happier than you can.*

He got to his feet abruptly and said it was time to go. Mattie begged him to stay longer, it wasn't even her bedtime yet, and hugged him around the waist. Susan told her to let go and picked her daughter's fingers off his jacket with extreme care, as if they were berries on a thorny vine. As if she would bleed if she touched him.

It was easy to say goodnight to Mattie, easy to tug her ponytail and rub his nose against hers. But what about his daughter? He glanced at the ceiling, she glanced at the floor; then they stared at his boxed gift, which he held against his chest like a bumper. He might have said, *I'm sorry for all the ways I let you down.* And Susan might've answered, *You were foolish sometimes, but I forgive you anyway. All that's behind us.*

But in the end they only said, "Good to see you," "You too," and Elliot hurriedly walked out.

On the street the air was brittle. He'd left his mittens somewhere, so he tucked his present under his arm and shoved his hands in his pockets. His car was parked a block away. At first he had trouble starting it and thought the battery was dead, but then the engine turned over. He tossed his gift onto the seat and flicked on the heater. Cold air blew into the car; he could see his breath. Where had he dropped his mittens? Barb's mitts. The ones she made. He'd have to phone Susan and ask her to look around.

The car was idling roughly, as if it were groaning. He grabbed the wheel and tapped the gas. His bare hands stuck to the wheel and a chill traveled through his fingers, up his arms and into his chest. He slumped in his seat and thought, I should've said, I love you. *Love you, Susan. Love you, Barb.* And if he'd said it just right, simply and honestly, straight from the heart, his daughter would be his friend and his wife would be at his side.

He got out and brushed snow and ice from the windshield. Then he settled into his seat, buckled up and drove onto the parkway. The wipers jerked across the glass—hup-lup, hup-lup—and he thought about how easy it would be to fall asleep at the wheel. He thought of the dentist he used to know who did himself in one day and no one saw it coming.

He turned on the radio. The forecast was for more snow and record-breaking temperatures. "No let up," the weatherman said.

No let-up-hup, no let-up-hup: his daughter was a stranger and his wife was living downstairs. And there didn't seem to be a thing he could do about it.

He turned off the Don Valley and onto the Lake Shore. Hardly any cars in sight. Everyone knew to stay home in hazardous conditions. The speedometer showed he was going fast and he meant to ease up on the gas; instead, he pushed harder. Then the loss of traction and the smooth streaming sideways that meant he was sliding on ice.

He took his foot off the gas and thought how slowly an accident happens: every moment held in time like a skater balanced on one foot. And then the other skate drops and a single second clicks by, and once again you are frozen on a sheet of time.

As the car spun slowly around, a concrete pillar loomed before the windshield, then disappeared. (One foot, the other foot; skating a lazy figure eight.) The post was like a spectator—here, gone, back again—growing larger and larger.

He wanted to hit it, he realized. His mind was laughing, streaking forward, testing the thin ice. *Hit it, hit it. Hit it hard.*

The car spun and his mind spiraled. Already his chest could feel the stab of a deep and bloody puncture wound. *The end, the end,* his mind sang, and he veered forward in his seat, willing the car to hit the pillar. Inches away, the car stopped: he couldn't even order his death.

His birthday present in its box flew off the passenger seat and landed on the floor mat. He leaned over, looked down. Beside the box were two mittens, hand in hand.

5

Angry

After a year of living apart, a funny thing happened to Barbara—she was no longer angry. She was happy in her own apartment where she controlled the heating and cooling and popped toilet paper rolls into the holder so the sheets ran sensibly over the top. Away from Elliot all this time, she finally understood an important thing: that she hadn't really left him because of his temperament or irritating habits. She left because of what had become of them.

When they were young, she thought now, they told each other everything. They shared fears and fantasies (heights, spiders, impotence; wealth, travel, world renown) and planned a perfect future of two careers, two kids, two cars, one house and a splendid retirement. When they were young they'd dance till three; they'd eat too much, drink too much, stumble to bed and babble sweet-nothings from sticky lips, their fingers writing heartfelt poems on each other's backs. But after many years together—years of work, responsibility, child-rearing, routine, daily disappointments and the wearing down that comes with age—something else was needed, a new way of speaking . . . and they found that they were tongue-tied.

When had she stopped talking—really talking—to Elliot? A long time ago, it seemed. Between the night he kissed her at someone's New Year's Eve party, swearing everlasting love, and the night he muttered to himself as he vacuumed ashes off the rug and loaded the dishwasher with party-stained goblets, "No fun talking to a bunch of people you hardly know." Between the time they told each other tales from their childhoods and the time there was nothing left to tell—they'd heard all those stories before—and anyway, they'd been listening to the children fighting all day and only wanted silence. By the time Dennis and Susan had grown up and moved out, they'd lost the habit of chatter. Something else was happening instead: Elliot reading the paper aloud or following her around the kitchen, quoting from books and magazines. He didn't want to discuss anything, just wanted her to listen and nod and agree with whatever point he was so insistently making. If Barbara said, "I think it's more complicated than that," he would drop the paper and walk out. If she tried to talk about something else— novels, for example, or classes at the Potters' Guild—his eyes would glaze over and she'd give up.

Slowly, over thirty-three years, she'd gone from feeling loved to feeling lonely. And if she was doomed to feel like that, she decided she'd rather live alone. There wouldn't be much laundry to do, hardly any dishes to wash, and no need to give in.

The funny thing was that now, a year later, she was thinking about his good points. Hard worker, for instance, and a first-rate provider; a smart, unpretentious man who delighted in music and art. He hated traveling and eating out, but nevertheless encouraged her to do those things with her friends. He was stubborn and foolish sometimes, had to be right and get his way—but no one was perfect. And though he'd changed over the years and they weren't as close as they once were, he probably—no, certainly—loved her in his fashion.

Away from him twelve months she could finally admit she loved him too, loved him in spite of everything. Despite the woman Barbara heard leaving his apartment once . . . and others she may not have heard. Because of the children and better days; because she missed him sometimes. Because of all their years together—their common, tangled history—and the fact he'd been a good father and was, at heart, a good man.

Only a few weeks ago she had still been angry enough to ignore Elliot's birthday. But now she was feeling generous and would make amends. They were driving to the country today for lunch in a charming restaurant they'd been to ages ago. The food would be hearty and plain and she intended to pick up the tab. She'd even give him a present. Then they would walk beside a river and talk. Really talk.

It was not clear who would drive. The car belonged to both of them so either could claim the driver's seat, but Barbara thought it should be her since she had planned the outing. Nothing personal, Elliot said, but he hated anyone else at the wheel. He'd never relax if she drove, and wasn't the whole idea for him to have a relaxing day—a happy belated birthday?

"Isn't it time you learned to just sit back once in a while and let someone else take charge? You'd be surprised how relaxing it is to let me worry about the road while you watch the scenery."

"I'd only be bored," he insisted. "I enjoy driving, honestly. It gives me something to do with my hands."

In the end she relented and let Elliot drive the car. Because they were doing this in honor of his birthday. And because of her long habit of giving in to her husband.

They drove east and then north. They hadn't been to the Maple Inn since 1965 when they'd come here to celebrate their second anniversary. That time was early June: the trees were yellow-green and the river high and burbling. He didn't complain about anything. The food was fine, the view great, their room (actually too small) had a squeaky bed with a soft mattress that rolled them together back to front, which Elliot thought was just the thing to encourage cuddling and fondling.

But he didn't seem to remember. When Barbara phoned to invite him to lunch and suggested the Maple Inn he paused to consult his date book, then answered coolly, "Good enough," as if he'd never heard of the place. And she was left to wonder why she'd made such a sentimental choice, especially if it wasn't going to please him anyway.

Just off the 401 they pulled over for coffee and gas. In the coffee shop they sat at a table on small swivel chairs so that Barbara faced the patrons and Elliot had a view of the road. This was how they always sat in coffee shops, she remembered. As if he couldn't wait to be back in the car, zooming off, and she needed to pause and imagine the lives of strangers. Was that couple nervous too? Did they have things to talk about?

Elliot spun his empty cup, glanced at his watch and stood up. This was how they always left coffee shops, she realized.

Back in the car Barbara read directions from a brochure. "Take the next exit," she said, "then right for three kilometers and left at the blinking light." At the light they turned left again, then drove for a long time. When the inn appeared suddenly at the end of a tract of farmland she said, "We've been here before. Doesn't it look familiar?" The car bucked slightly as he played with the gearshift, and she knew all at once that he did indeed remember.

"We were so young," Barbara said, "twenty and twenty-one."

He stopped the car in front of the inn and switched off the engine. Barbara opened the passenger door and stepped into the frigid air, but when she turned around he was still in the driver's seat, his forehead against the wheel.

He was thinking about that weekend. It all came back to him in a rush—spring, the river, filet mignon; the bed that was too short, the mattress that was too soft; Barb lying under him, her eyes wide and worshiping. . . . When Elliot got out of the car he walked quickly past her, his eyes on his winter boots.

They got a table with a view. Mostly they saw the white road but also a screen of trees—evergreen and bare-branched maple, birch and sumac—and the elbow of a frozen stream. "Isn't this nice?" Barbara said, but Elliot only gazed out. The room was half empty and the waiter stopped to talk to them. He suggested the daily special, roast beef and baked potatoes, but Barbara was in the mood for fish and Elliot ordered bread and soup. "I'm not very hungry," he said.

Her eye twitched in annoyance. All this way for a bowl of soup? Why bother coming if he wasn't going to eat or talk?

They stared out the window at the stiff trees and rutted road. He began tapping his spoon on the table to a staccato beat and her forehead tightened. "Look," she said, "I'm sorry I didn't see you on your birthday. But I'm trying to make it up to you with a nice lunch in the country. I thought you'd be delighted."

Delighted, Elliot sniffed. After she destroyed their marriage, then ignored his birthday. "Delighted?" he said aloud. "To come back to this place, a place where we were happy? To come here—back here—after what you've done to us?"

"You don't understand."

"*You* don't." He smacked the spoon against the table and fixed his eyes on hers.

The whites of his eyes were red-veined, the irises muddy, the pupils deep . . . so deep that peering at them she felt drawn under a wave. Her lungs were actually hurting when she drew a breath.

She turned toward the window and that curve of water in the trees. She wanted to cry—was going to cry. . . . Wouldn't cry. Not here. But it wasn't fair, it wasn't right! The idea was to spend the day in a place sweet with memories so it could be like old times—chatter, laughter, tenderness—and later they would drive home and things would be better between them. Instead he was making her feel bad.

The waiter had already brought their food, turning cold in front of them. The sauce on her fish was thickening, and the steam from Elliot's bowl of soup had long since risen and dissolved like a blown cloud. The waiter came by to ask if everything was all right and Barbara nodded glumly: they were making him unhappy too. For his sake, she ate some fish and a forkful of vegetables, whereupon Elliot dipped his spoon. They'd always been considerate of other people's feelings.

The waiter took their plates away and brought mugs of coffee. Barbara smiled and paid the bill. She drank her coffee steaming hot, while Elliot tried to stir his cool. Around and around his teaspoon went, playing a sharp, tinny song against his cup.

"Why don't we go for a walk?" she said. "Across the road,

beside the river? As long as we're here we might as well."

Elliot didn't disagree. He blew on his coffee, drank it down. She left the waiter a big tip.

At the door they put on their jackets and hats. Barbara pulled on leather gloves and Elliot slipped on mittens she had knitted for him one winter. They crossed the road without speaking and found the path to the river without having to pause to look around. Their feet still remembered the trail. They walked slowly and steadily, as surefooted as donkeys. Elliot's eyes were unfocused, filled with sun, green leaves and sparkling water from long ago. He heard the roar of rapids. But when they reached the water's edge it wasn't a river anymore, only a sluggish, icy stream.

Barbara stepped off the path and climbed down the frozen bank. She plucked a rock from the hard ground, tossed it over a border of ice and into a pool of water. It landed with a decisive plop. Then she broke a small hole in the ice with the heel of her boot and reached down to touch the water, shockingly cold. Under her clothes she was shivering. There was nothing for them to talk about except their estrangement, she realized. Lunch in the country was a mistake. And maybe she was wrong about other, more important things. Maybe they couldn't keep living separately under the same roof. Maybe she ought to move out before things became worse. These days the rooms seemed to be tilting and shifting, as if supporting beams had been cut. Floorboards whispered and the walls bulged with secrets. If they got away from the house, she'd thought, even for an afternoon—if they got out of the damn house! She threw another rock in the stream.

Elliot watched her throw stones. What was on her mind? he wondered. Good news or bad news? Had she brought him here to soften the blow of a final declaration—*I'm moving on, I want a divorce*—or to promise future happiness? *We were happy once, we'll be happy again. I don't want to live alone anymore, I want you back.* What would he do if she opened her arms and said they should try again? Hug her tightly, cheek to cheek, then pick up where they'd left off? Or stand silent, frozen, thereby letting her know he can't be won back easily?

She lifted a rock so heavy she could barely straighten up, then lobbed it onto a patch of ice. It sank through the splintering ice, water bubbling up to the surface and pulling the boulder down. Quietly it disappeared and Barbara was disappointed. She had wanted noise—a great crash—and a plume of ice and water. Not a slow slipping away. She turned to look for Elliot, who had wandered farther along the path. Was he thinking about when they were young and his birthdays were happy? When his wife still lived with him and hadn't yet ruined his life?

She heard the faint crackle of his boots on the frozen trail and had the urge to follow him, to run after and grab him. *Don't be angry,* she wanted to say. *I left you but I still love you. Don't hate me, Elliot.*

As a child she had borne the shame of being illegitimate, endured snubs and name-calling, the scorn of her schoolmates and the pity of her teachers. Later she would ache for a father she had never known. Then one day Elliot appeared and changed everything. She was happy in the glow of his love. But as he grew busier and more distant over the years, she filled up with grief again, back to where she'd started. And even though it was her idea to live apart from Elliot, even though she had new friends and was building a new life, she couldn't let go of him altogether. Couldn't stop hoping that the only man who'd ever loved her might still love her again as wholly as he once did.

But if they got back together, would anything be different? Would he change his habits? Love her better?

Well, maybe for a while. But soon he'd stop deferring to her, and she'd step back into the shoes of a recently retired teacher and discontented housewife as if she'd never been out of them. Barbara would begin to disappear again, cell by cell.

She climbed up the bank and waited. Better to leave things as they were.

The trail turned away from the bank and Elliot lost sight of the stream. He was deep into the woods now, surrounded by evergreens and bare, glistening branches. Barb thought he hated trees, but that wasn't it at all; he hated looking after them, the pruning, patching and raking. The two in their front yard he'd just as soon chop down. The maple shed seeds in June and dry leaves in November which Elliot had to rake and bag, and the droopy branches of the spruce had to be trimmed regularly. In the backyard the apple tree was awkwardly tilted toward the sun and no matter how he braced it, the trunk refused to grow straight. Scarred apples dropped in the fall and had to be collected and buried in the composter. Branches had to be carefully pruned and, on top of everything else, the tree was subject to bugs and diseases he was expected to deal with.

But out in the country, where the trees took care of themselves, he admired their endurance. In fact, he wished he were tree-like himself, durable and thick-skinned. A tree exists. It's purpose to grow and propagate. Nostalgia and loneliness, confusion and resentment have nothing to do with anything. A tree just continues. It doesn't want and not-want at the same time.

He walked a little farther and then, as if he'd reached the end of a long leash, turned back. Barb was at the start of the trail, a hand cupped over her eyes. When he got to her he kicked a bit of hard snow with the tip of his boot.

"Did you have a nice walk?" she said.

He dug his boot into the snow. "Just fine."

"I'm sorry about all this."

Sorry that she missed his birthday? Sorry that she brought him here, or sorry that she broke up their home in the first place? She had a lot to be sorry for. "Let's get going," he said. "It's too cold to be standing around." His eyes and mouth were scrunched against the wind as they headed back.

They got in the car. Elliot started the engine and turned on the heater. Barbara took off her hat and gloves and fluffed her hair in the small mirror glued to the visor. She stared at the glass and cleared her throat. "Maybe you don't want it but I made you a present. It's in my bag. I wasn't sure when to give it to you. What about right now?"

Politeness eased his face into a neutral expression: "Why not?" He turned to her as she flipped up the visor.

She pulled her tote bag out from under the seat and poked around inside. Out came a long, thick package wrapped in silver foil. "Happy birthday a little late."

A hand-knitted scarf. She'd made him a scarf. Same blue-and-gold and the same V-shaped pattern as the mittens he was wearing. As he looked down his vision blurred (chevrons swam in circles, like fish in a sunny pond) and he thought he must be crying. But his eyes were dry. "That was nice of you," Elliot said.

"I worked like a fiend, day and night."

He laid the scarf and torn paper on the seat between them.

"Aren't you going to put it on?"

"No," he said. "Not now. Don't forget your seatbelt."

Then he put the car in reverse, turned around and drove back the way they had come. A scarf to match his mittens? What the hell was she trying to say? Did she love him or didn't she? Maybe she was toying with him, keeping him on a hook in case things didn't work out. In case she decided down the road she was miserable and wanted him back. That no other man she'd met—no one she was likely to meet—was half as good as Elliot.

But he was not to be trifled with. *Make up your mind!* he wanted to shout. *Live with me or move out altogether, out of my sight. This has gone on long enough!* But Elliot was silent as he drove onto the 401.

Traffic was heavy for this time of day. Maybe there'd been an accident, or maybe hundreds of couples had decided it was a great day for lunch in the country and now, fed and happy, were returning to their cozy homes.

At least the cars were moving. He saw an opening on his left and pulled out of the middle lane and into the fast one. But only a few minutes later that lane slowed down and he changed to the middle again. When that one came to a dead stop he veered to the left again, cutting off a Sunfire that honked loudly and swerved right. The car slid up alongside and the driver gave him the finger.

Moments later the Sunfire was behind Elliot, on his tail. Deliberately he slowed down and the Sunfire squealed, lurched right, then cut back into his lane, inches ahead of Elliot now. On the passenger side a blonde swung around in her seat to look at him and stick out her tongue. The driver had springy hair that bounced up and down as he jerked his middle finger in the rearview mirror. Then on came the car's brake lights— red as fire, red as blood—and Elliot had to stop short. Behind him a horn blared. Barb whipped forward and the contents of her tote bag spilled over Elliot's feet. "Are you okay?"

"Get away from that nut," she said. "He's probably drunk."

Traffic was moving steadily now. He switched lanes and switched again, edging into the slow lane. Barb reached around his leg to pick up some of her dropped things. When she brushed his pants his leg stiffened. "Get it later," he said. "That's dangerous."

She leaned forward and picked up the scarf from the floor mat, then folded it neatly on her lap. "I'm sorry you don't like it," she said.

"I didn't say that, did I?"

"You didn't say anything."

"I don't get it, that's all."

He pressed down hard on the gas and hopped into the middle lane. The Sunfire was beside them again. The blonde rolled her window down and motioned for him to do the same. "Don't do it," Barb said, but he opened his window anyway.

"Hey, asshole!" the blonde yelled. "You're a fuckin' asshole!"

"Fuck you too!" he answered. "Fuck you both!"

The car zipped ahead and he followed it into the fast lane. Pain exploded over his eye and vibrated under his skin, as if his forehead were a gong struck and ringing. He wanted to fix the blonde and the man with the coiled hair. Scare them, hurt them, *get them good.*

He caught up to the Sunfire, shot forward and butted the bumper with his own. The car jolted, swayed and shook; it leaped ahead. He drove close, tapped the gas and hit it again. "What're you doing?" Barb screamed. "You'll kill us! Are you out of your mind?"

He gritted his teeth and bore down. The Sunfire swerved from lane to lane, then alongside the shoulder, and he matched its every panicky move. All around cars were honking. He leaned on his own horn, mocking them with its nasal song.

Barb grabbed the steering wheel and turned it toward the shoulder. He jerked it back, she pulled again, and the car wobbled back and forth. "Stop it, stop it, stop it!" she cried, wailing and tugging at the same time.

Just ahead was an exit ramp. They each struggled with the wheel and he couldn't tell whose strength it was that finally, safely steered the car up the ramp, around a U and into a shallow ditch. He shut off the engine and glanced at his wife. She was no longer crying but was slumped against the back of her seat, twisting his knitted scarf in her hands.

Elliot was panting. The windshield was steamy and the car wheezed and shuddered with the fierceness of his ragged breath. He thought his heart would bang forever; he thought he'd never be calm again. He thought he would stay in the driver's seat, an arm's length away from his wife, gulping rage, unable to speak . . . and this would just go on and on.

6

Handle and Griddle

Susan said, "She missed his birthday."

"Only by a few weeks."

"Just the same, it hurt him."

"He said that?" Natalie asked.

"Well, no, but I could tell. He came for dinner Saturday and was out of sorts the whole time."

"We saw him the next day—"

"Sunday afternoon."

"—and he seemed fine. He was happy to see us." Susan saw the dark side of everything, Dennis thought. Of course Dad would rather have seen Mom on his birthday, but he was a man to make the best of a bad situation. Much like Dennis, he would not give in to melancholy, he wouldn't sulk.

"Sure he was better the next day, it wasn't his birthday anymore."

Natalie leaned forward, stretching an arm over the coffee table, dipped tortilla chips in salsa and sank back into the couch. Susan was at the other end, a large, necessary space of empty cushion between them. Dennis sat opposite, squeezing a glass with both hands. Later in bed he would grind his teeth, keeping her nervously awake, and tomorrow she was on call: another night of poor sleep.

"Anyway," Dennis said, "she did finally take him to lunch."

"And now they're barely speaking!"

Dennis fixed his eyes on the bottle of wine on the table: he hadn't heard about that. But what if they'd had an argument and weren't talking, so what? Every couple bickers and pouts and ignores each other now and then. Certainly he and Natalie do. Imagine being married for as long as Mom and Dad have—and living in different apartments to boot. All things considered, they were doing well. As far as Dennis was concerned the main problem was Susan, who examined their every move. *Get on with your life*, he wanted to tell his sister, *and leave them alone.*

"But I spoke to your mother and she said they had a good time."

"That's not what she told me. She said he hardly said a word and coming back he drove like an absolute maniac and nearly got them both killed."

Dennis reached for the Chardonnay and filled his glass. "Dad's too good a driver for that."

"He's got a temper—or haven't you noticed?" He *wouldn't* notice a thing like that, Susan thought. Her brother had a knack for never seeing anything nasty. Like years ago, driving north, her parents in the front seat of the old Ford, bickering: "I *told* you to take Exit 10"; "Maybe if you told me sooner, I would've been in the right lane." Dad hunkered over the wheel, passing every car on the road, slicing in and out of lanes until her mother said through her teeth, "Are you trying to get us all killed?" Yes, killed. Like roadkill. Like skunks and squirrels and raccoons. Her stomach cramped as Susan thought, Dad's going to kill us. But later, when she spoke to Dennis, he said he hadn't heard a thing.

Natalie reached for another chip. "Good lunch, bad lunch. Whatever happened, they'll work it out. Don't forget they're grownups." She was sick of all this endless fretting about her in-laws. Her own parents were trouble enough, divorced since she was in high school and now leading ridiculous lives. Her father lived with a woman only three years older than Natalie, while her mother kept lining up for cosmetic surgery—her eyes, chin, belly and breasts. Next to them Barbara and Elliot seemed well adjusted. They'd work things out or not. They'd move back together or they'd sell the house and get divorced and finally make a clean break. Either way her life, Dennis's life and the lives of their children wouldn't change one bit.

Dennis crossed his legs and sipped wine. "Well, of course they will. Fundamentally Mom and Dad are well matched."

"Except they can't live together," Susan said.

"They've made a little adjustment. After thirty-odd years of married life you have to expect that."

Natalie covered a yawn with her hand and kicked off her shoes. Imagine being married to the same person all that time. She didn't think she and Dennis would stay together half as long. Someday when the kids were big and things slowed down a bit they'd look at each other blankly and try to remember what it was that attracted them in the first place. They'd sit and wonder what on earth there was left for them to talk about. She hated to admit it, but sometimes she thought of him coldly as her first husband, father of her children. Never as her mate for life. There were young doctors she worked with who flirted with her, made her laugh; made her wonder why she'd picked a man as tame as Dennis.

"Which reminds me," Susan said. "We ought to start thinking about their thirty-fifth anniversary. Especially if we're going to book a hall, we have to do that soon."

"An anniversary party? But you said they're not even talking." A dumb idea, thought Natalie. Besides which, the last thing in the world she had time for was to rent a hall, hire caterers, choose flowers and all that.

Dennis took his glasses off and wiped them on the hem of his shirt. He hated social gatherings. Only as a boy did he have fun at parties, and then because of Susan, who'd pull him into dark rooms, behind doors or under tables draped in hanging linen where they'd eavesdrop on conversations, giggling into their cupped hands. But now, too big to steal away, he'd have to stay and shake hands with people he'd never met before, make silly chitchat and smile till his jaw hurt.

He put his glasses back on. "They don't even live together. How can we celebrate a marriage like that?"

Susan looked from her sister-in-law to her brother and back. "You talk a good show but you don't believe they're going to work out anything, do you? You don't believe they'll still be married a year from now—but I do. And whether they're living together or not, I don't want them thinking we forgot their anniversary."

"What about what they want? Do you really think they'd like to spend their anniversary waltzing in a crowded room?"

"You think I'm being selfish. You think I want to organize a big party for my sake—isn't that what you're saying?"

Dennis slid back in his chair and smiled noncommittally at a spot over Susan's head. That's exactly what he thought. The point of planning a party was to win their parents' approval, to make Susan look good. She'll never give up trying to be the favorite child.

Natalie said, "Elliot might go for it but not your mom, she's not the type."

"I've known her longer than you and she *is* the type," said Susan. "She'd love being fussed over. She'd love the chance to kick up her heels and party the night away."

"Just because you've known her longer—"

"Mom respects tradition, though she doesn't always act in a traditional way," Susan said.

Natalie glanced at Dennis, who was grinning at the chips as if he expected them to break into song. Wouldn't it be nice if he told his sister to fuck off? Certainly he never would—though God knows someone should. He lets her get away with things he'd find rude in anyone else.

A small voice piped up from the stairway behind the couch. "I can't sleep," Stevie said, and Natalie stood up, thinking she'd rather deal with her six-year-old than a grownup who acts like one. But when she started toward him, Dennis leaped in front of her. "I'll tuck him in," he said. "Why don't you stay here and relax?" They walked upstairs hand in hand, the hem of the boy's loose pajamas dragging on the carpeted steps, and Natalie turned back to Susan, her lips compressed to hide a yawn.

"We'll keep it small," Susan said, "fifty friends and family. We could rent a hall, hire musicians. I know a good florist and a woman who runs a very successful catering business on the side."

"Surely we don't need a hall. That special room in your building would do very nicely."

"The dark little party room? There's nothing special about it. I can't imagine celebrating anything down there."

Natalie was too beat to argue with her sister-in-law. Back-to-back patients all day, then she made her hospital rounds, rushed home, hugged the boys, had cold meat loaf and carrot sticks while Dennis put the kids to bed, answered the phone—it was Susan—and was now trapped in her living room discussing plans for a party that would probably never happen for a couple who seemed quite content to have as little to do with each other as possible.

"But maybe you're not interested in doing something special for them."

Natalie sat a little straighter. "Of course I'm interested. They've always been important to me."

"I mean, you've got your own parents. So naturally I don't expect you to take the initiative. . . ."

"If there's going to be a party, I'll do what I can to help—though God knows where I'll find the time. But really, Susan, something small would be more appropriate."

"It has to be a special night, a night they'll remember. Maybe if they're still living separately a year from now, this could be the very thing to bring them back together."

"Aren't you being sentimental?"

"A night with friends and family to remind them what matters more than all their disagreements."

"What do you mean?"

"I mean love!" Susan threw her arms apart and brought them together in a wraparound hug. "The love they still feel for each other, that keeps them from getting divorced or moving out of the same house. Maybe all they need is the right kind of encouragement—"

"An anniversary party?"

"—to make them finally realize that deep down they're crazy in love and want to be together."

"I see," said Natalie. "Crazy love."

"Yes, *love*." Susan said the word in a throaty, impassioned way that made Natalie scoop up chips and crunch down on them loudly. Love this, love that: she was always going on about some deeply felt emotion, dropping her voice and waving her arms. You never knew what to expect from the Queen of Expressed Feelings.

Dennis walked back into the room in his stockinged feet. Brown pants, Natalie saw, and white socks with a large hole in the left toe. It was hard to love a man who wore dark pants and white socks in dire need of mending. He had a new three-pack of brown socks in his dresser drawer, which, incidentally, she had bought for his birthday, but Dennis would never think to coordinate his colors. Or comb down his cowlick. Or clean his glasses properly. Some women found absentmindedness and boyishness attractive in their husbands. Natalie did not.

Dennis said, "He's still awake, but I think he'll fall asleep now. The little guy's overtired. He runs around in day care, they can never get him to sit still."

"And Raymond?"

"In dreamland."

"Sounds wonderful," Natalie said.

Susan said, "While you were gone we worked out some of the details. We're looking at a caterer, live musicians, fifty guests...."

Susan kept talking. Dennis stared at the blank wall between his sister's head and his wife's and saw himself as a child in a grainy home movie, in the doorway of Susan's room. He heard her nasal breathing and the squealing sound she made in the panic of a nightmare, her Raggedy Ann pressed flat as a saucer against her chest. Young as he was, he knew to pat her hair and whisper in her ear, "Shush now, it's only a dream." And she would turn and nuzzle his hand, a half-wakened puppy.

"You with me?" she interrupted. "The anniversary party for Mom and Dad's thirty-fifth?"

Dennis slipped his fingers under his glasses and rubbed his eyes. "We're still on that?"

"We're not sure about a hall. But I can make a few calls anyway," Susan said, "to see what's available and how much."

Dennis lifted his wineglass, sat back in his armchair and watched his sister over the rim. She was holding a glass too and sat twisted away from him, turned toward Natalie. In this light, at that angle, her face looked even sharper and thinner than usual. Perhaps she was losing weight. Although, as he remembered, she'd always been rawboned. They used to play a game in which she'd climb a tree in the backyard, then jump into his waiting arms, and it would be like catching a spear. Back in university she once dated a friend of his who told him indiscreetly that sleeping with Susan was like lying on a bed of nails.

Rawboned and high-strung. You had to watch out with Susan.

Dennis believed in breathing space and keeping people at arm's length—although the distance varied. Between him and his mother there was often just the slightest space, because of a long-standing affinity between them. A fixed space existed between Dennis and his wife as they negotiated daily chores. It shrank those evenings they found time to read in bed and (if they weren't exhausted) grope under the blankets. Though his eyes were red and burning and his senses might be dulled after a day at the ministry, he never failed to be startled by the softness of her bare skin.

With Susan he tried to keep the biggest possible breathing space. Her brain was a fire pot with toxic emotional fumes constantly escaping. But she wasn't easily shaken off. From the time she could crawl she would grab their parents' ankles and demand that they pick her up. When she started to talk she would scold them if they put her in a playpen and walked away. She grew up angry and mocked her brother's company even as she followed him from room to room. She'd be Tinker Bell to his Peter Pan, Juliet to his Romeo, then accuse him of being unemotional and boring. Why did Mom and Dad want her to be more like him? she'd ask. Who'd want to be a drip, a tin man without a heart?

But it wasn't true that he felt nothing. When he saw her asleep sometimes, a doll locked against her chest between her scabby elbows, he wanted to cry. When his college friend told him what it was like to sleep with Susan, he wanted to crush the guy's balls. He whooped with joy when his friend and his sister broke up.

For all her bluster and glowering, Susan was fragile. Dennis had always known that. And so, despite his need for space, he never refused to help her. Dennis was the one she called when she got pregnant at eighteen and wanted to have the baby. Dennis was the one who talked Dan into marrying her and giving their baby a good home. And after Dan walked out and Susan swallowed a bottle of pills, Dennis was the one she phoned, the first to get to Emergency to see if she lived or died. And he knew that interminable night that it mattered to him even if it didn't matter to Susan.

Natalie yawned audibly and didn't bother to cover her mouth. "You'll have to excuse me. It's been such a long day."

"I should be going anyway, it's past Mattie's bedtime." Susan glanced up the stairs and heard the tinny warble of a television laugh track coming from the playroom.

"Don't hurry," Dennis said. "Finish your wine."

Natalie shot him a hard look. Susan swiveled her wineglass, still more than half full, and settled back.

"I don't want to be rude but I have to go to bed. I'm beat." Natalie stood up, brushing crumbs from her skirt. "I'm sure you can carry on without me." She nodded at her sister-in-law, blew Dennis a short kiss, picked up her shoes and went upstairs. Moments later a door closed sharply at the end of the hall.

"Maybe it's time. . . ."

"Your wine first."

"At least let me tell Mattie to turn down the TV."

"In two minutes she'll be snoring, and nothing can wake Nat when she's overtired. She sets three alarms to ring at five minute intervals starting at six."

"Doesn't that drive you crazy?"

"I'm up and out of the room before the second one goes off."

"You don't mind getting up early?"

"It gives me time to read the paper before I have to deal with the kids."

Susan laughed. "If she woke you at four, you'd find a reason to like that too. You're just the obliging type."

"Nothing wrong with that," he said. "Especially in a marriage."

She set down her glass and pushed up her sleeves. "And what would I know about that?"

"I wasn't referring to you and Dan."

Susan scratched her elbow. "At least one couple's still together in this family."

"You have to work at a marriage. You overlook certain things and try not to hold a grudge. You think about the children."

She stopped scratching, licked a finger and dabbed her elbow, because she'd actually drawn blood. "Sounds like a lot of fun."

Dennis rolled his wineglass between his hands. "I know you think a relationship has to be intense to count. In fact, the ones that last any length of time never are."

"And that's okay with you," she said, "having a friend and not a lover for a wife?"

He dug his heels into the carpet and pushed back his chair. "Natalie and I are compatible in many ways. We like the same music and art, same books, same food. We respect each other's careers and we want to do what's best for the kids."

"And happy? Are you still in love?" Her voice became husky: "Do you feel love when you look at her?"

"I would say . . . I believe—" His gut was making water-sounds, as if it had turned to slush. "Content. I'd say I'm content."

"So you settled for contentment. You always were a wimp, Dennis."

Now there was pressure in his gut. Casually he dropped his hands over his abdomen and thought he felt his bellybutton bulging under his thin shirt, a short cork about to pop.

"Daddy, I can't sleep." Stevie was on the stairs again, small, pale and phantom-like in oversized white pajamas printed with faded sailboats.

Dennis put his glass down and snapped to his feet. "I have to deal with Stevie."

"Wait a minute," Susan said. "I didn't really mean that. I don't think you're a wimp at all. I think you're smart— smarter than me—because you've found a way to live, a way to be comfortable. The truth is I'm envious."

Dennis paused at the foot of the stairs, his ears hot and probably red. He was neither smart nor comfortable. "I'll send Mattie downstairs."

Stevie's warm hand felt pulpy in his own as he led him back to his bedroom. "Stay here," he told him. "I have to say goodbye to Mattie, then I'll come tuck you in."

Dennis went to the next room where Mattie lay face-down too close to the TV. "Time to go," he patted her head. "Your mom's waiting downstairs." She turned off the TV and pushed herself up. She was thin and flat like Susan and walked like her mother too, quick and light and slightly hunched. He followed her to the top of the stairs, suppressing the urge to reach out and pull her against him. Mattie didn't like to be held by anyone but Elliot, who could still bounce her on his knee. But if

Dennis, Barbara or even Susan merely brushed her shoulder, she would hug herself and shrink away. And yet there was something nervous and familiar about the girl that made him want to comfort her.

From the bottom of the stairs she said, "Goodnight, Uncle Dennis." Susan murmured to the girl, and then he heard a slippery sound like the whisper of silk as they passed through the front door.

For a minute the house was eerily still and he wanted to call them back. *Sit down*, he wanted to cry out. *Sit down and I'll tell you everything!* But how to begin, and what to say? *We're too tired at the end of the day. We're too busy and too tired to love each other properly.*

The gloom of the darkened hall slid over his body like a gloved hand. He squinted into the gray tunnel. At the far end of the hallway the oak door of the master bedroom was firmly shut. Sleep tight, he smiled at the door, but the sentiment was as dry as his lips.

He turned into the boys' room, dusky and orange with the faint glow of night-lights. The walls were papered with teddy bears in turn-of-the-century costumes and the room seemed overcrowded. He would have preferred a celestial pattern of planets and constellations, but his wife had said bears were more appropriate for young boys.

Raymond slept soundly on his small bed beside the wall, curled up against the pleated trousers of distinguished bears. Across the room, Stevie was on his back now on top of his quilt, breathing softly and regularly. When Dennis slipped the quilt down and tried to cover the boy up, Stevie blinked his eyes open and said, "Daddy, I'm not cold."

Dennis took a step back and Stevie said, "Don't go. Tell me a story, I can't sleep."

"Move over then," he said, and the boy made room for

his father on the side of the bed. "What do you want to hear tonight? *Snow White and the Seven Dwarfs? Rip Van Winkle? Rumpelstiltskin?*"

"Make something up. Tell me one of yours."

He held his son's sticky-warm hand on his knee and closed his eyes.

"What're you doing?"

"Thinking."

Stevie puckered his mouth and said, "Can I have a cookie? I'm hungry."

"I'll tell you a story with food in it. A story that'll fill you up so you won't be hungry anymore. The story of ... Handle and Griddle."

"I know that one," Stevie said. "That's not what it's called."

"You don't know it, I made it up. And that's what it's called, 'Handle and Griddle.'"

Stevie rolled onto his hip and inched up to his father's thigh. "Once upon a time," said Dennis, "there was a boy named Handle and his sister's name was Griddle."

"*Gretel*, Daddy."

"No, Griddle. And the boy was exactly your age and the girl a little younger, so Handle looked after his kid sister and tried to protect her from bad things."

"What things?"

"You know—wolves and witches and hairy beasts."

Stevie put his thumb in his mouth and fisted his other hand in his father's palm. "They lived in a house in the country," Dennis went on, "with a mother and father who worked in the village and came home late at night when the kids were already sleeping. So they didn't know that the children's nanny was very wicked and very mean and made them suppers of boiled cabbage, pig's feet and spinach juice. One day Griddle, who was hot-tempered and outspoken, told the nanny she'd had enough and ran off into the woods. Handle hurried after her to bring his sister safely home, because the woods were dangerous with poison ivy and wild boars."

Stevie drew his breath in with a wheezy sound and chewed his thumb.

"But he couldn't find his way back. So Handle and Griddle walked all night, deeper and deeper into the forest, terribly lost."

"But what about the breadcrumbs? Hansel dropped breadcrumbs so they could find their way home."

"Not in my story he didn't. No one dropped anything and Handle and Griddle got totally lost."

Stevie pulled his hand out of Dennis's hand and played with the quilt, bunching it and patting it flat.

"But the very next morning—what do you think!— they found a house made of bread and cakes and ate until their tummies hurt. And an old lady came out of the house and fed them milk and Oreos and put them to bed in the cottage."

"But she was really a witch," said Stevie with a pouty lip.

"Who locked them up in cages and fed them Coke and pizza until they were as round and soft as overstuffed teddy bears."

"And then she tried to cook them!"

"She made Griddle light a fire outside the gingerbread house and told her to lean over and see if it was hot enough, then pushed Griddle into the flames."

"But she jumped out and ran away."

"No, no," Dennis frowned, "that was the problem. Griddle was attracted to fire and would've stupidly fried to death if Handle hadn't escaped his cage, pulled his sister out of the flames and rolled her around in the dirt."

"Mommy says we shouldn't play with fire."

"Mommy's right, of course. Griddle was very foolish.

Good thing her brother was there to keep her from hurting herself."

"Did she say thanks to Handle? Mommy says you should say thanks when someone does a nice thing."

"Can you believe it?—she didn't thank him. Griddle was angry at Handle! She said she would've jumped out herself when she got too hot and Handle was always spoiling her fun."

Stevie sucked hard on his thumb. "What about the witch?" he mumbled.

"What do you think happened to her?"

"They threw her in the fire and she burned up."

"Exactly."

Stevie rolled over and popped out his thumb. "Are there more witches in the woods?"

"She was the last of her kind. Today witches are extinct, so you never have to be afraid if you're playing in the forest."

"Is Griddle still mad at Handle?"

"Yes, I'm afraid so."

"Don't they go home again and live happy after? Don't the parents fire the nanny and stay home with their children?"

"There are many ways to end a story."

"End it a nice way."

"All right, let me think."

The boy closed his eyes and said, "I'm cold, Daddy. I'm cold now."

Dennis tugged the quilt down, slipped in beside his son and covered them both. He curled his arm around the boy and pulled him against his side. "That better?" Stevie nodded. "Now here comes the ending. . . .

"After the witch burned to nothing, Handle and Griddle filled their pockets with money and jewels they found in the house. They also found a road map and walked safely out of the forest back to their own home. When they got there the nanny was gone: she'd been fired for negligence when the children went missing. So Handle and Griddle stayed up late until their parents came home, and there was great rejoicing. Then the children emptied their pockets and rubies and emeralds rolled on the floor, and now the family was so rich the parents didn't have to work, and they all lived happily ever after."

Stevie's knees were hard apples pressed into Dennis's thigh; his head was a melon on Dennis's arm. His eyes were closed and the boy was snoring.

"Then Handle and Griddle climbed into bed on opposite sides of the children's room, and their parents kissed them goodnight and retired to their own room. Griddle turned to her brother and said, 'So now you want me to thank you for saving my life back there, even though you know I'm sick and tired of playing damsel in distress to your hero. One of these days I'll save you and then maybe you'll see what it's like to make up your mind to die and someone comes along at the last minute and says no, you can't do it, I won't let you, I need you to live.'"

One possible ending. In another one she falls into her brother's arms and whispers in a voice weak with feeling, *Thank you, thank you, thank you.*

Dennis closed his eyes then and darkness poured over him. His tongue relaxed and floated like a log in a black pool. "Don't mention it," he said, and didn't know if he had spoken aloud or not.

GOODForm

Elliot was keeping busy. Trying to stay focused. He cooked and cleaned and shopped for food, saw Ivan, saw his kids, played the sax, groomed the cat—and kept his mind fixed on whatever he was doing. In this way he stayed in check, like oil in a tanker or a laced shoe.

One of his favorite pastimes was practicing Tai Chi. It toned his body, cooled his brain. So two afternoons a week he packed a purple T-shirt and loose black sweatpants—the uniform of his Tai Chi club—and took a streetcar downtown to an old three-story building. Some days the walk up the steep, narrow stairway to the top-floor gym felt like more than enough exercise. Panting, he would change his clothes, then bow and enter the main room: a moment when his blood rushed hot and tingling to his cheeks no matter how many times he'd done this over the past year.

Elliot was a good student. He'd learned the form in record time and soon felt part of the group, so that even his instructor, a sturdy, solemn young man, remarked on how well he was doing, a compliment that pleased him. And yet, despite his efforts to stay calm and focused, he was often embarrassed because he was old, clumsy and soft where others in the class, more experienced than Elliot, were young and firm and fluid. Of course he told himself it was foolish to compete with twenty- and thirty-year-olds who'd been training for years, but reason had nothing to do with it. He felt ashamed of his age, that his hair was thin, his flesh doughy, his neck puffy and wrinkled; that his gums were receding. He felt ashamed that a stick of a boy or a girl-sized young woman could unbalance him easily and send him tripping to the floor with a twist of their hips and thrust of their arms. To see it all reflected in the mirrored walls of the dusty gym was to see his humiliation played out on an oversized screen . . . but still he kept coming back.

It wasn't very long before Elliot perfected his form, learned breathing exercises, simple meditation techniques and the basics of pushing hands. He started feeling bolder. One day he decided it was time to take his hobby out of the overcrowded gym and into the world. Though he was not a man who liked calling attention to himself, he would do the form in his neighborhood park on a stretch of grass surrounded by trees and if someone saw him, so what? People ran and biked in the park, they played soccer and volleyball, beat drums and power-walked, and no one paid them any mind.

The morning of his debut was cold and damp, with a flicker of sun, a teeth-chattering day though the calendar showed it was April. He wore a windbreaker over a sweater, and under that the purple T-shirt and black sweatpants of the club. He walked briskly to the park, along those wide, tree-lined streets of stately homes and rolling lawns without even seeing them, because his pulse was beating hard and fitfully behind his eyes, so that his eyes were watering and he was partly blinded.

For this, his first appearance, he chose a hidden clearing in the woods behind the park gate, more a patch of dirt than a field. There was no one around. He found a hard, flat spot and got into position: feet spread, knees relaxed, pelvis tucked and arms at his sides. But he couldn't begin. What if someone happened by and stopped to watch? Wouldn't he look like an idiot waving his arms and pivoting in a ring of trees; dancing, as it were, without music or a partner?

All at once, from nowhere, a leathery-faced old man sat down on an empty bench a few feet away. He was wearing a toque with a pompon and holding a paper bag. The man cleared his throat and spat, his phlegm pooling on the ground. Elliot crossed his arms and stiffened.

Soon after, along came a woman with a shopping bag in each hand. Thick red ankles showed between the hem of her coat and her open-toed slippers. She stopped at one end of the bench, set down the shopping bags and spoke to the bench in a foreign tongue.

The old man cackled. "The lady's talking to the bench."

Elliot ignored him.

"Hey, darlin'," the man said, "does it look like your hubby?"

She sat down and babbled on, incomprehensible. The old man moved aside. "Shin-dinny rubadub!" he mocked her.

After that a young man in a suit and tie walked by, a cellphone pressed to his ear. He circled Elliot and the bench, then paused just behind it, speaking loudly into the phone. "Milk . . . right. Turnip . . . right. Or do you mean rutabaga? No, they're not the same thing. One's big and yellow, while the other's small and white with an understated flavor. . . ."

The old man tipped his head and put a fist against his ear. "Rutabaker, Studebaker!" He trembled with laughter. Then he scooped pieces of bread from his paper bag and threw them in an arc at his feet. There were no birds or squirrels in sight, but he leaned forward, clucking, snapping his fingers. When no animals turned up he slid back and waited. At last he looked at Elliot and said sharply, "They'll come."

Elliot backed away from the bench.

The man wagged a finger at him. "You must be a jogger. They never stay in one place, they're always bouncing up and down, even at the red lights. You won't be here when the animals come. You won't get to see anything."

Elliot paused. "I'm not a jogger. I came here to do Tai Chi."

"That some kind of board game? I used to play backgammon before my fingers got stiff. What about you?" he said to the woman. "Ever hear of Tie-Gee?"

The bag lady smiled and repeated something to the bench.

"Me neither," the man said.

"I'll show you," Elliot said, regretting the words as he spoke them.

The guy with the phone glared at him, then resumed his conversation.

Elliot couldn't remember why he wanted to do his exercises outdoors in the first place. Nor did he know why he offered to perform for an audience of strangers. But even as his mind was scolding him to stop and go home, he straightened up, stepped forward and moved into position.

Slowly he raised his hands and started the form. He got as far as Slant Flying when the old man called out, "Hey, I know what's going on, I saw that stuff on TV. A milk commercial, that's what. Everybody stretching their arms like they were ready to take off. Reminds me of 'The

Flying Nun.' Do you remember that show?" He slapped his thighs and hooted. "A crazy bunch of flying nuns!"

Elliot opened his mouth to yell at the old man to shut up, but squeezed his lips together instead and concentrated on his moves: Brush Knee and Push (four times); Carry Tiger to the Mountain; Step Back and Repulse Monkey (left and right, three times); White Crane Spreads Wings; Needle at Sea Bottom. . . . Minutes later the man said, "What do you call what you're doing now, flapping your arms like a seagull?" He moved his arms up and down, imitating Elliot. "Does it have a name, that thing you're doing?"

"Wave Hands Like a Cloud," Elliot said through his teeth. Then he was into the kicks: right foot, left foot, turn body and kick with heel. . . . When he glanced around he saw that the guy with the phone had disappeared. The bag lady, silent now, was curled on the bench with her eyes closed.

Suddenly the old man got up and shook his legs, then hopped from one to the other as if he were crushing grapes. Under his feet, pieces of bread flattened and muddied into brown gruel. "How am I doing, Tie-Guy? Think I can get on TV?"

Anger rose in Elliot like a spurt of blood. Trembling, he stopped moving and clenched his hands. He wanted to grab the old man and break him across his knee. He wanted to shove handfuls of dirt down his scrawny throat—fill his mouth with sand and hear him coughing, choking.

The old man finished his dance. Then he skipped away from the bench, showing more agility than Elliot thought possible in someone so weathered and bent. He hop-skipped across the field, waving his paper bag behind him like a kite. The bag lady stretched out and rolled over on the bench, her back turned to Elliot.

He stood very still now, his lips pressed tightly closed. His throat ached and he worried that if he opened his mouth he might cry. Or howl like an animal. There was no telling what would happen next if his feelings escaped. Something terrible, no doubt. Maybe he would grab a stone and cut open his veins till his blood mixed with trampled bread and predators came out of the trees to feed on his anguish.

As he stood there it began to rain. Not a casual dizzle but a sudden, stinging downpour, smacking the dirt with a whooshing sound, erupting in spray and puddles. In the noise and blurry wetness he opened his mouth and a scream came out, as loud as the rain. Another followed that one, and still another after that. But then his shouts became sobs. There was no stopping them. The sound he made now was a gulping, slurpy weather-sound, as his tears trickled into rain.

He listened to his crying. Then, in a shower of rain, he held out his hands, palms up, and they were washed empty and clean.

Drippy-haired and soaked to the skin, he posed in proper Tai Chi stance and started the form all over again. He focused on his breathing and emptied his mind of all thought. One movement after the next: his body knew the sequence. Slant right, slant left, turn, push, step back, kick, punch, cross hands. . . . Traffic rolled by but he heard only a distant hum. His eyes were staring, seeing nothing: the world a sheet of dim shapes and washed-out colors, like a backdrop on a stage. But though he saw nothing clearly, his concentration was intense.

Well into the form now (Golden Cock on Left Leg, Golden Cock on Right Leg), he began to notice objects. Tree limbs, small buds, pools of water, scored mud; the brown, sodden bread at his feet. By degrees they became distinct. And then something else happened—everything ran together again but kept its essential shape, as if the trees, water and dirt had banded into a broad ring that rose over his head till he no longer saw them.

Instead he saw an empty light, and his brain felt hosed down. Weightless and silent. The world had quietly disappeared and even his body, spinning through the last movements of the form, had lost its solidity and moved of its own accord.

Slowly he completed the form and then he stood still with his feet apart, fingers curled, eyes closed and face relaxed. Here was a man without a plan. Without expectation. He didn't know what would happen next in his new, uncertain life, but that didn't matter right now. A momentarily free man who was only sure of the second he was living in.

It was still raining steadily and his body began to cool. Rain made him chilly and slick, but Elliot was not afraid. A man without a vision of the future who was unafraid? How could that be?

It could only be for a moment. But such a singular moment of insight and self-possession was not to be sneezed at.

He opened his eyes, rubbed his hands together and stretched. He ached all over now, cold and heavy in his bones. His toes were numb in his wet socks and he wanted to be home already, dry and warm. He jogged to the park gate and started back at a half run. A line of houses, trees and hedges streaked by like stripes of rain.

A dog shot out from behind a bush and snapped at him as he hurried by. "No!" he shouted, "go home!" but the dog closed in on his heels, only a growling breath away. He imagined the animal's saber teeth piercing his skin; felt the bite, pictured the blood. He'd have to go to Emergency, where a doctor would stitch the wound. He might develop rabies and would have to be admitted for tests and painful shots in the stomach. Then he'd lie in a hospital bed for days—maybe weeks even—before his wife or children even noticed he was missing and inquired as to his whereabouts.

Elliot ran across a street and the dog stopped chasing him. He was breathing so hard his chest hurt. What if he had a heart attack—a massive coronary right here, right now, alone on a drenched street? What if he fell face-down on a slimy square of concrete, the dog chewing his wet pants?

But he didn't have a heart attack; his breathing gradually slowed down. And the dog had crawled under a car and was energetically licking a tire. Elliot started walking again at an unhurried, moderate pace, pretending he enjoyed rain. His sneakers slapped the sidewalk with a squishy, almost playful sound and he anchored his mind to that. One, two, three, four . . . one, two, three, four. . . . He would not think as far ahead as the mail slot in his front door. He would not think about getting home, a message on his phone machine or how he would spend the night. There was no peace in giving in to the mind's endless casting, so he wasn't going to think about what might happen next.

He absolutely would not.

8

SNAPSHOTS

On the plane to New York she wondered
what on earth was she doing there. What could she have
been thinking? Wasn't it enough that the last time she'd
been here, arm in arm with Elliot, someone had grabbed
her purse? If she could be attacked walking next to her
husband on a residential street at dusk, what would happen on her own?

It was Brad's idea in the first place. She'd gone to his
store to buy supplies and ask about some bowls that had
cracked in her kiln. Talking shop with Brad was a pleasure she'd discovered in his pottery classes last year and
then continued in the store. No one knew more than he
did about the physics of clay or the chemistry of glazes. It
was during their chat about her bowls that he mentioned
he had just returned from a trip to Manhattan. She told
him about the time she went with Elliot and got mugged,
and he told her to give the city a chance. "Go by yourself,"
he encouraged her. "It won't be the same."

His hands were spread on the counter and she stared down at his knobby knuckles powdered with white dust. His hands that could make the most amazing shapes from wet clay. She had the urge to lick them clean, a notion that embarrassed her: he was young enough to be her son. She had the urge to ask him along . . . even as she imagined him nude and going hopelessly soft in a midtown hotel room at the sight of her stretch marks and fifty-two-year-old breasts. She imagined flying home alone, the reel of their ruined sex playing over and over on the screens of her eyelids.

"I'll think about it," she told him.

But she hadn't thought about it enough. She bought her ticket impulsively, deciding it was high time she traveled alone. She planned to tell Elliot she was going away for a few days, so that he wouldn't worry if he didn't hear her coming and going and creaking about her apartment—but in the end she took off suddenly, without a word, as if her courage would fly from her mouth if she opened it.

And now she was thousands of feet in the air. Barbara tried to calm herself as she gazed out the window at the gray wet cloud of her solitary future. Fear travels with you, she thought, whether you're alone or not; whether you fly across the border or enter a dark room in your own home. Fear is what she felt when she slipped into bed at night and heard unfamiliar sounds, faint and repeating, in another part of the old house. Fear was her response when she thought it was the distant noise of Elliot's tumbledown bed squealing under the rhythmic weight of two bodies making love.

Elliot and someone else. If it hadn't already happened, it would happen soon.

They'd been living apart just two months when she heard that woman in the hall; when she peeked through her door and saw someone flushed on her way out. Now she had to admit she was most afraid of turning around and seeing him on the plane with his arm around some bimbo.

No, no, it wouldn't matter where she went or who with. It wouldn't matter whether or not she took cabs and buses to avoid riding the subway; stuck to busy thoroughfares or followed a whim and turned down a godforsaken side street. Anything was possible at any time, any place.

She lifted her camera from her lap, aimed it toward the window and clicked at the livid sky. Striations of blue and white. Not an interesting shot, she knew; it would lack perspective, definition. Still, it would remind her that she'd left the ground and touched the sky despite the obvious dangers.

She checked into the same hotel she'd stayed in with Elliot and took a room on the sixth floor, the same floor as last time. Her room was tiny and smelled of disinfectant and paint. She cranked open a window, then sat down on the quilted bed and unpacked her carryall. She pulled out a sewing kit, hair dryer and travel iron, the section of the paper with the long-range forecast and a small selection of guidebooks. A wave of whirring and beeping noises blew in through the window with the day's heat. She smoothed open a map of a walking tour of midtown and stabbed her finger at the Empire State Building on Thirty-fourth.

Out on the street the roar and chug of jackhammers was painful, the air thick with exhaust fumes and the dust of construction. She felt grit between her teeth. Her bare feet were slippery in her sandals as she walked along, and every loud rumble seemed to vibrate under her skin. She raised the camera around her neck and paused to take a picture, but someone walked in front of the lens and what she got instead was a gray swatch of shoulder.

A wide ring of people circled the Empire State Building. Barbara elbowed her way into the air-conditioned lobby, where an usher waved her downstairs and she wound up on a snaking line in the hot, window-less basement.

Tourists in front of her, tourists behind. The line inched forward slowly, like syrup oozing from a can. Finally she turned a corner and saw an arrow far ahead aimed at a flight of stairs. "You get your tickets up there," an usher pointed at the stairs. "Then you ride to the top, but you can't stay because of the crowds. You want to hang around up there, come back in November."

The line lurched and seemed to pull apart into sections. The air was sweet and heavy with the smell of sweat and perfume, and Barbara felt lightheaded. She bumped into someone's shoulder, apologized and straightened up. In the winter, she recalled with a jolt, a gunman opened fire on the observation deck of this very same building. Innocent tourists were wounded and someone killed. It could happen again, happen to her. She could wind up a sad statistic, a half-remembered victim.

She stepped out of the lineup and doubled back the way she'd come. In the air-conditioned lobby she grabbed hold of a velvet rope, lowered her head and breathed deeply until she felt cool enough and steady enough to go outside.

From there she caught a slow, wheezy bus traveling uptown in bumper-to-bumper traffic. She got out at Forty-ninth and walked through Rockefeller Center, then rested on a low wall surrounding a dry fountain on the Avenue of the Americas. All around were office towers like tall, gray cereal boxes lined up one behind the other on a white shelf. It was Monday, lunch hour, and people poured onto the street like identical Cheerios rolling out of their cartons. Men in open-collared shirts and women in smart sundresses perched around the fountain. They were chewing sandwiches, sipping coffee, not seeing the middle-aged woman balancing her purse on her knees and looking unsteady on the edge of the wall.

A bearded man in a shapeless hat sat down on her left side, his thigh against Barbara's. She swung her purse over her shoulder, hugging it under her right arm, and inched away. The man slid even closer and brought his face up to hers.

"Hot day."

He smelled sour. She jumped up, joined the stream of people on the sidewalk and was pulled briskly along until she lost sight of the fountain and bearded man. Finally she stepped aside and pointed her camera at the receding towers. Snap, snap, snap, snap as people jostled her, hurried on, and Barbara spun like a turnstile jerked around a notch at a time. The shots would be nothing more than lopsided slits of glass and dark streaks of concrete.

Then she turned north again and walked to the Craft Museum, feeling the last of her energy leaking out of her sore heels. Once inside the museum she fell into a chair in a dim, empty room with a grainy video playing on a small screen. The film was about a young artist weaving willow branches into something that most resembled an oversized wasp's nest. The giant display itself was behind the last row of chairs. Barbara watched the video over and over again, massaging her blistered feet, then moved to the back of the room and stepped into the sculpture. It was faintly lit through a hole in the top. The walls were rough-textured and close, surrounding her like dense woods. She sat down on the webbed floor in a space only large enough to accommodate her jutting knees. In the quiet gloom of the woven nest she felt like a larva in the intricate mesh of a thick cocoon. Carefully she touched the walls. A stillness in her all at once, like the stillness she felt at her wheel sometimes, when consciousness moved into her hands and she was aware of nothing but the strength of her fingers.

She stayed there even after the moment passed and weariness returned like a weight pressing down on her head. She closed her eyes and slipped back ten, maybe twelve years, to the summer's day she walked in the woods of Northern Ontario, climbing among lichen-covered boulders and scraggly pines, and discovered a shallow cave where she hunched up just like this and listened to the drone of bugs, the drip of water, patter of leaves. There were snakes in the forest, stray foxes, wasps, bees and whatnot; night was fast approaching, she was hungry and thirsty, getting cold, and unsure of the way back. But there, alone in the polished cave, her mind relaxed for a while and she felt still.

It was already dark when the spell broke and she started back in the general direction of the cottage they had rented. She took several wrong turns and was breathing hard when she ran into Elliot in a clearing, waving a flashlight at the trees. By then she was glad to see him, but didn't let on.

"Are you out of your mind?" he scolded her. "Alone in the woods at this hour? You said you'd be gone ten minutes."

"I was just on my way back. I would've been home shortly."

"You would've been here all night wandering in circles if I didn't come and find you!"

"You didn't find me—I wasn't lost."

She strode past him, swinging her arms. But later that night she would curl up against him on the musty-smelling mattress and cry.

Now Barbara sat up and opened her eyes. She climbed

out of the sculpture and toured the rest of the museum, glimpsing rows of display cases filled with pots and lidded jars. But what she would remember best when she looked back on her visit was the silent nest.

Back in her hotel room she kicked off her sandals and fell across the double bed. It was late afternoon and her room was sunny, hot and stale. She closed the window and turned on the air conditioner full blast. She opened her legs to the shoot of air and spread her damp hair on the bed. Yes, she'd done it, gone alone, and here she was at the end of the day, stunned and exhausted, with no one to talk to. What was the point of all this?

She rolled over, reached for the phone and dialed a number: Elliot's. She didn't expect him to be there. It would've been enough to hear his buzzy, flat message on the answering machine, but he picked up at once and said, "Where are you, for godssake?" when he recognized Barbara's voice.

"Midtown Manhattan. The same hotel we stayed in three years ago, as a matter of fact."

The line crackled. "You're alone?"

"That's right."

"And didn't tell anyone where you were going? Not even the children?"

"I'm telling you. I'm telling you now."

"No one even knew you were gone. Didn't you think we'd worry when we found out you disappeared? Didn't that occur to you?"

"I didn't disappear, I just decided to take a little trip. You probably didn't even notice I was missing till I phoned. And now you won't have to worry, you know where I am."

"I suppose you want me to fly down and rescue you."

"Rescue me!"

He paused. "Are you all right?"

"Of course I am. Just tired." She laughed. "Don't you remember how exhausting Manhattan is?"

"When are you coming home?" he said.

"I'm not sure. A few days."

"I could fly down anyway," he spoke in a quieter voice. "I'm not doing anything."

"I don't want you to do that. I want to do this on my own. I just called to let you know." Which wasn't the whole truth, but as much as she wanted to tell him.

The next day she went to places she'd been to with Elliot: the Metropolitan, Guggenheim, a bookstore on Lexington; a bakery with fresh bagels close to the hotel. All day long she thought of him, which wasn't supposed to happen. The way he'd walk up to a painting until he was nearly touching it, then back away carefully, considering it from this angle and that as his perspective changed. They could've spent a morning in a single room of the museum. He would choose a book in the same way, turning it over in his hands and flipping pages one by one, as if there were no other books in the store.

She thought of him again when she entered the bakery: the way he'd marched back and forth eyeing bins of bagels—garlic, onion, seven-grain—before choosing pumpernickel; then up and down the glass counter, deciding on the right filling—not salmon or chopped herring, chopped liver or tofu, but ordinary egg salad. How he sat across from her at a bistro table by the wall (the very same table she was sitting at now, alone), his mouth stretched wide to accommodate the bagel while a dollop of egg salad fell to his plate. How she herself had to put her bagel down and pause for breath because her throat was squeezed shut with a tenderness she couldn't explain.

An old man suddenly appeared at her table and said,

"You don't mind? There's no other chairs." Barbara nodded, "Be my guest," as he sat down and noisily chewed his sesame-poppy seed-caraway bagel with cream cheese. She beamed a smile at his lowered head, waiting for him to look up and make conversation, but the man kept his eyes on his plate and wolfed down his bagel. Finally she asked him if he'd lived here his whole life. Was he married? Any children? Did he play chess in Washington Square? Feed the pigeons in Central Park?

He wiped his mouth on the back of his hand, then pulled a photo from his shirt and slid it across the table. It showed a plump woman and child. Black-eyed and button-mouthed, they wore the same tight-waisted, puffy-sleeved party dresses and flowered hats. "Very pretty," Barbara said.

The man picked up the picture and rubbed it against his cheek. Then he put the photo away and jabbed a finger at what was left of the whole wheat bagel on her plate. "Never get the plain," he said, "if you can have the fancy for the same price."

She paused to consider this advice. Was it meant philosophically? A cryptic bit of wisdom like a message in a fortune cookie?

He took her hand and patted it. "The seeds get in your teeth but it's worth it, every damn one."

"I'm not sure what you mean," she said.

Whereupon, like a courtier, he kissed the back of Barbara's hand, bowed and left the table. All the way back to her hotel she felt the gentle pressure of his dry lips on her startled skin.

That night she slept fitfully under the taut bedclothes and dreamed about a gallery with portraits of old men. She dreamed a picture of Brad, too, his ponytail and open shirt and unbelted raincoat, a tuft of hair showing just below the hollow of his throat—the way he looked the afternoon he stopped by her house unannounced and they stood on the street a while, discussing grog and crazing. The way his fingers shaped the air as he spoke quickly, fired up.

In another shot Brad was lying naked with splayed feet, his long, even toes like the keys of a piano; his hands still moving. Barbara murmured in her sleep. But later, as the air conditioner clanged and rattled on and off, Elliot filled the frame of her dream, bucking and bouncing on a bed. It pained her to wake up to a gray morning, all alone in a chilly, sour hotel room.

Her third day in Manhattan she decided to ride a ferry to the Statue of Liberty. At Fifty-first and Lexington she sank step by step into the tunnel of the subway. Just past the turnstiles a bag of hot, muggy air closed around her head and she struggled for air. But the train itself, when she got on, was cool, clean and quiet. Passengers read newspapers, dozed, knitted, stared at nothing, bounced to the beat of their headphones. It all seemed perfectly harmless and Barbara relaxed in her seat.

She changed for the local and got off at South Ferry. Then she bought a ticket for the boat to Liberty Island and lined up beside the dock. It had started to rain, a fine mist, which meant that the view would be lousy, but also there'd be fewer tourists to sidestep.

A man appeared from nowhere with an armload of umbrellas and sold them all before she found a five-dollar bill in her purse. Umbrellas opened around her like flowers spreading their petals as she yanked her windbreaker over her head. Another man in a straw hat parked to one side of the line, pulled a banjo from a case and began playing calypso songs. On a dry, hot, sunny day it might have been appropriate, but not today, not in the rain. Why was he playing in the rain? Water dripped from his elbow and from the corner of his hat as he sang about banana boats and nights in Jamaica. The crowd shifted uneasily and stepped away from the troubadour. After a while he passed a hat, which came back nearly empty. The man scowled. "What? Don't you like my songs? Don't you like how they make you feel?" He thrust his hat in someone's face. "Then show me you like what I do. Is that so much to ask, a couple dollars for my trouble? Man, you see it's raining out? You think I want to be here?"

Barbara pushed through the line and put her five-dollar bill in the man's hat. He grabbed her hand and began singing slowly and quietly, as if for her and no one else—a song she'd never heard before about a girl with beautiful hands. She shivered in her jacket. Then the man gave her his card ("available for anniversaries, weddings and bar mitzvahs"), hoisted his banjo and left.

The ferry arrived and she got on. As soon as they reached the island, she bought a poncho decorated with little green Liberties and slipped it on. Then she followed the crowd to a rectangular plaza where people stood in two lines leading to an entrance at the foot of the statue. Barbara went to a doorway where there wasn't any lineup at all. "This is for the elevator," a guide explained. She could wait outside in the rain for hours to climb winding stairs to the crown or ride to the top of the pedestal in seconds flat.

Barbara took the elevator. The operator told her you couldn't see very much from the crown in this kind of weather anyway.

She walked around the pedestal as if she were wading through a cloud, reading the walls with her fingers as she inched along. It was windy on the platform and her statue-studded poncho billowed and flapped like a parachute. She circled round a few times and then, in a moment when the fog thinned and blew apart, stopped to take a shot of New York. In the distance the city was a humped shape against the sky, a mound of clay. She lifted her camera, pressing its eye against her own, and held the lumpy skyline between her hands.

On her last day Barbara took a Circle Line boat tour. Another rainy day, but she'd brought an umbrella this time. She climbed to the upper deck and stood under her wide umbrella, watching the city drift by. There went the Chrysler and Empire State buildings, the World Trade Center and the skyscrapers of Wall Street. New Jersey on the other side and then, as they entered the harbor, the Statue of Liberty once again, her torch blurred in a pillow of mist.

"May I share your umbrella?" a woman said, and Barbara made room for her. The woman ducked beside her and snapped a shot of the statue. "Oh, I know it's corny, but she always makes me choke up." The woman glanced at Barbara's face. "You're teary-eyed too."

"Just the rain," said Barbara, but it wasn't rain in her eyes and it wasn't the statue that was making them water. It was Elliot again—she was thinking about her husband. Because the view of Wall Street had made her think of finance; which made her picture him reading the business pages in the *Globe*, and how she interrupted once by plopping herself down on his knee; and how he slid his hand under her skirt and squeezed her inner thigh; and how they stretched out on the couch in a crinkle of inky pages and thought how lucky they were for the safety and affection of each other's arms. That had happened years ago . . . but not so many years ago. Too many years ago.

"Have you been to Liberty Island?" the woman asked.

"Yesterday."

"Never want to go there myself—too many tourists. Poor Lady Liberty, you wonder how it makes her feel, alone on the water and surrounded by strangers."

"Very lonely, I suppose."

The boat entered the East River, slipped under the Brooklyn Bridge and sailed past the U.N. The woman pointed toward shore. "See that building over there? That belonged to Jackie O. I bet she was lonely too."

"I don't think so," Barbara said. "She knew so many people, and her children and the Kennedys—"

"Lonely in *here*"—the woman pressed a large hand over her heart. "It doesn't matter who you are and how many people you know—everyone carries a bag of grief."

The landscape turned treeless and bleak as they went past Harlem. Then an eruption of green as they wound through the Harlem River, swung into the Hudson and sailed by the Cloisters.

The woman started talking again. "So, are you married?"

"Yes," Barbara said, "but my husband and I live separately."

"You're separated?"

"Not exactly. We live in separate apartments in the same house."

"You get along?"

"We get along just fine. Sometimes we meet for lunch, see a movie, go for a drive—"

"And then what?"

"Do we have sex? Is that what you mean?"

"I didn't mean—"

"Everyone wants to know that. It's the first thing people ask."

"You don't have to answer."

"Not anymore," said Barbara. "It wasn't . . . it didn't work out."

By and large she'd gotten used to no sex. She'd been getting used to it slowly when she still lived with Elliot and their lovemaking was infrequent, uninspired. And yet, when she saw an attractive man—a man like Brad, for instance—desire returned as quick and sharp as a stitch in her side. If she ignored it, it went away. But memories of better times, of certain nights with Elliot, stuck together under the sheets, were harder to set aside.

"I was also married once, but that was so long ago I can't remember his face anymore. You never think that you'll forget the features of your husband. . . ." The woman shrugged. "But then you do. You remember things he said or did, but not exactly how he looked. Someone else becomes important, crowds his picture from your mind—or else you just get on with your life and fill your head with other things."

Barbara squeezed her eyes closed and there was Elliot plain as day: his thin hair and thick neck, his face screwed up in bafflement. *You'd really forget me?* He mouthed the words. *After all we've been through?* When she opened her eyes to strangers and the drizzle-coated upper deck, she felt relieved.

The woman was watching her. "Would you mind taking my picture?" She held out a camera and went to stand by the wet rail. Barbara laid her umbrella down, swung her own camera aside, then aimed and focused the other one. Probably the woman was as old as Barbara's mother, but unlike Dora in her black sweaters and gray suits, she wore a yellow raincoat, a blue plastic rain bonnet and red boots. Dora would rather be soaked to the bone than be seen in such an outfit.

In the viewfinder the colors were distinct and riveting. Barbara looked through the glass square, her finger on the shutter button pulsing but steady, and the colors seemed to enter her. They came in through her finger and moved up. Her eyes fluttered shut again: colors and shapes behind her lids, but Elliot was nowhere in sight.

She peered into the camera. The woman posed at the ship's rail with bluffs in the background. She stood as still as a sign flashing red, yellow and blue, then disappeared in brightness. The brilliant colors swam in the air, unaffected by the rain. When Barbara clicked the shutter button she reappeared.

The woman turned toward the cliffs. "Life is full of special moments," she said over her shoulder, "and they can be enough, you know."

The boat rocked on the water. After a while the woman said, "Let's take one of you now," and Barbara passed her the cameras.

With Riverside Church in the background she stepped up to the guardrail. Rain fingered her gleaming hair and spattered on her bare arms. It touched her brow, nose and chin and pooled at her collar like the lips of a lover on her neck. A warm rain that polished her skin as slick as mud.

"That's a good one," the woman said. "You look glad to be here."

Barbara stood very still in the rain-softened moment. Next week she would hold the picture gingerly in the palm of her hand. She would study her features carefully, as if she were seeing them for the first time. She would notice that the camera had caught her shy and open-mouthed, like an infant astonished by her unaccountable hunger. She would see herself shiny and wet, sliding into the arms of the world.

9

RELATING

In the gloom of the movie theater, Elliot worried about his hands. They seemed to have a will of their own. They seemed imbued with the memory of how he behaved as a teenager sitting next to a pretty girl in a darkened room. The left wanted to slide across her back to rest on her shoulder, while the other one had bolder ideas. The right hand was straining to inch under her short skirt, to slither up her stockinged thigh and dive into the V of her crotch— and was pulling at the end of his arm like a dog on a leash.

Fifty-three years old and he still had these urges. Elliot laced his fingers, squeezed his hands together in his lap and sat stiffly, motionless. He could not follow the movie. Someone had been killed—there was blood on the screen and a naked corpse—and now a cop and suspect were rolling and bouncing and panting in bed, which wasn't helping anything, neither the plot nor his twitching hands. Elliot tucked his fingers under his thighs and flattened them with his weight.

Beside him Celia was eating a bag of popcorn, her eyes as round as doorknobs. The chomp she made as she chewed and the crinkling of the popcorn bag keyed him up even more. If he kissed her he would silence her; then, going further, trade munchy-crunchy sounds for slipping and slurping as he probed her with his fingers and tongue. Something stirred and he looked down: the shiny zipper of his fly bulged and dipped like the tracks of a roller coaster.

Shit! What was he thinking? Could these be the true thoughts of a steady, still-married man out for an evening with his buddy Ivan, Ivan's girl and her wide-eyed friend Celia? Is this what usually happens when you press the leg of an older man against the unsuspecting thigh of a woman in a miniskirt—even if she's twenty years younger and a stranger?

He turned toward Ivan, who was sitting in the next seat, but Ivan's back was facing him. Ivan's arms were lost in the dark shape at the end of the row, his girlfriend Ramona.

"You need distraction," Ivan had said. "You're spending too much time on your own. Come with us to the movies, we'll find you a date. And maybe you'll get lucky."

"Why do I need a date?"

"You want to get over Barb or not?"

He'd thought about her trip to New York; he'd thought about that overly friendly young man with the ponytail and the fact that Elliot hadn't slept with anyone in sixteen months, then told Ivan he was ready, he wanted to meet someone new. But now he wasn't so sure.

Celia leaned into his shoulder and offered Elliot popcorn. "No thanks," he whispered, "it gets stuck between my teeth." The most he'd said to her all night. When Ramona introduced them outside the cinema he'd said, "Nice to meet you," and Celia shook his hand and answered, "Nice to meet you too." Then Ivan jumped right in, telling the plot of the movie and what the critics had to say, until it was time to go inside. Now he felt he owed her at least another sentence. "Also you could break a crown biting down on a kernel." Hating himself immediately for mentioning his damn crowns, which would only remind her of his age.

Behind him someone hissed "Sssh!" and Celia snickered into the bag. Was she laughing at Elliot? Because someone shushed him or because of his crowns? She was old enough for crowns herself—he'd fitted them for teenagers! Old enough for root canals and even a partial bridge. He'd seen plenty of cases in his long years as a dentist. But that was behind him now.

Celia crumpled her popcorn bag and dropped it casually under her seat. From the corner of his eye he watched her lick salt from her fingers. Suddenly she stopped with her fingers stuck to her lower lip and stared at the screen. The same cop and suspect were making love in the back of a car. He noticed the similarities of darkness and cramped seats, a skimpy skirt and bare thighs, and wondered if Celia had too, as her leg moved against his, her hand brushed across his knee and she made a mewling sound in her throat.

The movie finally ended with a fanfare of gunfire and screaming tires. Lucky for the horny cop the long-legged suspect turned out to be innocent, and they fell into bed again as the credits rolled. When the lights came on Ramona said, "It was just so *violent*. We should've seen a comedy. I hate all this violence," and Ivan stroked her shoulder and kissed her cheek.

Out on the street they headed toward Ivan's car two by two, the men up front, the women behind. Ramona was wearing thigh-high leather boots with tall heels that clacked against the sidewalk. Celia said to her, "Well, but you liked the cop, didn't you? He was so cute."

Ivan quickened his step, pulling Elliot by the elbow, and widened the gap between the pairs. "What do you think of Celia?" he asked when they were out of range.

"I hardly know her," Elliot said. "We haven't exchanged a dozen words."

"But she looks great, doesn't she? If you ask me, that's a good start." He elbowed Elliot in the side—"Makes the old libido jump."

Elliot moved away from him. "Your car's just across the street. Why don't we wait here and let the girls catch up."

Ivan stopped dead in his tracks. "Something's bugging you, I can tell. This isn't about your wife, is it? You're not feeling guilty?"

Not that exactly. More just . . . peculiar. At odds with himself. But that was too complicated to talk about with Ivan. "I'm not thinking about Barb. And yes, Celia's attractive. It's just that she's so young, and I'm out of practice."

Ivan patted him on the back as the women walked up to them. "It all comes back to you, just watch."

Ramona was dragging her right foot. "I stepped in something back there." She hopped to the curb and scraped the sole of her boot against the sidewalk. "Stupid dogs," she grumbled. "You can never get the smell out."

"It's not the dogs," Celia said. "They're doing what comes natural."

"Ha! Stupid fleabags. They should all be rounded up and shot."

"They have as much right to live as you do," Celia said. She crossed her arms and stuck out her hip. "When I was growing up we had a poodle named Snowball and we never let her do her business out in the open. We always kept her on a leash and cleaned up after. You can't blame the dogs. It's the owners who don't look after them properly that should be shot."

Elliot gulped down a lump of nausea at the back of

his mouth. Why was he listening to an inane discussion of dog shit? Why would he want to spend the night with an animal rights activist who probably adored baby seals? They crossed the street and Ivan unlocked his car. "Elliot's a dog person too," he told Celia as they climbed in and buckled up, Ivan and Ramona up front, Celia and Elliot in the back. "What kind?" she asked Ivan. He started the engine, pulled away from the curb and drove northwest. "Big dogs. Any kind." He looked in the rearview mirror. "Isn't that right, Elliot?"

"Newfoundlands are my favorite," he answered the mirror.

"Big dogs frighten me."

She stared out the side window as Elliot put a hand on her knee. Look what his hand was doing now!—his foolish, unthinking hand with its own base agenda. He expected her to push it off but she didn't move. "They're smart, friendly animals," he said in a kindly tone, squeezing her knee for emphasis. The sleekness of her stocking against the pads of his fingertips made him stiffen under his fly. His hand began to rotate around the hump of her kneecap. He scolded himself—*she's not your type, you know nothing about her*—but his hand wouldn't stop. Without so much as glancing at him she put her fingers over his and together they massaged her knee. He could hardly believe the brazenness of what they were doing.

Ivan parked in front of a café and they got out. Inside it was so dark that Elliot walked into a stool. Celia laughed and took his arm. They found a table in the back, ordered drinks and nachos and vegetable sticks for Celia, who was watching her weight. "What are you watching your weight for, you're thin as a bean," said Elliot.

"I work at it," she answered. "Aerobics and weight lifting and being careful what I eat." Celia flexed her biceps and Elliot gave her arm a pinch. The feel of her hard muscle under the softness of her blouse was a provocative sensation.

"Celia's a gym teacher, junior high," Ramona said. When she named the school where Celia worked, a nacho lodged in Elliot's throat and he hacked loudly into his hands. Ramona looked scared. "Is he okay?"

Ivan passed him a glass of water and told him to drink. When he looked up, his face burning, Elliot grinned stupidly. "It's just, my wife—before she left. . . . My wife used to teach there."

"Your wife?"

"His ex-wife, he means."

"I thought you might've known her. I thought maybe you worked with Barb, maybe you were even friends."

"Barb who?"

"Rifkin. She taught art to Grade Eight."

"Grayish hair, pulled back, sort of like this?" Celia yanked her blonde-streaked hair into a ponytail. "Dark eyes, medium tall, a little on the plump side?"

"Curvy, I'd say, not plump—but that sounds like her, all right."

Celia stirred the ice cubes in her drink with a swizzle stick. "I didn't know her well," she said. "I was only there a few months before she retired, but I know who you mean. We met in the staff room once or twice and chatted about this and that."

The temperature of Elliot's skin rose even higher and his earlobes began to pulse. "What did you talk about?"

"Just things."

He laughed a false laugh—"Me?"—and Celia looked at him blankly.

Ivan ordered more drinks. Ramona excused herself and hurried off to the washroom, clickety-clacking her way across the pine floor. Celia chewed a carrot stick and gazed over Elliot's head. "Well, did you?" he pursued.

"Can't remember," she said, "but I'm sure it wasn't personal. Probably just school stuff."

"Let's drop this," Ivan said when the waitress put their drinks down. "It's not going anywhere."

Celia stood up and said she was going to the bathroom too. As soon as she was out of sight Ivan hissed at Elliot, "Are you some kind of schmuck or something, going on about your wife? You want to get laid or don't you?"

"I want to get to know her a bit. I was trying to make conversation."

"Didn't we agree that if you're going to forget Barb, you have to sleep with someone else?"

"But she knew her, she talked to her. If Celia and I—if we actually made it—Barb would be in the room too. I'd be wondering what they said about me."

"Didn't you hear Celia? She hardly knew Barb and they never said anything personal. You're really blowing it, Elliot. She wants you to squeeze her biceps, she doesn't want to discuss your wife."

When Celia and Ramona returned, they swallowed their drinks quickly and finished the food. Something dripped on Ramona's skirt and she had to run to the washroom again to rub it with soap and water. Ivan talked about baseball while Celia played with her swizzle stick and Elliot shivered to think that his wife might've told a stranger things about their sex life. As soon as Ramona came back Ivan suggested they call it a night, and everyone followed him out the door.

They got in the car and Ivan asked Celia where to drop her off. She gave him an address and minutes later he stopped in front of a featureless apartment house. Her hand already on the door, Celia turned and signaled to Elliot with a flick of her head. When he hesitated she took his hand and tugged him out behind her. He could hear Ivan's laughter as he drove off.

"Thought you'd like to have a drink and see my apartment." She led him through a small lobby with two chairs and a sofa chained to a wrought-iron railing. He followed her around a corner and onto an elevator. "I didn't just want to say goodbye and maybe never see you again."

"Why would you want to see me again? It's not as if the evening was a great success."

"I'd like to get to know you." She pushed Twelve and the doors closed. "You seem like a nice guy."

The walls of the elevator were panels of speckled glass and he stared at their reflections in the harsh light. Her hair was brown with yellow strands, her face blotchy-pink and smooth. His own complexion was ghastly pale, his skin puffy, scored with lines, and what remained of his hair was gray. Why would anyone want to get to know him? "Twelve's my lucky number," he said, the first thing that came to mind.

The elevator doors opened and Celia jiggled a ring of keys. "You just got lucky, didn't you?" She winked one of her big eyes.

Her apartment was done in white with bold colors here and there like unexpected ink blots. White sofa, white chairs, white table and curtains; a red pillow, green planter, blue lampshade, purple vase. An uninviting room that spoke of a longtime single occupant. A room that made him feel sad. She left him in the living room and vanished into the kitchen. "Go sit down," she called out, but he couldn't possibly do that. What if his new jeans stained the moon-white upholstery? What if he got a nosebleed? "It's okay," Celia said. "Everything's done in Scotch Guard."

He sat on the edge of an armchair covered in some nubbly fabric that seemed a shade or two darker than everything else. Celia brought him a glass of wine, also white, and one for herself. She flopped down on the thick rug directly in front of him, her legs tucked under and her skirt hiked up her thighs. "So tell me about yourself."

He could say he shouldn't be here, he wasn't ready after all to be alone with a pretty girl, but his hands clutched the arms of the chair and he stared dumbly at her thighs.

"Ramona said you used to be a dentist. Was it interesting?" Elliot mumbled something and she grinned, showing crooked teeth. "Maybe if we become friends you can do something about my smile."

"I'm not an orthodontist," he said.

"Maybe you can straighten me out." She giggled at her little joke, then put aside her wineglass. "You don't talk much, do you?"

"I'm not interested in your teeth."

"So what are you interested in?" She swung out her legs, drew them up and hugged her slightly parted knees, so that Elliot got a glimpse of the dark cave between her thighs. A throb and flutter in his groin: she wasn't wearing panties. Maybe she took them off in the kitchen, maybe in the café when she went to the bathroom. Or maybe she'd been bare-assed even in the movie theater, wet and waiting all night long.

"Come sit over here," Celia patted the rug.

He finished his wine and lowered himself slowly down beside her. She pulled his head to hers and he kissed her glossy, puckered mouth. "I'm interested in this," he said, one hand darting under her blouse, "and this," as the other slithered under her skirt. His mind interrupted with a warning that they hardly knew each other and should talk more; that Barb had told her intimate lies; that she was just a few years older than his daughter. That his condoms were in his wallet, tucked into his back pocket, and how could he get one discreetly? That at any moment Celia might laugh, push him away and throw him out, flexing her beautiful biceps. But the blood pulsing in his ears was louder than his worried thoughts, and his fingers just kept moving.

She helped him take her clothes off. Her breasts were bumps with pink nipples no larger than nickels. Hard stomach, narrow waist, hipbones sharp and prominent: a woman who never had children.

She unzipped Elliot's fly and reached for his penis, as hard as a seventeen-year-old's. He groaned, falling back on the rug, and Celia undressed him quickly, throwing his clothes onto hers. Her mouth was all over him as he worked his wallet out of his jeans and pulled out a condom. Then he was on top of her, kissing her and murmuring and fumbling with the condom. Then he was jammed deep, up-to-the-hilt inside her.

He never guessed he would be like this—so vital and excited—and it thrilled him, it stilled his mind. He never guessed that her smoothness, her wetness and tightness would stir him into a frenzy: hair in his eyes, his fingers slick, his belly slap-slapping her own. A stud, a brute, a satyr . . . until she groaned for more and cried for him to stop at the same time.

When he plucked off the condom, slippery and full, it slid through his fingers and emptied on the white rug. Celia grabbed it and ran off. He heard a toilet flush with a growl and water splashing into a sink. He sat up on the soiled rug and kneaded a tender spot on his back.

When Celia returned she was wearing a terry bathrobe. She frowned at the wet spot, knelt down and rubbed the stain with the hem of her robe.

"Sorry about that," he said, meaning the spill.

"Don't be sorry—you were great! I really appreciate older men."

Elliot froze. So that's it, he thought sadly, Barbie Doll

149

likes geezers. Because they're grateful, no doubt. Because they last a long time. Because they spend money on you and treat you like a lady—and every other cliché about older men he could think of. Then he dug through the pile of clothes and pulled on his boxer shorts, jeans and socks.

He picked up his bunched shirt and flicked out the wrinkles. Not because she honestly liked him, wanted to get to know him better or thought he had a nice face, a sexy voice, a kind heart. Elliot's chest sank as he slipped on his shirt and buttoned it. Anyway, he wasn't really old, he was only middle-aged.

Celia rocked back on the rug and wrapped her arms around her knees, her robe falling open from the waist down. He looked away.

"What's the matter, Elliot? Why are you getting dressed? You don't have to go yet. I want you to stay—I mean it."

He was cold and clammy in his clothes and wanted to sleep for twenty-four hours. He wanted to be out of there, in a taxi on his way home. In his kitchen, drinking warm milk; in a hot shower, washed clean; under a blanket in his own bed. He wanted someone to hold him and stroke him and whisper his name. Someone older than Celia.

She got up and hugged him, pressing her breasts into his back. "We can do it again if you like, just don't go yet, don't leave. I want to spend the night with you. I want to lie with you and watch the sun come up in the morning. Wouldn't that be wonderful?" Gently she massaged his neck and shoulders and his tight scalp. "You don't really want to be alone tonight, do you?"

He jerked away from her touch as if her fingers were ice picks.

"We'll help each other out a little, give each other

comfort. Even just for one night."

"For godssake, you're not my wife! I don't even know your last name. Why should I help you with anything?" He strode to the door and opened it.

"You didn't help *her* either, did you?"

He swung around. "What was that?"

She crossed her arms and jutted her hip. "I'm talking about your ex, Barb. She told me you can't expect a man to cure your loneliness . . . and now I understand what she meant."

Elliot didn't stop to think that Barb's remark was ambiguous. He stared at Celia open-mouthed, his back hurting, shoulders bent. Then he turned and staggered out, like a drunk or a baby or an old man in need of a cane.

He slept in till ten-thirty, something he hadn't done in years, and woke up hungry and dazed, only to discover he was out of bread and coffee and the fridge was nearly empty, the cupboards bare. Not even a box of cereal or a lousy egg. He drank some close-to-sour juice, changed into a tracksuit, combed his fingers through his hair, brushed his teeth and went out.

A cloudy day in September. The summer had been especially hot, and now the street looked wilted and dull. All around were parched lawns, gray sidewalks, faded bricks. Rows of droopy leaves on the trees reminded him of loose teeth. Even though it wasn't cold, he buttoned up his cardigan, hunched his shoulders and ducked his head. He blamed the weather for his mood. He blamed Barb and Celia and the treachery of women.

The coffee shop was the farthest away and that's where he headed first. He bought half a pound of beans, ground extra fine, and a cup of the house blend to go. When the coffee cooled he slurped it down. Walking south, he picked up bananas and grapefruit. The young clerk at the register wished him a nice day and Elliot snorted in reply.

Next he stopped at the supermarket for cornflakes, milk and eggs. On line at the checkout he spotted a familiar woman talking to the cashier and bagging her groceries. Maryellen what's-her-name, his former cooking instructor. Wallow, Woolen . . . *Whelan*. He called her name and waved and was relieved, when she turned around, that Maryellen Whelan seemed to recognize him too.

She waited for him just inside the front doors. "Good to see you again," she grinned, and he was struck once more by the fine whiteness of her teeth. Her straight, evenly spaced teeth that needed no fixing.

"How long has it been?" he said.

"One year and five months," she counted on her fingers. "Are you still doing Tai Chi?"

"Absolutely. Every day. I know the whole form now." His ears burned as he recalled the time he brought her back to his apartment for a demonstration and wound up tripping over his own feet.

"Too bad I never got to see it," Maryellen said.

He couldn't tell by the tone of her voice whether she was mocking him, fishing for an invitation or shrinking at the thought of that silly, bungled afternoon. He bumped his plastic bag of groceries nervously against his knees and wondered what to do next. But when she picked up her grocery bag and pushed through the exit, he simply followed her out and fell into step at her side. "I'm off to the butcher," she said.

"Okay if I tag along? I want to buy some cold cuts." When she nodded agreement, a single coil of red hair bounced on her forehead. He tried to picture the rest of her hair, tucked under the bowl of her hat (wavy, curly, long or short?), but the memory escaped him. He wanted to ask her to take off her hat, but what he said instead was, "Are you still teaching 'Cooking for Men'?"

"Oh yes, 'Basic Cooking.' I just finished another course."

Her lips were as purple-red as when she was his teacher, her face still freckled and smooth (though noticeably rounder); her eyes as friendly as ever. And yet she seemed smaller and tired and moved heavily down the street. Was it solitude that weighed her down, or just the accumulation of years?

"I keep busy during the day," she seemed to answer to his question, "but the nights can really drag on."

"Nights are the hardest," he said. "I try to go to bed early, but then I lie awake for hours."

She touched his arm lightly. "Herbal teas are excellent if you have trouble falling asleep. Passion flower or chamomile."

They entered the butcher shop. Maryellen walked back and forth across the creaking floor, examining the glass case, then chose chicken legs and a pound of lean ground beef. For his part, Elliot bought slices of ham and bologna. "Is that all you're getting?" she asked. "What about the good things you learned to make in my classes? Beef stew, meat loaf. . . . I hope you haven't forgotten. I hope you're eating properly. Do you take a multivitamin?"

"Well, no."

"You ought to. I started doing that myself just last winter and haven't had a cold since."

Next he followed her down the block and into a health food store, thinking that he'd had more colds and flus than he could count since he and Barb split up. Maryellen bought granola, yogurt and a strange grain that smelled like paint; buckwheat honey, black beans, organic kale and oatmeal soap. Elliot got an expensive bottle of vitamin-mineral tablets that Maryellen suggested.

"So how've you been?" she asked when they were out on the street again. "What have you been up to?"

"Oh, this and that," he said.

"Did you and your wife get back together?"

"No."

"Didn't think so. I could tell by the way you shopped. When people live alone they forget to take care of themselves." She stopped to arrange her grocery bags. "Me and my ex will never get together again either." She looked up and squinted at something in the distance. "Five years now and I'm still not used to it. Do you ever get used to living alone?"

Elliot didn't respond, though he thought the answer was probably no. Who could ever adjust to silence, one table setting and an empty bed?

When they started walking again she said, "Of course there's lots to do if you want some company. Volunteer work in a shelter or soup kitchen, reading out loud to the blind. I thought I might look into it."

"Sounds like a good idea."

"You were a dentist, weren't you? You could visit schools and talk to kids about flossing and tooth decay."

"I'm not looking for things to do."

"As people grow older—especially if they live alone— they get a little peculiar. They talk to themselves, forget how to dress"—she smiled at the torn, sagging knees of his sweatpants—"and watch too much TV. They can't relate to anything except cats and houseplants."

Elliot thought of his cat Hammer (who shared his bed most nights), the ivy in his kitchen and the spider plant in the bathroom, and his mouth shrank.

"If you're by yourself you have to get out and talk to people every day or else you get old inside, too. Your blood turns to sawdust."

Speak for yourself! he wanted to say. *He* wasn't like that. Maybe he was a poor dresser and overly attached to his cat, but he didn't own a TV, he saw his children regularly and related well enough to tempt a young woman like Celia—who'd made his blood roar and made him feel seventeen again. He wasn't old and turning strange . . . just a little lonely.

But he never got the chance to speak because his hand—that willful hand!—reached out and touched her fingers carrying a shopping bag. His hand rested lightly on hers, then moved stealthily toward her wrist, her smooth knuckles rubbing his palm. When she drew a breath and slowed her pace, his heart gurgled to his ribs.

They came to a bakery and Maryellen ducked inside, but he decided to wait on the street. Did he have the courage to ask her out? Could he admit that it would mean a lot to him to spend time with a sympathetic woman? More than anything else he wanted to sit in her big, bright kitchen and watch her fix a simple meal, the way she did when he was a student in her cooking class. He wanted to see the heat of the kitchen turn her neck and face pink and bring her freckles boldly alive, just as he remembered. He'd say, *I know the last time we got together turned out bad. . . . What you must think of me,* he would laugh, *showing off my Tai Chi and falling on my ass like a clown!* But then he'd get serious, his voice dropping an octave. *Give me another chance,* he'd say. *Let's get to know each other and find whatever comfort we can.*

When Maryellen came out of the bakery he blurted, "Can I take you to dinner sometime? Next week? Saturday? I mean—do you want to?"

In answer she reached into a sweet-smelling paper bag and pulled out a pumpernickel bagel, his favorite kind. She held it up, flashing her teeth, and he grabbed a piece of the brown bagel, their fingers pulling opposite ends as if they were breaking a wishbone. "It's warm," he said. "It's still warm."

They watched each other while they chewed. Her upturned face was round, freckles scattered like chocolate chips, and pink with reflected heat. And in her eyes—her gleaming eyes—he saw the golden flames of a hearth.

10

Hot and Cold

"**Dad's got a girlfriend,**" Susan said, her voice scratchy on the phone. "They go to the ballet."

"Ballet? Your father?"

"He says he's drinking herbal tea and taking multi-vitamins."

"People change, I suppose."

"What do you mean 'people change'? How can you be so blasé?"

Barbara moved the phone receiver slightly away from her ear. "What do you expect me to do?"

"Get angry at least!" said Susan. "I give you infuriating news and you don't react."

"You think I don't know what's been going on?"

"He told you?"

"He didn't have to tell me."

"Then what?"

A silent pause. Barbara imagined Susan twisting the phone cord around her wrist.

"You don't mean you *hear* them? You actually hear her upstairs?"

"It's his apartment, Susan. He can do what he likes."

"How can you stand it? You should bang the ceiling, kick his door—"

"Really, I have to go now. Gran's coming for dinner and I haven't done a thing yet. Let's talk another time." Barbara slapped the phone down. She only hoped her mother wouldn't harp on Elliot's friend as well.

She went to the kitchen, breaded veal, peeled potatoes, washed lettuce, then sat down to wait for Dora. But no sooner did she arrive, hang up her coat and take a seat than she started in. "He didn't have to tell the children—it's not like it's going to last. Dennis is beside himself."

Barbara filled a pot with water and started the potatoes. "How do you know it won't last? Maybe they're a good match."

Dora pushed up the sleeves of her sweater, baring her arms. "Susan said he brings her upstairs to his apartment. What's wrong with a motel? Or what about her place?"

"You spoke to Susan already?"

"I tell you, it's about sex. A man needs sex. But his heart still belongs to you."

Barbara heated a frying pan, fried the veal on one side, turned the slices over and poured a creamy sauce on top. She poked a fork in the new potatoes boiling at the back of the stove, then finished making a salad. She hadn't talked to Elliot in weeks now—two months!—ever since he started dating Maryellen what's-her-name, and didn't know if he even bothered thinking about her anymore, let alone what he felt in his heart. It was nothing she wanted to dwell on.

"I warned you," Dora said. "I told you dividing the house would only lead to no good. I told you he'll want someone in his bed again before long—not to mention home cooking and clean socks."

Barbara set the kitchen table, put down the salad bowl and a covered dish of potatoes, then served the veal straight from the pan. Her mother watched through narrowed eyes. "It's not too late," she said. "One word from you and he'll drop that hussy in a wink. Remember, Barbie, you're his wife. The wife has the last word."

"Elliot's free to do what he wants—sleep around, become a monk—it's his choice. One of the reasons we live apart is so we can make our own decisions. Whether or not I like his decisions is beside the point." Barbara cut her veal into bite-sized pieces and slipped a portion into her mouth. It tasted like leather and the sauce wasn't right either. That was her mother's fault for breaking her concentration.

The front door clicked shut and they heard footsteps, soft and heavy, on the stairs to the second floor. They heard Elliot's thick voice and a woman's lighthearted laugh. "It's her," Dora whispered. "He brought her back to spend the night."

"You don't know that," Barbara said. "Besides, it's none of our business."

Dora banged the handle of her knife on the table. "Don't pretend you don't care. Don't pretend he hasn't cut you to the quick." Of course she was thinking of her own affair with Marvin Wilkes and all the grief it caused her. So long ago, but she still remembered how it felt when he said it was over, the breath-stopping pain. She was pregnant with Barbie at the time, which didn't sway him one bit. No, he'd never leave his wife, he couldn't hurt his family. So he hurt Dora, badly, instead. Two years later he was dead from a stroke, and she thought that it served him right.

Barbara played with her fork, pushing potatoes around

her plate. "I've got my own life now," she spoke very slowly. "New friends, interesting work. . . . I can spend a day throwing clay and not know where the time went."

"Where's the satisfaction in fooling around with mud balls? Look what it's doing to your hands—they're all chapped."

Overhead the ceiling groaned. Dora stopped talking and looked up. Bumps, thumps and scraping sounds, as if Elliot and his friend were rearranging furniture. "What on earth do you think they're doing?" Dora said.

"I'm not listening."

Minutes later the upstairs door squealed and slapped shut; then there were footsteps going down. "Stay here," her mother hissed. Before Barbara could stop her, Dora popped up from the table, ran out the apartment door and into the hall. She heard her mother's sharp voice, Elliot's deeper, muffled one, and a lighter, quieter murmur. The front door opened and closed. Another moment and Dora was back.

"I told them I was just going to check for mail."

"At this hour?"

"And then I asked Elliot to introduce me to his friend."

"As if they couldn't guess what you were up to. How embarrassing!"

"I'm happy to report you have nothing to worry about. She's short, on the heavy side"—Dora made a big circle with her hands—"and definitely middle-aged. Forty-something, I'd say. And judging by her conversation, not very clever."

"What did she say, 'Nice to meet you'? That's what your opinion's based on?"

"Why are you taking her side?"

"I'm not taking any side. I'm just being sensible and grown-up about this."

"That's what I get for being helpful." Dora turned her

back to Barbara, cleared dishes from the table and stacked them on the counter.

"You're not being helpful. I don't want to hear about Elliot's friend, but you won't talk about anything else. You're no better than Susan."

Barbara washed and her mother dried. Steam rose from the filled sink, water splashed, dishes clinked and bubbles rocked on the surface. "Dinner was lovely," Dora pronounced, but Barbara only shook her head and said the veal was too tough. She peeled off her rubber gloves and swatted a strand of wet hair stuck to her forehead.

Dora put the dried dishes next to the sink. "I think they were going out to eat," she said absentmindedly. "I heard her tell Elliot there was nothing edible in his fridge."

"There you go—'edible.' She used a three-syllable word so she can't be as dumb as you think."

"I didn't think she was dumb, I only thought she wasn't as smart as you. But at least she knows a good catch when she sees one, I'll give her that."

Barbara filled the kettle for tea and put it on the stove to boil. "Any man you haven't lived with seems like a good catch."

They watched the kettle until it steamed. Dora was remembering how much she'd envied Marvin's wife, who lay with her husband every night, and how much she envied them their Sunday dinners and evening walks . . . while she exhausted herself waiting for him to call her into his office and lock the door.

She turned off the burner. "Not for me, not tonight. Suddenly I feel tired."

"I made muffins for dessert."

"I couldn't eat another thing." She hugged her daughter, got her coat. "Next time I'll stay longer."

Barbara saw her mother out, then rushed back to her

apartment, glad that Elliot and his friend hadn't chosen that particular moment to reappear. She went to her bedroom, stripped off her clothes and stared at the floor-length mirror on the closet door. Living independently had noticeably aged her. Her breasts were heavy, hips wide. There was more gray in her hair than brown, and her skin had lost its freshness. Two years ago she wasn't sure what a jowl was, but now she knew precisely—that loose, puffy ridge under her lower jaw. Elliot's fortyish girlfriend, no matter how short and round, could not look any worse than this.

She turned away from the mirror and pulled on a robe. So what if she was losing her looks—life was better than ever! She had her clay, her wheel and kiln, her friends, freedom, privacy and, of course, the children. Anyone would say she's lucky. Anyone would envy her to have as much as all that. *Lonely?* they'd say. *Who isn't?*

Back in the kitchen she made tea and had a muffin, still warm. Tomorrow morning she'd drop by Rita's studio downtown to look at her ceramics and, if her friend was free, they'd go somewhere nice for lunch. At night she was babysitting for Dennis and Natalie, and Sunday she could spend time with Susan and Mattie if she liked—go skating, see a movie, visit a museum.

But Monday she'd be on her own, back in the basement. She'd bury her arms in wet clay, trying to focus on her work, and imagine she was hearing grunts of tenderness from upstairs.

A clock ticked loudly in the silence of the shadowed room. Barbara put her cup down and stared at her hands, which were shaking. Dora was right, they were red and raw—totally ruined for the sake of bowls nobody needed.

Again she heard the front door, laughter in the hall and the trill of footsteps skipping up a flight of stairs: Elliot and his friend were back. Despite herself, she strained to hear a snippet of conversation, but their words were slurred and gurgling, like the sound of a running stream.

She heard them in his kitchen, which was over hers. Pipes crackled in the walls as they ran water in his sink; the fridge door softly whomped, a chair scraped against the floor, and here and there a footfall. Suddenly her arms tensed. Her fingers clenched of their own accord and struck the table once, twice.

She crossed her arms and trapped her tight fists in her armpits. But even though she breathed deeply, told herself that what she was feeling was irrational and visualized a tranquil beach, the bad feeling hung on. She sank heavily into her seat, although she knew she ought to get up and go to a room where she couldn't hear the two lovers overhead.

Now they were climbing the stairs to Elliot's bedroom-study on the third floor. If she listened very carefully, she might hear the springs creaking, on and on and on and on.

Her tea was cold and dark flecks had long since settled on the bottom of her cup when Barbara pushed herself up and went to the bathroom. She emptied a hamper of dirty clothes into a laundry bag, which she dragged to the kitchen. She heaved the bag onto a chair and threw in a set of stained placemats, two limp dish towels and an apron she hadn't washed in months. From upstairs a slight rasp that could've been . . . anything.

Her cheeks were hot and she puffed for breath, her heart shaking the bars of her ribs. She went to the sink to splash her face and wrists with cold water, but when she opened the tap only a thin trickle came out. They were running water upstairs.

In a house as old as this one, the pressure was lousy. You were careful not to flush a toilet, wash dishes or use the hose if someone was taking a shower. Because if you ran hot water, the person in the stall would freeze; if you ran cold he'd be scalded.

She washed herself as well as she could, then closed the faucet and sat down. Water dripped from her chin to her lap, darkening her thin robe. She leaned over and wiped her wet hands on the laundry bag. She would leave the kitchen, do a wash. Stop thinking. Keep busy. Get through the night.

But then there was a burble and gush in the wide, rusty drainpipe that ran through the broom closet on its way to the basement, which could only mean that someone was indeed taking a shower on the second floor. Maybe that was a giggle she heard, maybe it was only something dropped on the tiled floor, but Barbara knew—was totally sure—that Elliot and his girlfriend were in the stall together.

Get out, get out. Get out of here!

She swung the laundry bag over her shoulder and hurried to the basement, where she turned on a dusty light over the washing machine, dumped her clothes into the tub and added a cup of detergent. The water level was set for high and Barbara turned the temperature to cold/cold. She pulled out the control knob and twisted it to the line that marked the start of Normal Cycle. Then she closed the lid and paused.

She imagined the two of them in the shower. At this very moment he was probably soaping her big breasts, higher and firmer than Barbara's. He was running a sponge over her waist, her apple-belly and cute navel, over the pink swell of her hips and into the black kinkiness between her thighs. And Barbara could feel the tension that was building in the woman's groin, the tingling that was shooting into her hands and feet and wouldn't stop. Could feel her legs buckling. Could feel his hard, slippery cock. . . .

But no, no, she saw nothing, felt nothing—didn't care! She lurched forward and slapped her palms on the surface of the white machine. She caught her breath and straightened up. Her hand rose and Barbara's fingers grabbed the dial and pushed it in. One click and the big contraption came alive. As cold water poured in and the washing machine began to fill, she thought she heard a woman scream.

11

ON THE Move

Barbara came home one night to find a note under her door: HAVE TO TALK TO YOU RIGHT AWAY. PLEASE COME UPSTAIRS. E.

No, she wouldn't do that. What if his girlfriend answered the door? That would be embarrassing. She'd call instead. But no, not that either. What if his girlfriend picked up the phone? Anyway, she didn't want to see him or speak to him, the two-timing bastard. So Barbara pushed a note of her own under his door in the morning: WHAT ABOUT? Then she went down to the basement, where she was making porcelain bowls and a series of elaborately textured and colored plates. Challenging work demanding her absolute attention.

After a while the phone rang but she didn't bother to race upstairs. Whoever it was could leave a message. Minutes later it rang again, and then for a third time. Anyway, she was building a bowl and couldn't stop right now. Didn't want to stop now. Not even when she heard a knock on her door.

This was more important. Thinking only of glazing the outside of the bowl white, the interior crimson. Smelling the mushroom scent of clay, feeling it slimy on her skin; her fingers moving with their own sensibility as something delicate takes shape. She will hold the finished bowl in her hands, gaze at its scarlet center like a small sun and feel proud. This is what she loves. *This.*

In the afternoon she went upstairs for coffee and a sandwich. She listened to her messages. All were from Elliot, telling her to answer the phone, talk to him, call back. On the floor by her apartment door was another sheet of paper. She picked it up and read the words, I WANT TO MOVE. LET'S TALK.

MOVE WHERE? she answered.

She was having another coffee when she heard rapping on her door. "I know you're in there. Open up. I want to talk to you face to face. Barb, this is important. Open the door, for godssake."

She put down her cup and sat still. Her breathing was shallow. *Go away, you sonofabitch! Go upstairs to your girlfriend.*

"Barb, can you hear me? At least tell me you're okay."

As still and silent as a stone. Let him worry, let him sweat. Let him lie awake at night, racked by guilt.

"I'm going now, you hear me? I don't want to tell you like this, but if you won't let me in, what else can I do?" He slipped another square of paper under her door. Then she heard him stomping down the hallway, hurrying out.

She picked up the note and read, I'M MOVING IN WITH MY GIRLFRIEND, HER HOUSE IS IN THE NEIGHBORHOOD. IVAN WANTS TO SUBLET MY APARTMENT. IS THAT OKAY?

She scribbled on the back of the page, IVAN IS AN ASSHOLE AND SO ARE YOU. LEAVE ME ALONE!—then ran upstairs and stuffed it under Elliot's door.

There was one more message after that: SORRY YOU WON'T TALK. LET ME KNOW IF YOU CHANGE YOUR MIND.

Early on a Saturday morning, two weeks after Elliot's notes, Barbara woke to a beeping horn. Then she heard loud footsteps going downstairs and across the porch. She peeked out from behind her bedroom curtains, holding her breath, and there was Elliot at the curb, talking to a round-faced redhead in a purple car, her head poking out the open window on the passenger side.

Barbara felt cold in her nightgown and bare feet so she turned up the thermostat, got into bed and pulled the covers up to her chin. The room smelled funky, like a stagnant pond. The radiator clanged and hissed as thick, steamy air wafted into her eyes and made them tear.

The front door opened and shut and Elliot bounded up the steps. After that she heard him slowly grunting his way downstairs. Carrying furniture? Not by himself. Most likely he was juggling suitcases, garment bags and sharp, bulky objects, wedged between wall and banister. He'd bump and scratch the paint and plaster, ruin the staircase, ruin the hall. He was ruining everything!

He stumbled out, came back, went up and down some more times; then Elliot tapped on her door. "I'm finished here and want to say goodbye. Will you let me in?"

Barbara was still in bed, still in her nightgown. Her face was puffy, her hair a mess and her mouth tasted like garbage. How could she let him see her like this, his last day living here? How could she send him off to his redhead in a shiny car with a vile image of his wife to call up any time he needed to remind himself he'd made the right decision? Besides, she was pissed off. If he wanted to move, let him. She had nothing to say to Elliot.

He knocked harder and raised his voice. "Look, Barb, I

know you're home, I heard you come in last night—so stop being childish. I won't walk away like this, I'll stand here till you let me in."

Barbara threw her blanket off, crawled to the end of the bed, reached out and turned on the television full blast.

Elliot began to shout. "I know this is hard on you—it's hard on me too, you know. That doesn't mean we stick our heads in the ground and ignore it. Can you hear me? Am I getting through? Turn off the TV!"

She sat cross-legged on the bed, watching a talk show. A woman was complaining that her ex-husband was no good—selfish, weak and untrue—and she was glad to be rid of him. Barbara laughed out loud.

Elliot was screaming now. "I left you the car—okay? If you need anything done around here, give me a call. I hope you'll phone anyway, I want us to stay friends. No reason we can't keep being friends, is there? Ivan has my number, he knows how to reach me. I really hope you'll stay in touch, but I know I can't force you to. You always do exactly what you want, that's the way you are—and while we're on the subject, let me remind you it was your idea to separate the house in the first place. So don't blame me for everything!"

The woman on the talk show had a female lover now. Sure, there were problems, but she knew they could work them out. You can talk to another woman like you can't talk to a man, she said. Men blew up, lost control. "Violent?" the host said. "That too," the guest replied.

Elliot kicked the door and thundered, "Listen to me, I'm going now! I'm going and I won't be back! This is your last chance!"

She waited till he stormed out and the front door banged shut, then switched off the TV. She went to the window and peered out. The sight of the purple car pulling away made her gasp. She turned her back to the window and decided she would wash up, get dressed, go for a drive. Nice of him to leave the Buick.

After she put on a jacket and boots she walked out the basement door and tramped across the snowy backyard, past the apple tree and under a tall evergreen, to the small garage that looked like the cottage of the Seven Dwarfs. The tin roof was covered with a thatch of needles and dry leaves that would no doubt slide off and fall on her head someday. A pair of low, paned windows were too grimy to see through, and the entry door was impossibly hung. She had to yank its handle several times before the door budged. Inside, the dim garage was crowded with tools, a lawn mower, garden hoses, ladders and, to one side, the Buick.

She opened the main garage door that faced a narrow laneway and got in the car. Her bare fingers gripped the wheel. She could see her breath. She tried to start the car but the engine wouldn't turn over. She tried again: no go. Maybe something froze or the battery was dead. If Elliot was here he would open the hood and poke around, jiggle this or that, get a boost or whatever. But Elliot was gone and she didn't have the know-how.

She leaned her head on the wheel and cried, a whimper at first, then noisy sobs that kept coming, wouldn't stop. He was absolutely gone!

In a while she left the car, closed the garage door and walked out. She backtracked across the yard, stepping on her solitary footprints in the snow.

It was late afternoon when the bell rang. Barbara rushed through the hallway and pulled open the front door, half expecting Elliot. But there stood Ivan on the porch, a knapsack on his back and a couple of satchels at his feet. Her arms dropped to her sides and she stared at him dumbly. She'd forgotten all about him.

"Can't find the key," he said cheerily. "Glad you're home." He held out a bag. "Give me a hand?"

Barbara backed away from the door.

"Well, howdy-do to you too." He dragged his luggage into the hall and started clambering upstairs. "You don't think he locked the apartment door, do you? Nah, why would he do that?"

"Take off your boots," she said. "You're getting snow on everything."

At the top of the stairs he opened the door and thumped his baggage inside. "See you later," he called out.

Back in her apartment, Barbara noticed Ivan was noisier than Elliot. His ringing footsteps overhead made the kitchen ceiling shake, and wasn't that a flake of plaster fallen in the corner? She'd have to speak to him again about taking his boots off.

She retreated to the basement but was too distracted to do anything. Even down there she heard him, dragging something across the floor, stamping back and forth like a goose-stepping soldier. Even with her fingers in her ears she heard him marching: there was nowhere to hide. Later, in the kitchen, she turned up the radio, but that didn't work either. One-two, one-two, her head throbbed in time with his steps. How could Elliot do this to her? Was renting his place to Ivan some kind of sick joke?

All she could think to do at the moment was get out. Leave the house. Go for a walk. Wait until she calmed down and figured out her next move. So she bundled up in her winter clothes and went outside.

Snow on the walk had been tramped down by Elliot and Ivan. She looked down and grimaced. From now on she'd have to shovel snow herself, throw salt, chisel ice. When the weather warmed up she'd be pushing the deafening lawn mower. If the roof leaked, pipes froze, the car stalled or furnace broke, Barbara would have to deal with it. Unless Ivan lent a hand, which, to judge by his careless noise and wet footprints in the hall, was highly unlikely. How could Elliot drop all this in her lap and vanish?

Barbara headed for the park. She passed a row of large homes with yellow-lit windows and white curtains that looked like the glowing faces of girls in frilly bonnets. Beside an old stone house she paused to imagine a fire in a fireplace, a wife knitting an afghan while her husband read the paper aloud, small children chattering, a couple of cats. The picture made her hurt inside. Although she knew if she were there she'd be swatting the husband with his paper before long and chasing the kids.

When she got to the park it was barren and white, its glaring starkness a relief. She took a snowy path among the gray trunks of oaks and maples, downhill to a frozen pond thawed in the center thanks to a small running fountain. She sat on a low concrete wall, coldness seeping through her clothes, and watched a few stubborn ducks circle round and round their constricted pool. They seemed happy enough, she thought. You can get used to anything.

She would get used to not phoning, not seeing Elliot. Not having him close by. She would get used to working hard, to silence and solitude, the path she has chosen.

And maybe she could get used to Ivan in his army boots clumping around upstairs. Like train whistles or traffic noise, certain sounds became so familiar after a while that you just stopped hearing them. And though they might pass in the hall, she'd never have to say more than a few words to Ivan or worry about his girlfriends. *Just slip the rent under the door*, she'd tell him, businesslike. Simpler and easier than dealing with her husband.

Barbara found crumbs in her jacket and fed the ducks. Then she jammed her cold hands in her pockets and trudged home.

When she got in she saw a note taped to her apartment door: PLEASE COME UPSTAIRS FOR A DRINK. YOURS TRULY, IVAN.

She tore the paper into bits and threw the pieces in the air. They came down like flat snowflakes, unmelting, unnatural; one by one.

12

And a Happy New Year

Dennis told Natalie they couldn't leave his mom sitting home alone on New Year's Eve—especially *this* New Year's Eve, with his good-for-nothing dad gone. But Natalie said she wouldn't know a soul at the party and would only wind up feeling worse. Dennis insisted just the same, so here they were in the sprawling house of Natalie's friends, the Gordons, introducing Barbara to people she'd never see again.

"Richard and I were in school together," Natalie told Barbara, who was shaking the hand of a good-looking man.

"Quite a tan you've got," said Barbara.

"I was in Bermuda."

"Dennis never tans," said Natalie. "Dennis burns."

Dennis hooked his mother's arm—"You should meet the Gordons"—and led her across the room to a slim, blond couple who looked enough alike to be brother and sister. "Dean is a podiatrist and Peg's a dermatologist."

"I'm Dennis's mother."

"A ceramist," said Dennis.

Barbara shook the long-fingered, limp hands of Peg and Dean. "We bought some interesting pottery in Central America," Peg said.

"Do you go there often?"

"Not very."

"Because of the sun," Peg said. "You can't be too careful."

"The pottery's in the den if you'd like to see it," Dean said. He pointed behind him with a digit like a whittled stick.

"I hope you stay out of the sun," Peg said to Dennis. "You're as fair-skinned as we are."

Barbara slipped away in the direction of Dean's finger, but stopped when she got to the bar. A teenage girl serving drinks poured her a glass of wine. "Having fun?" Barbara said. The girl shrugged.

"Me neither."

The girl passed a drink to a black-haired, white-faced woman under thirty in a dress that barely covered her ass. Her black-stockinged legs seemed as long and straight as flagpoles. Barbara watched her walk off, then she said to the teenager staring blankly at the scene, "You know how many years it's been since I wore a miniskirt?"

"Nuh-huh," the girl said.

"I'm probably the oldest person here. Do you think maybe that's why I'm not having a good time?"

"You married?" the girl said.

"People keep asking that—and what difference does it make? My husband hates parties. If he was here now he'd be hiding in a dark room, and I'd be feeling a lot worse."

Barbara gulped her wine down, then held out her glass so the girl could refill it. "He stayed home tonight?" she said.

"I don't know *where* he is tonight, but he's not with me."

"That sucks."

Barbara drank some more wine. "I do know, actually. He's spending the night with his girlfriend. That's who he'll kiss at twelve o'clock."

"That *really* sucks," said the girl. Then she got busy serving drinks to three or four people at once. When the bar cleared, she was surprised to find Barbara still there. "Why don't you divorce him?" she said. "I mean, like, I would if it was me."

"What are you—sixteen?"

"Seventeen," the girl said.

"You're too young to know anything. Life isn't black or white, wrong or right. What the hell would you know about being married thirty-four years!"

The girl shrugged.

"Where's the den?" Barbara said, then followed the girl's glance toward another part of the house.

She wandered through corridors, up and down tiled stairs, in and out of four bedrooms—one of which was occupied by a sleeping man in a striped suit—back-tracked, turned again and finally arrived at the den. There were multicolored pots in different sizes around the room, but she fixed her eyes on a couple busy necking in a corner. Mainly she had a rear view of a long-legged young woman, the one she'd just seen at the bar. When her partner pushed her against a wall, Barbara saw them in profile, their faces contorted by the action of their mouths and jaws, the collision of their noses. The woman's breasts were half-exposed, her skirt hiked up to her crotch, and the man's hands were moving fast. He was suddenly familiar: his leanness and ponytail, those big-knuckled hands. . . .

She backed out of the doorway, ran to the central part of the house and looked for Dennis in one room after another. Loud music she'd never heard before was play-ing wherever she went. She counted at least eight speakers, each of them blaring the same thing. She pressed her hands over her ears and heard her wildly beating heart.

In the jam-packed main room Natalie was still laughing and chatting with her doctor friend. She was wearing a beige silk blouse that molded her large breasts, and Barbara thought another button was undone at her throat now. But maybe she was imagining that. Maybe she was just imagining Brad in the den, too, and this whole miserable evening.

She found Dennis sitting on a sofa in a dark room. There were several people in the room, but he wasn't talking to anyone. The seat beside him was empty and she sat down. "I want to go home," she told her son. "I want you to take me home now."

"You only just got here. Why don't you give the party a chance? At least stay till midnight."

"I can't stay another minute."

"It's not easy for me, either, making silly chitchat with people I hardly know. These are all Natalie's friends, they don't want to speak to *me*. But I try my best, I make an effort. People will be friendly if you show a little friendliness first."

"There's someone here—a man I know . . . and don't want to talk to."

"Someone you don't like?"

"No, I like him very much. But I don't like what he's doing."

"You're confusing me," Dennis said.

She stood up. "I'll take a cab."

"You won't get a taxi tonight. If it's so important I'll drive you. Just let me tell Natalie."

In a corner of the main room, Natalie and Richard Blotsky were still talking head to head. They'd been doing that nonstop for almost an hour now. What could be so interesting? Dennis tapped his wife's shoulder and had to say "Excuse me" twice before she jumped and spun around. For just a second he could swear she didn't even know him. "My mother wants to go," he said. "I'll take her home and be right back, it's still an hour till midnight."

"I told him she wouldn't enjoy herself," Natalie said to Blotsky. Then to Dennis, "All right. I'll see you when you get back."

"It's snowing hard," Dennis said, but Natalie had already resumed her conversation. "I'll drive slowly," he spoke to the back of her head.

His car was parked a few blocks away from the Gordons' house, and Dennis had to steady his mother on the icy streets. Then she had to steady him. They weren't wearing winter boots, but thin-soled dress shoes that slid across the sidewalks like runners on a pair of sleighs. Nor were they wearing hats. Snow whitened and flattened their hair, filled their collars, stung their cheeks. His overcoat was too thin and Dennis trembled violently. The wind coiled his mother's long skirt around her ankles, so that she walked with teeny steps, slowing them down even more. He thought they would die of exposure long before they reached the car. And yet someone looking out an overhead window would probably find them a pleasing sight, Currier and Ives-like: white-dappled revelers in wind-whipped fancy clothes on their way to a party.

Eventually they got to the car and sat in the front seats like shivering wet puppies while the car idled noisily and the heater blew cool, then tolerably warm air. His mother asked for a tissue and he passed her a wad from his coat. At first he thought her eyes were running because of the snow and cold, but then he saw she was crying. A swollen feeling in his gut, as if he would burst if she didn't stop. It was hard enough when his sons cried, but this—his mother—was worse. He was the one who should be crying. He was the one whose wife had hardly spoken to him all night. He rubbed his mother's shoulder. "What's wrong? Why the tears?" Then he remembered. "That man at the party? The one who was doing something?"

"Making out in the den with a half-dressed little tart!"

"That happens at parties, Mom, when people have been drinking. . . ."

"I *know* him. We're friends."

"Okay, he was kissing someone. Why should it bother you so much?"

His mother started whimpering. "You're right, you're right, it shouldn't matter—shouldn't matter one bit. . . ."

He put two and two together. Even though she was in her fifties, Barbara was attractive. If Elliot with his bad back and balding head could find a lover, why couldn't she? But the thought made him sick. Somehow it wasn't right—his own mother, for godssake!

He'd never really understood his parents' living arrangement—and then his father made things worse by moving out of the house. (How would he ever get used to *that*, Dad arm in arm with a lady who wasn't Mom?) Enough changes! Enough already! It was one thing for Barbara to live in her own apartment, another thing entirely to take up with a new man . . . even though his useless father had led the way.

He tried to speak calmly. "How long have you and this man. . . ?"

"How long have we what?"

"You know."

She stared at him wet-eyed, a tissue mashed against her cheek. "We're not lovers, if that's what you think. He's not much older than you are."

"So why are you crying?"

"Not that I haven't thought about it, dreamed about it sometimes. . . ." She turned to face the windshield. "It just took me by surprise. A hard dose of reality."

"You're confusing me again."

"Let's go," his mother said. "The car's warmed up enough."

The streets were empty but slippery, so Dennis drove carefully. His mom was quiet at his side. He kept his eyes on the road and his hands on the wheel, but his mind was stuck on Natalie. Was she still talking to Blotsky? Did she dream about *her* friend the way Barbara dreamed about hers . . . or had it gone even further?

All of a sudden he wanted to get back to the party quickly. He sped up. When they came to a stop sign he hit the brake too hard and the car fishtailed left and right. They almost nicked a parked car, but his mother didn't protest. When he turned a corner sharply the car skidded again, but he didn't care, they were almost there. In a few minutes she'd be home and he could start the trip back.

Then his mother spoke up. "I was talking to a girl at the party, the one who was tending bar. I told her about your dad moving in with his girlfriend and she said I should divorce him. Do you think I should do that?"

"Dad's an idiot," Dennis said. "He had no business running off."

"Divorce him and save face? Make a break? Start clean?"

Much like Susan, he had hoped things would work out and his parents get together again. Maybe Dad was acting out some adolescent fantasy or suffering male menopause and would come to his senses soon, return home. But now he feared it was too late, too much damage had been done; their marriage was past saving. Nevertheless he told his mother, "Don't be impulsive. You haven't seen the last of him yet, just wait and see what happens." It was New Year's Eve, after all, so why make her feel lousy?

When he reached the house he double-parked and helped his mom along the snowy, unshoveled walk to her door. Coldness worked through the soles of his shoes and his toes curled up in pain. She opened the door and turned to him. "I won't do anything right now . . . not for the moment."

"That's good," he nodded. He gave her a peck on the cheek and then he was out of there, back in the car and driving recklessly all the way to the Gordons'.

Through the oversized windows of their oversized house, he saw that the lights had been dimmed. When he opened the door and walked in he heard schmaltzy music—something by Guy Lombardo, he guessed. Couples were doing the two-step. Peg Gordon swept by in the arms of a man he didn't know, while across the room her husband Dean was grinding against a young thing in a dress the size of a handkerchief.

He went to the bar and ordered Scotch from a flat-chested teenager. When he finished the drink he had another. What the hell. His hair was still wet from the snow and he smoothed down his cowlick. "Dance with me?" he asked her.

"Nuh-huh," the girl said. "Gotta stay behind the bar."

"I want to dance with my wife," he said, "but she's dancing with someone else."

"That sucks," the girl said.

"Damn right." He emptied his glass.

Then he turned back to the room, his stomach hard and noisy, like a pot of boiling water. The music was low and slow now; couples were humped together. A pair danced in front of him, and he heard the woman ask about the man's niece's birthday. "I want to send her a card," she said, "something with flowers, she loves flowers. And what about your brother, doesn't he like golf?" Dennis pictured a card in bloom and one with clubs and golf balls. Here was a loving wife who remembered her husband's relatives—maybe even distant cousins—and

181

no doubt invited them all for Thanksgiving dinner. Did the guy know how lucky he was? Natalie wouldn't cook for a crowd or send cards to anyone—not for Christmas, graduations, birthdays or illness, and certainly never lesser cards like GOOD LUCK IN YOUR NEW HOME or BON VOYAGE. "Don't have the time," she'd say, and Dennis would have to mail them himself. Sometimes he wished that his wife was more domestic; sometimes he imagined her sending a THINKING OF YOU card. Not to a friend or relation—but to him. She would send it to him. *Thinking only of you, dear.*

He stepped around the dancers and searched the room for Natalie. She was moving in the undulating shadows across the floor, dancing with Blotsky, their bodies swaying in accord, like synchronized swimmers. He pushed his glasses up his nose, marched up to Blotsky and slapped him on the shoulder. "I'd like to dance with my wife now, if that's all right with you."

Slowly Blotsky straightened up and blinked at him several times, as if he'd just been wakened. His hands slid down Natalie's blouse, and Dennis heard the crackle of static electricity. "Sure thing," he said. "I was just keeping her warm till you got back." Then he walked away and was lost in the crowd. Dennis pulled his wife close and they danced in a circle.

"Aren't you going to take off your coat?"

"What was that about?" he said.

"What was what?"

"You and Blotsky."

"Richard and I were dancing."

"And talking together all night."

"Why shouldn't I talk to him? He's an interesting man."

The music changed to a waltz and he led her around the floor, one-two-three, one-two-three, bumping couples out of the way. "I'm tired," she said. "I can't do this."

"Pretend you're dancing with Blotsky. That'll perk you up," he said.

"I'm dancing with you—and I want to stop. My feet are killing me."

But he held her tighter, moved faster, squeezing her fingers with one hand while he pressed the other into her back. She was like a beanbag in his arms, heavy and shapeless. Her left arm fell from his waist and swung lifelessly at her side. She had not been like this with Blotsky, he was sure.

"Almost midnight!" Peg screamed, and suddenly the music stopped, the dancers stopped, his breath stopped. He gazed into Natalie's eyes, which were sinking bit by bit as she slumped in his hold. He pulled her fully upright. *Love me, think only of me*, he burned into her retinas with a fiery look.

"Ten, nine, eight, seven . . .!" the Gordons hollered, whipping their arms like orchestra conductors.

"Six, five, four, three . . .!" Everyone was shouting now.

Dennis parted his lips and mashed them against Natalie's, using his tongue to open her mouth. He licked her teeth and gums and the smooth flesh of her inner mouth, but everything was dry, inert. Like running his tongue around the inside of an empty jar.

He pulled his face away from hers and clapped his hands on her shoulders. Her blouse was partly undone and he saw the half-moons of her breasts quivering over the top of her bra as he gave her a shake. "What's wrong?"

"I'm tired now. I want to sit down."

He shook her again. Her breasts jiggled, her eyes closed. He watched Natalie disappear into her own thoughts and gripped harder, shook harder—harder than he meant to. He was only trying to bring her back. "Stop that," she said, but he couldn't stop. Could have. Didn't stop. Because he didn't want to. Because he liked the feel of her bones, the silky thinness of her blouse, the bobbing and shuddering of her chest.

But all at once they were pulled apart and someone was kissing him. "Happy new year!" people yelled. Someone was kissing Natalie, too, though he only got a glimpse because a woman turned his face away and was pressing her sticky mouth to his, her lips tasting fruity. She was giggling and jabbing him with her tongue, reaching into his throat, it seemed—when suddenly she was gone and another woman took her place, and someone else after that. He smelled of booze and perfume as he spun from face to face and was grabbed, twirled, pinched and chewed. Red lips, purple lips, an orange mouth, a pink one: a chain of interlocking rings.

Dennis couldn't catch his breath. He was losing his balance. Dizzy and gasping, he stumbled into the new year.

13

TOGETHER

After he moved into her house, Maryellen
followed him around asking questions. For instance, she
wanted to know if he always slept on his left side. She
wondered why he liked to read the morning paper out
loud. At breakfast she asked him, "Is that all you're having, cereal and coffee?" And Elliot felt nervous to realize
all they didn't know and had to learn about each other:
shoe sizes, hat sizes, styles, habits and preferences; personal histories, anecdotes, sexual secrets, family ties; the
meaning of a look, a gesture or half-completed sentence,
and all the intricate ways in which a man and woman
communicate without actually speaking. It would take a
while, he reasoned, before they stopped worrying and
settled down.

In the meantime Maryellen worried about idleness
and thought he should get out more. Instead he lay down
on the couch, put on a classical CD and lit his pipe. She
worried about Elliot's health and fed him daily tablets of

vitamins A, C and E, a multimineral supplement and large cups of ginseng tea. She cut back on meat and poultry in favor of fish, beans and grains, and served lots of vegetables and local fruits in season. She begged him not to smoke indoors and even mixed his coffee with decaf, thinking he wouldn't mind—"Can you really tell the difference?"—but he held his ground on that one: fresh-brewed and caffeinated, drunk cold.

Despite her careful regimen, Elliot got a bad cold soon after he moved in. "Your body is discarding toxins," Maryellen explained, but he had no idea what she meant. She gave him several kinds of teas—licorice, echinacea, cayenne and elderberry—and had him sniff eucalyptus oil from a vaporizer. *Is this better? Is that better? Can I get you this, can I get you that?*—tucking him firmly into bed and feeding him homemade chicken soup; her face flushed and freckles bold as she pulled his head to her plump breasts. And again he thought, How round and soft; how much like Barb.

His brain was wooly, his tongue thick, his nose raw and running and his throat sore. But the press of Maryellen's hand on his forehead was heavenly, and the way she held a cup to his lips or rubbed his back with mustard oil almost brought tears to his eyes. *What do you usually do for a cold? Have you tried catnip? Rosemary?* There was endless fretting and questioning for eight dreamy days while the cold ran its usual course, and then he was cured.

Except for his insomnia. Elliot missed his old apartment (only a few blocks away), especially his huge bedroom-study on the third floor and the double bed all to himself. Though Maryellen's house had a big, bright kitchen with a greenhouse attached where she grew herbs, the other rooms were small and dark, particularly the master bedroom, facing north. He didn't sleep well there; he felt cramped, a mouse in a hole. She asked if he wanted a blackout shade, soothing music, white noise, the room cooler or warmer. "Or is it me?" she lowered her eyes. "Do I make you uncomfortable?" He didn't know what to say. Because his stubborn wakefulness *did* have something to do with her. Here was a man who'd only shared a bed with his wife most of his life, then got used to sleeping alone, and now was lying tensely beside a virtual stranger, having to match his movements to hers, afraid to wake her with his snores, shock her with his morning breath, offend her with a stray fart. Just the thought of going to bed at night made his heart shake.

Nevertheless, he believed the problem would pass in time. "Let's just wait a while," he said. But Maryellen was restless. She brewed various herbal teas—passion flower, skullcap, chamomile, valerian—and gave him a cup of one or another at bedtime. Subsequently, he was up peeing three times a night and finally refused any liquids after 6:00 P.M. Eventually, after a number of weeks, he did indeed get used to having Maryellen at his side and slept through the night.

Their days together went like this: up early, followed by a high-fiber, low-fat breakfast and a brisk walk. Home again, Maryellen would go to her study upstairs where she was writing a cookbook, while Elliot read, listened to the radio or puttered around the kitchen. Sometimes they made love—and it was pleasant, perfectly fine, if not quite magical—after which, Maryellen would shower and go back to work and he would take a short nap.

Two afternoons a week he went to his Tai Chi club. The rest of the time he practiced at home, played his sax, tidied up and ran the old vacuum cleaner if Maryellen was done for the day. "Why do you clean so much?" she asked. A shame that she was allergic to cats and he couldn't bring his tabby, Hammer, who shed hair year-round and had to be chased with a Hoover. Then she might've appreciated his hygienic habits.

The afternoons she taught cooking classes he would leave the house, rather than hide on the second floor or face curious students who would glance at the holes in his track pants and wonder what he was doing there. He would go to his favorite greasy spoon, order coffee and rye toast and talk to the waitress if she was free. "You want I stir the coffee?" she might ask in broken English. "You want I don't butter the toast?" And his eyes would well up at her willingness to please him. What a lucky man he was, surrounded by agreeable women.

After, he would shop for groceries, buy a paper, walk in the park. But now it was the dead of winter, a snow-coated, freezing day, and he hurried along with his head down, ice crunching like peanut brittle under his feet. He squinted at his dirty sneakers, aware of tingling in his toes, which were already half numb. ("You don't have winter boots?" Maryellen had asked, incredulous.)

He lingered in the supermarket, drugstore, greengrocer and finally the health food store, pondering his choices. Regular tofu or extra firm? Light soy or dark soy? Spinach pasta or whole wheat? A sleepy-looking young woman sat by the register, reading the afternoon paper. "What's the forecast?" Elliot asked.

"Snow today, snow tomorrow, snow for the weekend."

He took that as a good sign: the dirty business of the world covered by a robe of snow while he busied himself indoors in Maryellen's cozy kitchen, making a pot of pea soup.

Peas. They were out of peas. He filled a bag with dried peas and plopped it on the counter next to his pasta and tofu. The woman bunched her paper and he tried to glimpse the headline. "Here, take it, I'm through," she said.

Another example, Elliot thought as he paid for his

groceries, of the natural generosity of women. He tucked the paper under his arm and pulled on his mittens—the lovely blue-and-gold ones his wife had knitted years ago. But he wasn't wearing the matching scarf, and when he stepped outside cold squeezed his bare neck like a tight collar.

How was she doing? he wondered. He hadn't heard a word since he moved out last month, though Ivan saw her shoveling snow and said she looked good to him, and Susan said her mom was all right, she was coping.

He walked through the park on his way home, moving as fast as possible with a grocery bag weighing him down and the icy, snow-spattered pavement sliding under his feet like an out-of-control treadmill. It wouldn't do to slip and fall and be laid up with a fractured hip, though Maryellen probably had a cure for broken bones too.

The sun was on the horizon when he turned off the walkway and took a shortcut through the trees. Soon he was over his ankles in snow, his socks crusty and soggy. His nose seemed to be clogged with ice, so he gulped the frigid air through his mouth, hurrying, hurrying home now. His throat stung, his feet were wet, but Maryellen would dry them and give him a soothing cup of tea. Then she would serve a comforting meal. And if he caught pneumonia, she would fix that too.

Dinner was around seven, unless she was teaching that night (in which case he'd fend for himself and she would have a sandwich). Often they had splendid meals with entrées, main courses, fruit, cheese and low-cal desserts. Maryellen did most of the cooking, because she was so much better at it. Elliot usually made stock, peeled potatoes, minced herbs, loaded the dishwasher, scoured pots. He no longer tried new recipes or cooked old favorites like goulash or chicken stew because she would pick at him—*it needs more of this, needs more of that*—or wrinkle her freckled nose and say, "But really, that's so *common*." Once he made ratatouille just as he'd learned in her cooking class, but Maryellen only sighed, "I think you've forgotten everything." As a teacher she was easygoing, tolerant and patient; as a partner she was more exacting.

But tonight was his birthday and he wasn't going to lift a finger. She'd peel vegetables by herself, mince, mash, pour and serve, set the table and clean up. Tonight she was going all-out.

When he got home from his wintry walk all sensation had left his feet, his neck was stinging, his hands clawed. Maryellen ran from the kitchen and hugged him in the hallway, trailing an intoxicating scent of lamb, herbs and yeast. "Oh, you're freezing!" she said as she squeezed him. Over her shoulder he glimpsed lit candles on the table, the wavering flames like dancing girls in yellow skirts.

In the living room she pulled off his sodden sneakers and wet socks and kneaded his feet in her hands as if they were shrunken loaves. She warmed his fingers between her breasts, rubbed his scalp and kissed his neck with lips as hot and soft and moist as fresh-baked muffins. "Flaming crown roast of lamb," she cooed the menu in his ear. "Roast potatoes with rosemary, green beans in mustard sauce, endive salad, muesli bread. . . ." His brain a bouncing bubble on the stream of her words. And then she helped him off the couch and sent him upstairs for a bath.

Soaking in the water he thought, Elliot, you're a lucky man. Elliot, you're in paradise. Last year at this time he was eating a meager birthday dinner at his daughter's: frozen lasagna from the microwave, not quite thawed, and a soggy salad. A cold, snowy, miserable night—and then he almost crashed on the icy, hazardous drive home. Barb, he remembered sharply, simply ignored his birthday. But now, only a year later, here lay a happy man.

When he went down to the kitchen again (in a clean shirt and good pants). Maryellen was pouring wine. She had changed into a black dress with a low neckline and long skirt. In the dim room her eyes and mouth were dark and her face glowed, much like the face of a carved pumpkin, lit from the inside. And he felt doubly excited, like a kid on Halloween night but also the birthday boy, as he circled the table, swinging his arms, not sure what to do next. "Sit down"—she pressed him into a chair—"and let's make a toast—to us."

"To us." He drained the glass. "To us!" And then he emptied another. "To good fortune and good food!"

Maryellen pulled a platter of lamb from the oven, splashed cognac over the crown, flicked a lighter and set it afire. Flames shot up, died down, and the walls bulged with changing shadows: an undulating dream-room. Elliot watched open-mouthed, his jaw heavy with wonder.

Dinner was a delight of spices, oils and sauces, hot bread, a variety of vegetables and the lingering flavor of roast lamb. "To me and you," they touched glasses. "To Elliot and Maryellen!" Knives and forks clicked an intimate song of satisfaction as they cut and chewed, swallowed and cut. Then, after a suitable pause, Maryellen brought out a long, thin, silvery box and a golden chiffon birthday cake with a single blazing candle for luck. The flame shimmied under his breath as his heart wobbled in his chest, and he thought, I wish, I wish, I wish. . . . But what more could he possibly want? His mind was blank. So he leaned over the nervous flame, his cheeks puffed with pleasure, and doused it with a spray of breath.

After cake and coffee, after chocolates and cognac, it was finally time to open his gift. He guessed his present was a tie, but when he looked into the shiny box Elliot saw a leather belt. It was hard not to feel let down. Not that he fancied a tie—which would've been the same sort of disappointing, impersonal gift you shouldn't give a man who practically lived his life in sweat suits. But maybe she was hinting it was time to change his wardrobe. Could it be that after less than three months in the same house, she wanted to make him over?

"Put it on," said Maryellen. "See if it fits."

He looped the belt around his waist. "Just right."

"I'm so glad. I wasn't sure what to get but you can't go wrong with leather. First I tried to buy slippers but didn't know your shoe size, then I looked at wallets, but you probably have enough of those."

Elliot put the belt aside and stretched out on the living-room couch, too woozy and bloated to move. Maryellen squeezed in beside him and opened his pants. She slipped her hand under his shirt, plucked at his chest hairs and kissed his swollen belly. "Did you like your party?"

"Mmm," he said.

She sang a chorus of "Happy Birthday to You" to his navel, then asked, "Do you love me?"

"Mm-hmm," Elliot said.

Her fingers circled his belly button, slid under his waistband and grabbed his dozy penis. "You never really told me, you know." His cock jumped in her fleshy hand. "You never actually said the words, 'I love you, Maryellen.'"

His cock slumped and she let go. "I need to hear it, Elliot. A woman needs to hear that."

Grateful, yes. Contented, yes. But love? Did he feel love? He liked her a whole lot, but didn't feel anything more. Maybe that would happen later; maybe it just took time. But it wasn't happening yet: it was too soon to love her. And of course that was terrible, since obviously she loved him—and the unfairness of it made his stomach knot, his face burn, his heart squeeze even tighter.

Elliot stretched his arms out and she curled against

his broad chest. "Let's rest," he breathed in her ear. "Let's have a little snooze."

"Wouldn't you rather make love?" She toyed with his cock again, but it lay there, lifeless. When she looked up his eyes were closed, and whether he was dozing or not she knew he was beyond reach.

Maryellen left him there and went to the kitchen to clean up. Later, when he got up, she would brew a pot of peppermint tea to help his digestion.

One Thursday evening in March, when Maryellen was busy with her "Basic Cooking for Men" class, he decided to visit Ivan in his former apartment. Elliot put on a thick coat, the scarf and mittens Barb had made, and even a wool toque, but still the cold stiffened him when he went outside; it flattened him in his heavy clothes so that he felt like a slice of Kraft cheese in a sandwich. Spring, spring, where was spring? He tried to recall if the ground-hog had seen its shadow last month, but his brain barely functioned in below-freezing weather. He could hardly remember his old address.

When he got to his former home, he blinked at it stupidly. Only a few months and already it looked peculiar. It loomed eerie, overly large and slightly out of focus, as if he were wearing 3-D glasses. And yet, as he approached it, there were details he noticed that he'd never quite seen before: the badly cracked walkway and the lopsided front porch; the balcony on the second floor missing several balusters. He walked up the steps lightly, afraid he might fall through, vowing to replace boards, to strip, patch, sand and paint, but then scolded himself, *Stop! You don't live here anymore. If she wants your help she can call and ask.* Anyway, there was always Ivan in a pinch. Or she could hire a handyman. It wasn't Elliot's problem.

He'd kept a set of keys, so he let himself in quietly.

Barb hadn't changed the lock, which he took as a sign that someday she might be willing to see him again or at least call him now and then. Susan phoned regularly—and once she even stopped by—but Dennis wouldn't call him at Maryellen's house, so he had to phone his son instead; and though their conversations were strained, Dennis never hung up on him. If he called Barb, Elliot feared, she would hang up right away and he wouldn't get a chance to say, *You don't even have to speak, just stay on the line a while and let me hear you breathing.* It was hard—no, impossible—to imagine not hearing her breath in his ear ever again.

The hall smelled of curry, and laughter sounded behind her door. What would he say if she came out suddenly and saw him? What would she do if he knocked on her door and asked how she was doing?

Slam it in his face, he figured. *How dare you! Who do you think—!* And so he went straight upstairs and called to Ivan, "Open up."

Ivan was wearing an expensive-looking cardigan that covered most of his large frame, but stood in the doorway slapping his arms. "It's freezing in here," he said. "I told Barb to turn up the heat and she said it was high enough. You have to bleed the rads or something. . . . I don't know what she's talking about."

"So you've seen her?"

"A few times. We pass each other in the hall, but mostly she keeps to herself. I don't think she likes me."

Elliot looked down and his eyes stopped at Ivan's boots and the muddy footprints in his wake: he was going to ruin the hardwood floors, and Barb would like him even less.

Ivan offered him pizza and beer. They ate and drank in the living room, where Ivan had already soiled the couch and stained the Scandinavian rug. What a stupid idea it was to rent his apartment furnished.

In a quilted armchair scratched to shreds in a far corner of the room sat Hammer, Elliot's big-headed cat. Elliot tapped his knee and called, "Here, Hammer, here boy," and the cat stretched, hopped off the chair and leisurely clawed a chair leg. Then he sauntered out of the room, dragging a thread behind him. Anger blocked Elliot's throat—*what about the scratching post, he always used the scratching post!*—but he swallowed it back. Surely it was Ivan's fault, his disrespect for property—or Elliot's own fault for having abandoned his sensitive pet.

"So how are you and Maryellen getting along?" Ivan said. He was on his second pizza slice while Elliot still chewed his first, already turned rubbery and cold.

"Fine, fine. No complaints. She's very nice, very thoughtful—not to mention a great cook." He laughed a thin, broken laugh. "She's spoiling me. No kidding."

"I like a girl who knows how to cook. Ramona's idea of a good meal is canned spaghetti and frozen peas."

"You mean you're still seeing her?"

"Nah, we broke up weeks ago. She said we never went anywhere, I just wanted to screw her." He narrowed his eyes at Elliot, who felt pinned down by his gaze. "I don't understand it. We'd go to movies and out to eat, then sure I wanted to sleep with her—Ramona was my girlfriend!"

Elliot put his pizza down on the ring-stained coffee table, picked up a beer and drank. What did women see in Ivan anyway, he wondered, aside from his good looks and full head of hair? Barb had never liked him much, but Ivan had a softer side others might appreciate. Although she never admitted it, Elliot thought she'd always been a little jealous of his friend, which made her too critical.

"So what about you?" Ivan laughed. "Getting it regular these days?"

Elliot wiped his mouth with his hand. "What do you think?"

"I bet you feel like a kid again."

"Not a kid exactly. . . ."

"Nothing like a new girl to perk up the old pecker."

He finished his beer and put it down on the ruined table. "I don't want you to think," he began, then stopped and tried again. "Barb and I were good together, I always found her sexy. There was nothing wrong . . . that way."

"Hey, she's a great-looking gal. Don't think I haven't noticed."

"You're not her type," said Elliot.

Ivan left his third slice of pizza unfinished and emptied a bottle of beer. "You think I'm missing something?" he said. "I look at you and say to myself, All those years with one girl, then he shacks up with another before he can catch his breath—there must be something to it, something good about settling down. Living with someone a long time, you don't have to put on airs, you don't have to go out at night. It must be nice and cozy to lie in bed with the TV on, eating chips and Chinese food or just talking about your day. I'm not a youngster anymore, I could go for a life like that . . . if only I found the right girl."

Elliot looked away because his eyes were suddenly burning. Not because of Ivan's speech, which he'd heard many times before, and not because of Maryellen. He wasn't thinking of her at all as he sat on his flattened, dirty couch, in this room, this house.

"Is that what it's like for you and Maryellen at the end of the day, you lie down and just talk?"

Elliot shrugged. "Sometimes."

They did and they didn't, he thought. They talked about her ex, Nick, who ditched her six years ago to run off with his secretary—which cost him the house and a tidy cash settlement. They talked about the book she was writing, which drove her crazy some days and made her happy other times. About her cooking classes and the students she liked, the ones she didn't and those who were utterly hopeless with a bowl and whisk.

They didn't talk about Elliot's days, which weren't very interesting. And he certainly never mentioned Barb: he didn't think he could speak her name without a quiver in his voice. He didn't talk about his kids or grandchildren either because, when he'd start in, Maryellen would interrupt. "Let's talk about us," she'd say. But she liked hearing about his mom, dead of kidney failure while still in her sixties, and about Elliot's father, who died a year later from a broken heart. She found the story romantic, a testament to the power of love, and he didn't contradict her. He didn't speak of his grief as he watched his mother slowly die, or how he felt about his dad—a man dependent on his wife, who had no friends, no hobbies, no inner resources; incapable of rearranging his life so he could live alone. A man who pleaded for his death. Elliot was not like that. Would never be that way again.

Ivan tapped his bottle on the table like a gavel. He was waiting for an answer to a question Elliot hadn't heard. "What was that? What'd you say?"

"You're always dreaming," Ivan said. "You should've been a poet, not a goddamn dentist."

From downstairs he heard a woman's bell-like laughter and Elliot's pulse bounded. Then he heard the slap and click of one door, then another. He shot from the couch to the bay window and looked down at the sidewalk. Barb and the skinny man in the moth-eaten raincoat were leaving the house, walking away, talking and gesturing and seemingly unaware of the cold. Barb was wearing her ankle-length coat, the one he'd always liked, unbuttoned and billowing, so that she looked as though she might be swept up, swirling, like a seed on a current of air. Long after they disappeared he stood at the window with his forehead against the glass, waiting for his heart to slow and his hands to stop trembling.

When he calmed down and turned around, Ivan said to him bluntly, "You should be over her by now. This is unhealthy. Here you're living with someone new, and who knows what Barb's doing—"

"With him—the guy with the ponytail? What've you seen?"

Ivan threw his hands up. "Nothing—I swear it. Okay? I was just thinking out loud. You said yourself she's sexy, and it's been a couple of years now. It's only natural for her to find someone else like you did."

Elliot sat down heavily in the clawed, quilted armchair and stared straight ahead at a wall, noticing how the wallpaper was streaked with grime. "I don't want her to find a loser in dire need of a haircut and a new coat." Then he got up to go: he couldn't stay any longer. It was probably a mistake to have come here at all. Hammer came out of another room and rubbed against Elliot's legs, coating his pants with stiff, ginger-colored hairs. Maryellen would start sneezing the moment he walked in.

"I'm not saying there *is* a man in her life—I was just talking. I didn't think you'd give a damn now that you're with someone new."

Elliot put on his hat and coat, his Barb-made mittens and scarf. "I miss cooking," he blurted out. "She hardly lets me cook anymore."

"Who? Maryellen?"

"I miss smoking my pipe indoors."

"Barb never liked it—"

"I like looking after myself without someone chasing me around asking questions. I miss having my own place."

Ivan put his feet up on the mistreated table and his boots landed with a thud that scattered hard pellets of mud. "You're talking to a bachelor," he said. "Don't expect me to understand why you went from one to the next."

Elliot started going to his Tai Chi club more often, three afternoons a week, then four, finally five. But Maryellen missed him and suggested that he find a hobby they could do as a couple. "Tennis? Cycling? Softball?" She worried that if they didn't spend more time together, they would drift apart.

But Elliot didn't like sports. Tennis was bad for the elbow, cycling made his knees ache and swinging a bat would undoubtedly dislocate his shoulder.

"I like doing Tai Chi. Besides, didn't you tell me to get out more?"

"I didn't mean every day—and always without me."

"But you write in the afternoon."

"An hour here, an hour there. In between I want to be with you, except you're never home. I'm not even sure where you are."

"Downtown, doing Tai Chi."

"And then you're gone in the evening."

"You *teach* in the evening."

"That doesn't mean you have to leave. Can't you find something to do at home?"

"I have a right to see my friend."

"You never ask him to come here. Because it's not just Ivan, you want to see the house too. You want to hear her moving about—and maybe, if you're lucky, you'll run into Barb in the hall."

"She won't even talk to me since I moved in with you." His voice was tight and sorrowful, which could only make things worse.

Maryellen stared at him, her eyes as white and flat as a pair of broad noodles. "After all these months," she said, "it's still her, isn't it? You can't stop loving your wife."

And still he could have protested, *No, no, it's you I love, I'm finished with Barb, it's over*—but the words hardened, sank in his throat, and Elliot was silent. Instead, he drew her into his arms and stroked her hair, red as a blush, and traced the shiny paths of tears running down her freckled face. A woman who forgave his faults and wanted to work things out. Who wanted the love he wanted to give, but could not. Just couldn't.

"I'll stay home," he said at last, "if that's what you want me to do." And Maryellen relaxed in his arms.

So once again he played his sax and ran the old vacuum cleaner whenever she wasn't writing. He practiced Tai Chi in the living room with the rocking chair and coffee table pushed aside, but soon he was back to lying around, reading, dozing, playing music, waiting for her to come down. Often her work wouldn't go well and Maryellen would stomp out of her study after a short while, eyes crinkled, mouth set, on her way to the kitchen for another cup of coffee, and he would follow at her heels, reading aloud from the *Globe and Mail*.

But she complained about that too. "Is this your idea of togetherness?"

"I thought you'd be interested, an article on cookbooks. . . ."

"Let's go for a walk, okay? I really need to get out of the house."

So Maryellen hooked his arm, led him to the closet and watched as he put on his hat and coat, his blue-and-gold mittens and scarf ("Do you have to wear *those* mittens?"), then tugged him outside into the damp, musky chilliness of early spring.

As they walked toward the park gates he noticed there were buds on the trees, snowdrops and crocuses and sprigs of yellow-green grass pushing up through matted lawns. The backyard of his former home would be dotted with purple and white flowers in the dirt borders on three sides, and the rest would be patches of new grass sprouting like soft, sparse hairs on a teenage face. Perhaps Barb would be outside raking the debris of winter into twiggy brown piles.

Quite automatically, he turned onto his old block, heading toward his old house, but Maryellen spun him around and pulled him to another street. "When are you going to stop thinking about your wife?" she scolded him, glaring at his bright scarf, and he said, "I happened to turn left. Force of habit, nothing more."

But of course that was a barefaced lie: he'd been thinking about her all day. Lying on the sofa with his feet up, pretending to read, while really he was wondering, What if I knocked on her door sometime, surprised her with a visit? Wouldn't she be glad to see me, too shocked to be angry? They ought to be on speaking terms, he'd say, for the sake of the children—and surely that would soften her. Then they would sit down in Barb's familiar, fragrant kitchen and have a long, intimate chat about the kids, home repairs or what they'd been up to lately (though he wouldn't mention Maryellen if at all possible). He missed their easy conversations, the fruit of more than thirty-four years of common history and ingrained knowledge of one another's habits. He missed her delight in simple things: a bird's nest in the window or the scent of flowers, fresh peas, strawberry-rhubarb pie. His girlfriend required more elaborate pleasures than his wife.

Once inside the park gates, she said, "Let's avoid the zoo. I hate the zoo this time of year. It's sloppy and smelly, don't you think?" She tightened her grip on his elbow and led him in another direction, up a steep, rutted road with rivulets of muddy water running along either side. "Aren't those oaks over there?" Maryellen pointed at a cluster of tall, straight trunks. "Isn't that a Scotch pine?" "Do you think the sap is running yet," she asked about some maples, "or is it still too cold?"

Elliot had no opinion on any of this. He was thinking how, most of all, he missed his wife's silences: there were no questions she had to ask, because she knew the answers. She could walk with him for hours on end and be there and not be there at the same time. Like being in the shadow of a low-hanging, shifting cloud—first a mountain, then a bird, then a bowl of oranges—but when you leaped and reached for it, your hand simply passed through.

"Did you hear me?" Maryellen asked. "Do you want to go on or turn back?"

Dear God, he wanted nothing more than to turn back . . . back to three winters ago, before they divided the house. How could he go on like this, his body in one place, his heart and mind somewhere else? Elliot started coughing to cover the low sound he was suddenly making in his throat.

"Are you coming down with another cold? I could make a pot of chamomile and fix you a lavender bath. . . ."

"I want to go home," he told her.

She hugged his arm as they left the park, as if keeping him close was enough to ensure their relationship. As if there were nothing left to do but hang on tight. But deep within her was the truth, unseen yet keenly felt, like a splinter lodged under her skin: Maryellen was losing him.

The evenings of her classes he no longer went out, but retreated to the second floor where he paced like a prisoner in his cell or sat hunched on the small balcony outside their bedroom and smoked his pipe. From downstairs the click and clatter of bowls and utensils, the whine of the Cuisinart, the whomp of knives against boards. At intervals the loud, urgent words of the instructor—"No, not like that, like *this*"—shot him back to a time when he himself was one of her students, eager to follow every command, to be refashioned, rescued. And above it all, like tolling bells, he heard the grieving voices of widowers and divorcés—men who mourned their former wives, former habits, former lives. Men who knew they were killing time as they whipped potatoes and cracked eggs.

At night, when everyone had gone, she'd come upstairs to join him. If he was in a chair, she would sink to the floor beside him, spread across his feet like ooze and drop her head into his lap. He'd feel the tired weight of her skull, touch her disheveled hair, and when she turned her face up he'd see that her eyes were red-streaked. "You're working too hard," he'd say, but they both knew that wasn't true. She was worn out by her terrible need, as visible in her flashing eyes as if they were double signs reading, LOVE ME, LOVE ME. And Elliot would kiss her brow, then move his lips to the top of her head, his face hidden in her hair, and murmur faintly to her scalp, "I don't want to hurt you. I don't want to let you down." His eyes stinging, wet with shame.

Why was it that he couldn't transfer his affections from his wife to his girlfriend? Why did he feel he was losing himself living with a woman who was always giving him something?

"Tea?" Maryellen said. "Shall I make tea? Do you want a snack? Are you comfortable? Should we lie down?"

And he shook his head no, no, his face still tangled in her hair; the strands a fragile, intricate web wrapping him from ear to ear.

One April evening when the weather was especially fine, Elliot snuck out of the house while Maryellen was busy in the kitchen with a large class. The air was fresh in his nostrils and the light had a velvety quality: he could almost feel it brushing his cheek. Sidewalks, stores and brick houses, one snuggling up to the next, were shiny and crimson in a last flare of sunlight. Elliot's legs tingled as he hurried along the polished streets. He knew where he was going.

Barb was in a wicker chair on the front porch of his former home, eating an apple as bright red as a child's balloon. She was wearing a blue jacket with a stand-up collar zipped to the chin. He tripped on a twig as he neared the porch, his legs tangling; oafish. When she saw him she stopped chewing and pulled her head partly into her collar, like a turtle, her mouth disappearing behind wool. Her eyes were fixed on the blue-and-gold scarf thrown around his neck.

He sat down on the top step, an arm's length from Barb's chair. All the way over he'd been practicing different openings—*so good to see you again; just wanted to say hello; no reason we can't be friends*—but now that he was actually here, nothing seemed appropriate. He gazed at his hands in his lap, at his slightly trembling fingers, and licked his suddenly dry lips.

"Are you waiting for Ivan?" she said through the wool. "How's that working out?"

"What—Ivan? He's okay. Makes a lot of noise and tracks mud in the hallway." She shrugged. "You get used to things. Why don't you go up and knock, I know he's in."

He circled his thumbs one around the other. "I didn't come to see Ivan."

She sank lower into her collar, leaned back in her chair and twisted the stem off her apple.

"I came here to see you."

She turned toward him, drawn to his voice. Slowly Elliot raised his eyes and Barbara drew her breath in, startled by what she saw. Such an unguarded look, full of sadness, full of need. If she had any sense she would go inside and leave him to stew in his own juice. She owed him nothing—not anymore. Certainly not loyalty, concern or affection: that was his girlfriend's job now. But she kept sitting on the porch, rolling the remains of her chewed apple in her palms, stabbing the pulp with her fingernails.

"I miss you," he said at last, his voice husky, eyes bright. Barbara angled away from him and looked out at the front yard. The spruce was droopy, gray-green, stubbornly resisting spring, while behind it clusters of small buds hung from the maple's slender branches like dark grapes.

He said, "I want us to be friends."

You already have a friend, she almost hollered, *so what the hell do you want from me?*

The ground was muddy under the spruce. Grass would no longer grow in the spreading darkness under its boughs, which was just as well, Barbara thought, since she didn't like mowing the lawn and Ivan had never offered to help with that or anything else. The house was really too much for one person to maintain. Sooner or later she'd get fed up and move to an apartment. And really, wasn't it better that way—out with the old, in with the new? But Elliot would make a fuss. Moving in with Maryellen what's-her-name was one thing, selling the house another. Maybe she should tell him now, *I've been thinking about the house....* Instead, she sat in the wicker chair and squeezed her apple to brown mush.

"I made a mistake, lots of them. But I learned a few things too." Elliot laced his fingers and cleared his throat. "I know how important you are. More important than anyone. I can't bear to think that you don't want to talk to me."

Her mouth came out of its wooly shell. "How can you expect me—?" but then she stopped short. He was free to live however he liked: that was part of the deal when they divided the house in the first place. Barbara wanted the same thing, so how could she complain when he exercised his freedom? She had no right to be angry, she knew what could happen ... although she could avoid him now and safeguard her feelings. So she ducked into her collar again.

"Couldn't we meet sometimes? Or talk on the phone like we used to? It's been several months now...."

It wasn't just the anger—she was hurt and confused too. Wanting to see him and not wanting to see him at the same time.

"We'll always be Dennis and Susan's parents. We'll always be grandparents. We have that much in common."

Wanting to turn the clock back or leap forward twenty-five years, into the muck of old age, when none of this would matter.

"I know we've changed in some ways, and certain things—our circumstances—changed too. But that gives us more to talk about, more to share. Don't you see? It'd be like getting to know each other all over again—except we wouldn't have to start from scratch, we already know so much."

So much and too little. They knew about betrayal and loss, bitterness and sorrow. But what did Elliot know about her struggle to be happy?

"We could meet for coffee once in a while, talk things over. Nothing more than that, okay? I just want—I need you to be part of my life again, the way you always have been."

She stood up, stepped to the rail and threw the ruined apple at the trunk of the spruce. "You want it all—everything!" she shouted at him. "Me, *her*—" But then her voice gave out, her head sank, shoulders sagged, her thighs bumped the railing and she swayed on her feet like a stalk in the wind. Didn't she want it all too—her own space, her own life, her husband living overhead in case she had a change of heart?

Suddenly he got up and moved close. She sensed him rather than heard him: the way his body filled the space directly behind her; his leafy smell and beaming warmth. Her own body like a reed, hollow and weightless.

She felt him coming closer. She felt so insubstantial that she had to grab hold of the rail to keep from blowing off the porch. A picture winked behind her eyes of Elliot stretching over her and pressing her into a mattress.

"Barb, please."

She whispered, "Don't touch me," knowing what would happen next: his hands on her shoulders. "*Don't*," she said again as he turned her around.

At which point the front door creaked open and smacked shut. In unison they turned their heads to see Ivan cross the porch, his boots clapping against the boards. Elliot's hands dropped to his sides and Barbara stepped away from him.

"Bad timing?" Ivan grinned. "But hey, I was just leaving." He clumped down the porch steps, hands in his pockets, whistling as he left the walk and turned down the darkening street. They watched his receding back and then the shadowy traces, like faint scratches in the air, of where he had been.

Night had descended suddenly, gloomy and cold. Barbara shivered, rubbed her arms and edged to the front door. Elliot took a step toward her just as she reached out and twisted the knob. The door swung open onto an unlit hallway. He stopped, uncertain, his eyes bewildered by the dark.

"Can I see you again?" he asked, but his wife had already gone in, locking the door behind her.

He looked through a door pane and saw a murky form in the hall. He saw it float away and fade, glimmer in a sudden flare of light from an opened door, then disappear entirely. His heart was beating in his throat: whatif, what-if. . . . What if he never saw her again?

14

THE EXTRA Man

Misty mornings, sodden days: April show-ers and all that. A month she'd just as soon skip, go right to the May flowers. The bricks of the house always wet, the rooms moldy-smelling and the walls spotted with mildew. Dampness all around as she worked in the base-ment—in corners of the concrete floor, in ceiling beams and narrow boards. Everything was mottled and rank. But still she hunched over her wheel, still making bowls and plates, flat-rimmed or rimless, some with simple rounded bottoms, some with feet. Trying to finish in time for the Mavis Hall Gallery showing next month.

Her first show. The thought of it made her eyes tear. Aha, more wetness!

When the phone rang she ran up. It was Rita calling from the tub, up to her chin in bubbles, she said . . . and oh yes, she was having a small dinner party Friday night and wanted her to be there. Her cousin was bringing a friend of his, someone she wanted Barbara to meet.

Seconds later Ivan phoned to let her know about a leak spreading on the third floor: water dribbling down a wall and bubbling the plaster. But she couldn't afford a new roof even if Elliot paid half. "Put a pot on the floor," she said and hung up.

She'd gotten used to his dirty boots and rattling footsteps overhead, his too-chummy notes on her door and boisterous greetings in the hall, but his helplessness in the face of dripping faucets and cold rads was too much. Why couldn't Elliot have rented his place to a handyman?

Back in the basement she finished up, washed her hands, cleaned up and washed her hands a second time. There was chafing from the water and clay, open sores from the chemicals: the hands of an old crone. She swept a string of hair from her face, hair that was rapidly turning gray, hurrying to catch up to her ruined hands. She was not in the mood for a party . . . but hadn't seen a living soul in two days. Holed up in her wet basement, nibbling tuna sandwiches, staring at towers of clay till their edges blurred and spun away. She was losing her appetite, losing her eyesight, losing her attractiveness.

She would make herself go to the party, talk, laugh, eat, drink. Rita was a great cook and always good company. Her guests were usually interesting. Her apartment was cozy, well lit and perfectly dry.

The door was unlocked and she walked in. Sitting in the living room were two couples Barbara knew—Jake and Ida Murray-Meyers and Leigh and Adam Falk—plus a frail man in thick glasses she'd never met. An old friend of Leigh and Adam's, Ida introduced him, Dr. Owen Martin. Or was it Martin Owen? Barbara couldn't get it straight. Her thoughts were fixed on Rita's cousin Adam and his wife Leigh, longtime acquaintances who hadn't been in touch with her since she and Elliot split the house. The

Murray-Meyers had phoned often to ask them over for dinner or drinks, singly or jointly, though neither of them ever went and eventually the calls stopped.

"That you, Barbara?" Rita sang out from the kitchen. "Make yourself comfy, I'll be there in a sec."

Barbara hung her jacket up and sat on the arm of the sofa. "Long time no see," Ida Murray-Meyers said, sitting beside her, craning her neck, then Leigh Falk looked her over and asked if she felt well. "You seem tired," she said from a high-backed wing chair across the room.

"Not at all," Barbara replied. "And how are you and Adam doing?"

"Busy, busy," Leigh said.

Adam stood behind his wife, his body mostly hidden and his head and shoulders seemingly riding the back of the chair. "Leigh has been training to be a sandplay therapist."

"Sandplay? What's that?" Owen-or-Martin was sitting in a chair by the sofa. He squinted through his glasses and tipped his head toward Leigh, his bald crown as tawny and smooth as the skin of a pear. He had a blemish on his pate and a fringe of white hair which he tugged at regular intervals, one section, then another.

"I'll tell you about it," Leigh said. "It's a nonverbal therapy that gives a client access to archetypal images stored in his unconscious. A medium for healing grief."

"Archetypal images?"

"Oh, you know," Adam said, his head still bobbing on the back of the wing chair. "Jung's primordial symbols? The collective unconscious?"

"Adam is a Freudian," Leigh said tersely.

Owen-or-Martin scratched the red blotch on his scalp. "I want to understand this. You mean you actually play on the beach?"

"Oh no—in a sandbox!"

"The same thing we played in as kids in the backyard?"

"Nothing quite as big as that. More like this"—Leigh spread her arms about two feet wide—"and not so high. You set it on a table in a room with little objects: tiny toys, plants, people, animals and whatnot. The client picks and chooses, then puts different things in the box to make a kind of psychological picture in the sand which the therapist interprets."

"Play therapy," Owen-or-Martin nodded, "for children."

"I'm talking about grownups! I'm talking about men and women making pictures, breaking them. . . . It's amazing how many feelings come to light in a sandbox."

"Just like in a dark bar—but I don't get dirt under my nails." At the end of the sofa, next to Ida, Jake Murray-Meyers looked down at his drink. He seemed to be sipping ice cubes, one clacking against the next as he raised and lowered his empty glass.

"One man I watched made a sandplay with monsters that symbolized his fear of women. There were warriors in the box, too, and a negative archetypal female. That showed his unhappy relationship with his mother and his struggle to free himself from the bonds of the unconscious."

"Grown men shouldn't play in sandboxes," Jake said as he poked ice cubes with his thumb.

Barbara moved from the sofa to an oversized pillow on the rug in front of a fireplace with a fake log burning blue. Owen-or-Martin got up and offered to pour wine from a bottle on the mantel. "The good stuff's in the kitchen," said Jake, but Barbara insisted wine was fine and Owen-or-Martin handed her a large glass of Burgundy, then lowered himself beside her, his knees cracking audibly. "So tell me, what do you do?" he asked.

"Potter," she said.

"Like Rita? My daughter's also a potter. Maybe you know her, Sylvie Martin?"

"Sorry." Quickly deducing his name: *Owen* Martin, not the reverse. "And you're a doctor?"

"Not a real one," Owen said. "A Ph.D."

"Psychology?"

"Oh no."

"I thought, because you know Adam—"

"We work at the same university, but not in the same field."

"Microbiology," Jake said. "He likes to look at teensy-weensy things through a microscope."

"And how's Elliot these days?" Ida changed the subject. "We never hear from *him* either."

Barbara glanced at Ida, leaning forward on the sofa. "Fine," she said. "Just fine."

"We heard he's living with someone."

Barbara took a sip of wine, the liquid quivering in her glass. Why didn't she ask Rita who'd been invited? If she knew Ida was coming, she'd have stayed home.

"Were you very shocked?"

"A little."

"You must've known the risks you were taking when you carved up the house. *I* knew all along your experiment wouldn't work out. Men are utterly helpless and you can't expect them to live alone."

"Because of their parents," Leigh said. "When clients play in the sandbox they often release memories of inadequate parents."

"Don't generalize," Adam said, though it wasn't clear if his comment was directed at Ida or his wife.

"Where's Rita?" Owen said. He stood up and crossed the room. "Rita, come join us."

"Another minute," she called from the kitchen. "Everyone having a good time?"

When Rita finally entered the room, Barbara's eyes went round as coins. Her friend's hair was blonde now, cut so close to her head it looked like a short beard. She was wearing a leather miniskirt, striped stockings, a fuzzy sweater and short, chunky-heeled boots. Abruptly she doubled over to fix a seam and tug her hem, then straightened up and squirmed in her sweater, which looked itchy and too tight. Her eyes were black-circled and her face powdered a bloodless white. She grinned at Barbara and stepped aside—"You haven't met Joshua"—and from behind her there appeared a young man in a black shirt, with hair down to his shoulders and a silver stud in his earlobe. Rita hooked his slender arm and bumped her hip against his while Joshua turned bright red.

"Isn't he cute?" Ida said. "They met a few weeks ago and haven't been apart since. Rita knows a good man when she sees one and holds on tight."

Barbara stared at Joshua. His lankiness and good looks reminded her of Brad, and her pelvis tightened suddenly. Couldn't be a day over thirty-five, she imagined, and Rita turning fifty in June. Well, good for Rita, good for her! Even if it didn't last. Even if he dropped her for a leggy twenty-two-year-old before her next birthday.

What else could an aging woman do for sexual excitement? The choices were limited. A brief affair with a young man or something less desirable with someone stooped and sixtyish, bewitched by microorganisms. Or last—and least—a platonic friendship with a guy like Brad. Friendship and fantasy instead of the real thing.

Rita and Joshua returned to the kitchen. Soon after, Joshua came back with a tray of fritters and bacon-wrapped chicken livers skewered with toothpicks. "He's in sales, isn't he?" Ida said to Jake as she swallowed something deep-fried.

Adam, sucking a toothpick, asked Joshua what he sold, and Joshua answered, "Lighting."

Rita appeared in the doorway. "We met in Ikea, he

was checking out their systems. That table lamp over there? He got it for me wholesale. He's going to do the lighting for my Ottawa show." She crossed the room, squatted next to Barbara in front of the fire and prodded the log with a poker, so that it spat orange sparks and grew yellow fingers of flame. "It's not just sex," she said softly. "It's so much more."

Later on they squeezed around a table in the dining nook. Owen sat on Barbara's right and Joshua was on her left. Owen asked about her work and Barbara told him what she was making for the show in May. He played with his hair as she spoke and seemed to hang on every word. Seen through his lenses, his eyes looked enormous and keen. When she asked politely what he looked at under his microscope, he mentioned plankton and protozoa and other things she half remembered from high school science. It got more technical after that, his speech peppered with jargon, but by then her mind was wandering. She found herself staring at the rose-colored spot on his crown, wondering what it could possibly be, a rash or infection.

Joshua hardly said a word. He dashed to the kitchen several times to fetch water, more wine, a platter of beef, a gravy boat, and then again to clear the table and carry out dirty dishes. But mainly he ate silently, glancing at Rita now and then, and once, when Barbara dropped a spoon and bent down to pick it up, she saw that they were rubbing knees. Barbara thought it was childish and couldn't account for the knot in her throat that made it hard to swallow.

"Eat something," Ida said to Jake, who hadn't touched his food. "The roast beef is wonderful."

He raised his glass, half-filled and crackling with ice cubes, and took a drink. "Certainly is."

"How would you know?" Ida sniffed. "You've drowned all your taste buds."

Jake probed his mouth with his tongue, as if trying to find and save the last of his taste buds.

"Drinking problems have to do with a difficult childhood," Leigh said. She put down her knife and fork and folded her hands on the table. "If a boy grows up without enough love from his mother, his ego will be damaged, he'll need constant gratification."

"No one gets enough love"—Adam flattened his hands on either side of his dinner plate—"and we don't all become drunks. You're always making preposterous statements."

Leigh twirled a section of her straight, sensible-looking hair draped in front of her shoulder. "I don't," she said. "I do not."

"I'm no drunk," Jake said. "Just not very hungry."

Rita and Joshua stood up and exchanged looks. "Maybe you'd like some coffee now," Rita smiled down at Jake, "and double-fudge chocolate cake. Joshua made it himself." She touched Joshua's elbow and they hurried into the kitchen.

"He's really something," Jake said.

"And you?" said Ida.

Jake shrugged. "Me? I'm a big nothing."

"No you're not!" Leigh said. "You're just feeling insecure. How can a child develop a strong ego without a mother's love?"

"I'm tired of mothers getting the blame for everything," Ida said. "Jake's mother was wonderful—a hard-working, no-nonsense woman with a sharp mind. She raised a pack of kids on her own and did a perfectly good job."

"I agree with you," Adam said. "A little less simplistic talk, a little more intelligent thought."

"I'm not simple," Leigh said.

"I didn't say you were, did I?"

Rita brought in the chocolate cake and cut it into wedges. Leigh, Owen and Barbara each had a slice of cake, but Adam, Jake and Ida declined.

Leigh finished her piece quickly and helped herself to another, which she wolfed down. Adam lifted an empty cup and Joshua popped out of the kitchen with a coffeepot. He stopped at everyone's place in turn, filling their cups.

Leigh swung around in her seat and rushed away from the table.

Rita set down a bowl of fruit. "Should I put something on Leigh's plate? Strawberries? A tangerine?"

"I don't think she'll be eating any more tonight," said Adam.

Leigh came back to the table looking dazed, pale and wobbly. Strands of shiny, damp hair had fallen across her forehead. With her chin lowered and arms crossed, she resumed the conversation. "You know, Adam, I've noticed something. Everything you say has a hidden message directed at me. You never miss a chance to embarrass me in public."

Adam rapped his coffee cup hard against its saucer. "Let's finish this at home."

Jake leaned back in his chair, so that it balanced on two legs. "My mother was a cold bitch."

"Sit up!" Ida snapped at him. "You're going to fall."

"Cold as ice." He shook his glass and the cubes tinkled like wind chimes. "Cold hands, cold heart. I didn't even like her."

"Have you thought about therapy?" Leigh said. "A therapist could help you heal."

"Why don't you just hand him your business card," said Adam.

Whereupon Jake's chair slipped and he fell over onto his back, his legs hooked neatly over the seat as if he were sitting upright and the rest of the room had shifted.

Owen jumped up. "Is he hurt?"

"Are you hurt, Jake?" Ida asked.

There were ice cubes on his chest and a wet spot on his shirt where his drink had spilled. Jake smiled and held up his empty glass. "Refill?"

Owen and Joshua helped him up, then Rita straightened the toppled chair. She gathered ice cubes off the floor and dropped them into the fruit bowl. Ida held a cup of coffee to Jake's lips and made him drink. Rita sat down again, writhing in her pink sweater, and squeezed a glass of red wine between her palms. Barbara wanted to go home and started making excuses, but Joshua touched her hand and his eyes pleaded *not yet*. "For Rita's sake," he mouthed the words. Again she felt her throat thicken. She wanted to rest her head against his slim arm.

Rita had nearly finished her wine when she groaned "Oh no!" and a purple stain spread across her sweater, just between her breasts, like a ruby pendant hanging there. Joshua reached out with a napkin to dab it as Rita shoved her chair back and ran into another room. He got up to follow, but Barbara said, "I'll go."

The bathroom door was unlocked. Barbara tapped, walked in and closed the door behind her. Rita was bent over the sink, scrubbing her spotted sweater. When she heard Barbara she straightened up and looked at her in the mirror. Rita's reflection shivered, though her skin was flushed. She was wearing a low-cut bra and her waist bulged above the tight band of her skirt. "What a mess," she said.

"The sweater?"

"No one's having a good time."

"It's not your fault," said Barbara. "Jake's a drunk, Ida's a bitch, and who knows the last time Leigh and Adam got along."

"I wanted you to have fun. You don't get out enough,

so I thought I'd ask you over and invite a few people, and Adam said he had a friend. . . ."

"I always like seeing you. And I liked meeting Joshua."

Rita hugged herself. "So tell me what you think of him."

"He seems very nice. How old is he anyway?"

"We don't talk about age."

"I have a young friend too. Brad."

"From the supply store?"

"Except that we're *just* friends. When it comes to carnal love, he prefers women his own age."

Rita emptied the bathroom sink, wrung out her sweater and held it up, still stained. "You're trying to tell me this is just a fling, I'm too old for Josh. But this time it's different, Barb. When everyone goes home tonight and the two of us are cleaning up, suddenly we'll drop everything, fall into each other's arms . . . and nothing else will matter."

Barbara couldn't help remembering how it was with Elliot—loading the dishwasher, emptying ashtrays, wiping spills and vacuum cleaning after yet another party; Elliot complaining that it wasn't worth the trouble. But there among the yawns and grumbles was something sweet and intimate too: the image of their friends around them, Barbara and Elliot at the hub, two halves of a single heart that pumped life into everything.

"Hand me that, will you?" Rita was pointing at a shirt on a hook on the door. Barbara passed her the blouse, then kissed Rita goodbye, saying she'd had enough of Jake and Ida for one night.

When she got back to the dining room, Leigh and Ida were bent over the table, giggling into their hands, while Jake recited a nursery rhyme. Joshua played with crumbs on his plate. Adam had changed seats and was now sitting next to Owen, discussing tenure and pension plans. Barbara said goodnight and went to get her jacket.

Suddenly Owen was at her side, guiding her arm into her sleeve. "May I walk you to your car?" he said.

"Well . . . if you want to."

Owen pulled a coat from the closet (just the sort of gray, limp thing you'd expect him to wear), then followed Barbara into the hall and onto an elevator. They faced straight ahead and didn't speak, though Barbara glanced at him sidelong. His glasses winked in the glaring light, his scalp shone. His coat hung large and loose, as if he were rapidly shrinking on the ride down.

He walked beside her to her car, parked close to Rita's building. He stood only inches away, his hands deep in the pockets of his unshapely coat, as she shook the contents of her bag and found her keys. When she turned a key on the driver's side all the doors unlocked, and she ducked down and swung into the bucket seat. She opened the windows and called goodbye as Owen yanked the passenger door and thrust his head into the car. A breeze blew his fringe of hair so that it swayed this way and that, like plants underwater. She thought of squirmy organisms—worms, larvae, one-celled creatures—trapped and studied on a slide, desperate to wiggle free while Owen watched them till they dried.

"I was hoping I could see you again. Buy you dinner sometime."

She pictured him in a restaurant, candlelight reflected off his endless brow and pale crown, glasses on the tip of his nose as he peered at the menu. He seemed like a bread-and-soup man: nothing to disturb his stomach, although he would be gracious and insist she order a full meal. *What would you suggest?* she'd say, and he'd name something expensive—filet mignon or swordfish—because, more than anything, he wanted to impress her. But what would they talk about after that? What could she possibly say to a man who lived in a miniature world where nothing was noisy, hot-blooded, impulsive or big?

"Maybe after my show," she said. "I'm so busy right now."

He dropped into the passenger seat. "I'm a widower," Owen said. "Maybe you didn't know."

That he was available? Harmless? Utterly respectable?

"And I know you left your husband."

Which makes her lonely and eager too? Is that what he was thinking? She jammed a key into the ignition and started the car.

"I'm alone, you're alone. It seems only natural—" and he lurched forward to kiss her cheek.

She saw it coming and turned her face, so that he planted a kiss on her jaw. "For godssake!" she hissed at him. "What was that all about? You don't even know if I like you."

"You're right. I apologize. I'm not used to this sort of thing, I don't know the protocol. I can't remember the last time I asked a woman out on a date."

"It's late and I'm tired," she said. "I think you should go."

"You're not angry?"

"Just tired."

Owen scrambled out of the car. "Goodbye for now. I'll call you."

Barbara turned the wheel hard, squealed out of the parking spot and drove off without looking back. She imagined him standing at the curb, his eyes stunned behind his glasses, hunched under his gray coat.

When she got to her house she slowed the car and parked on the street. It was drizzling again. April showers. Rain hit the windshield and ran down in winding lines like cracks in the glass. She turned off the engine, turned off the lights and sat there for a moment. Rain played a melancholy song on the roof. No rush to go inside to her damp, dark apartment, eerie in its silence.

No hurry to get into bed between musty-smelling sheets cold against her bare skin.

If only Brad were in her bed: *Surprise, surprise! I changed my mind. Why can't we be lovers too?* Or even Elliot—yes, him. *I couldn't stand to be away from you another minute.*

She wouldn't want him there in the morning, lumpish and grumpy, expecting her to whip out of bed and fix him a big breakfast. But she wanted him now.

Barbara sighed, got out of the car. Her freedom was precious, but she was spending too much time in the basement, too much time at the wheel, too much time on her own. Ruining her eyes, ruining her hands. She ought to get out more, be with others; join a choir, a gardening club, see the children regularly, go places with Rita. Now that her life was finally hers, now that she was working hard, following her own course, why was she also feeling deprived? It seemed unfair that she should come this far only to miss things she'd left behind.

When Barbara walked into the house the hall was dark. Light filtered in from the top of the stairs, where Ivan's apartment door was ajar. Ivan himself was standing on a stool in the narrow hall, removing the glass shade that hung from a chain in the ceiling. He was wearing tight jeans and his ass made a round silhouette. "Bulb burned out," he said. "Mind if I change it?"

"Turning over a new leaf?"

"Just trying to be helpful."

She couldn't squeeze around him, so she leaned back against the door, waiting for him to finish. "Here, hold this," he said, handing her the amber shade. He unscrewed the old bulb and passed that to her as well. Then he got a new one and stuck it in the socket.

She gave him the shade and he put it back. Her hand was unsteady and she shoved it into a pocket. "How's the leak?" she asked as he hopped off the stool.

Ivan grinned at her in the suddenly yellow-bright hall. "The pot works real well. Come on up and I'll show you."

"Another time," she said. "It's late."

He looked at his watch. "It's early." His shirtsleeves were rolled and his arms big and hairy. His collar was spread open, three buttons undone.

"No, really. I'm very tired."

"How many times have I asked you?" He shook his head. "How many notes on the door, how many personal invitations? Here we are in the same house and you won't even have a drink with me. But maybe you don't like me."

When Barbara didn't answer he started upstairs with the stool, glancing over his shoulder. "Last chance," he called out.

She couldn't say why she decided to go, but she followed slowly, step by step, looking behind her as she climbed, as if searching for something she'd left below. Her legs moved heavily, as though she were underwater. By the time she reached the third floor, her lungs felt waterlogged and she could barely catch her breath.

She would catch her breath, look and leave. She would not sit down, take off her jacket, have a drink.

He turned on a table lamp and showed her the stained ceiling, the blistered paint and wet plaster that smelled like chalk. In a corner, close to the molding, was a blackened pot with a broken handle and uneven bottom. She crouched down and saw about an inch of murky water in the damaged pot. "Looks bad," she said, "but I can't afford to fix it now."

Ivan shrugged. "Want a beer? I was just going to have one myself."

"I can't stay. Really."

When she straightened up and turned around, Ivan cupped her face in his hands and kissed her wetly on the lips. His tongue pushed into her mouth. When she pulled away she was gasping.

She expected him to say, *I've been wanting to do that a long time.* She expected him to whisper her name, touch her hair, kiss her again. *You do like me, don't you?* Instead, without a word, Ivan walked to the bed and undressed. In the pink light from the table lamp his skin was rosy, youthful, though she knew he was exactly the same age as Elliot. He was broad-shouldered, long-limbed, soft-bellied and hairy, a dark line of curls from his navel to his bushy crotch. His penis glistened, half stiff.

She could say nothing, turn on her heel, march haughtily downstairs. Or say, *Put your clothes on, don't be ridiculous* and *Let me remind you who I am,* then walk away disgusted. She could roll her eyes, shake her head, even laugh.

She could take off her jacket, shoes, stockings, dress, bra and panties . . . walk up to him very slowly, belly in and chest out, his eyes on her nipples, on her groin. She could rub against him, warm and wet, his fingers grabbing her flesh as they fell onto the mattress and he spread her legs and pushed into her, hard and deep. . . .

She didn't want to be kissed again. Didn't want to see him—so she closed her eyes, pretending she was sleeping with a stranger, a man who didn't know her name and wouldn't ever see her again . . . but who would touch her just so. And oh yes—*yes*—it was good, it was good, it was just right.

She opened her eyes as he rolled off. They got dressed side by side, their backs turned.

"Elliot's my friend," he said. "You won't tell him, will you?"

"Of course not. What do you think?" And then she hurried downstairs.

She took a hot bubble bath and got into bed between the cool sheets. On her nightstand was a photograph of

Elliot and the children, taken many years ago. She was not about to mutilate an old family snapshot—but now as he looked at her sternly, she had the urge to cut out his face or ruin it with an inky mustache.

It's my life, she glared back. *I do what I want, just like you.*

And the photo answered sheepishly, *Forgive me. Forget it.*

"Forgive and forget," she said aloud to Ivan, Owen and Elliot. Then she closed her eyes tight and saw only the black, blank underside of her eyelids.

15

Soup Bowls

The Mavis Hall Gallery comprised a big front room with a second, smaller room at the back. One area led to the next by means of an archway. The main room had windows facing the street along the east wall and a desk in the northwest corner where a staffer sat, smiling vacantly at the guests. Beside the desk was a table with crackers, cheese and crudités, bottles of water, pop and wine. Reflected in a window, Mavis Hall herself was talking to a man wearing a coat like a patchwork quilt.

Around the room were white shelves with the work of several ceramists, formal, functional and ornamental pieces. Porcelain vases decorated with crackle and sgraffito; raku ware in metallic colors; a covered jar on rococo legs; an assortment of pots with cutout shapes and clinging whimsical creatures; a series of earthenware cocoons; a lustrous bouquet of ceramic flowers; a bronze and stoneware object, wheel thrown and hand built, and various other sculptures on tables or the floor.

The potters hovered near their work, wearing black, stretchy suits or skimpy, silver-threaded dresses that showed off their young figures. They were eager to explain symbol, metaphor and inspiration to anyone who cared to listen. The potters could be overheard using such expressions as "circuitous simplicity," "ethnographic continuum," "organic divergence" and "tonal disparity." For them, clay was a medium of aesthetic transcendence and potting was a death-defying, spiritual activity that renewed as it reaffirmed, a wall raised against the creeping emptiness of existence.

People clustered here and there, munching broccoli flowerets and cheese cubes and sipping wine, examining different pieces or gossiping among themselves. They were friends and family of the artists, fellow potters, dealers and those who simply saw an ad in the paper and showed up. The room was noisy, crowded and hot. Someone opened a window and a sweet breeze parted the guests, reminding them that outside the night was fragrant with May flowers and musical with the tiny cries of reawakening insects.

A few curious visitors passed through the archway to peek at the adjoining room, filled with bowls and plates, but the space was intimidating. No windows, no snacks, subdued lighting and silence, as though they had entered a sanctum. The artist herself was middle-aged, her hair in a bun on top of her head with gray strands escaping; an assured-looking woman in a long dress and loose vest, tall enough to be imposing. The guests nodded and circled the room, mainly speaking among themselves, but sometimes asking questions which the artist answered simply in a soft voice.

Some of her dishes were bunched and stacked in sculptural arrangements, while others were displayed singly, the better to accentuate their shapes, colors and patterns. They'd been stamped, carved or paddled to achieve different textures. Some of the thinner porcelain bowls with crimson interiors seemed to be holding sunsets. The plates, either flat-rimmed or merely thickened at the edge, were delicately shaded pools. A plaque on the wall read, "Wheel thrown or hand built, porcelain or stoneware, these bowls and plates are conventional in form only. Their surface decorations and subtly altered structure challenge one's perception of the nature and function of familiar domestic objects." The potter's name was Barbara Rifkin. Her work was impressive, but no one had ever heard of her.

As the outer room filled up, more and more visitors poured into the alcove, as if by osmosis, leaving a trail of cracker crumbs, empty glasses and toothpicks. Soon the older potter was enclosed by young admirers. One of them she recognized and gaily embraced: a lanky man in a ponytail, wearing an open raincoat despite the balmy weather. They spoke in buzzy whispers and her face became pink, her eyes gleamed; her voice grew higher pitched while her hands made sinuous gestures. They spoke about tools, slips and glazes, dominant surfaces, line and motif, and now and then she'd giggle into her palm like a schoolgirl. When Mavis Hall entered the room, silk pants swishing and a wineglass raised like a beacon, Barbara introduced Brad as her former instructor, but Mavis already knew him, his pottery supply store and excellent ceramics. "Isn't Barbara's work exciting?" Brad said, and Mavis agreed: "Truly amazing."

Meanwhile, in the front room, two couples had arrived and were grouped around the snack table, drinking wine. One of the women was small and thin, wearing a trim, corporate-looking brown suit; the other was in a low-backed, tight-fitting black dress, a head taller and chesty. The paler, heavier man was rubbing circles on her bare back. "Dennis, please, don't," she said. "Don't touch me, it's too hot." The man removed his hand at once, then pushed his glasses up his nose, took off his suit jacket and folded it neatly over his arm.

"So where is she?" the other man said. He was more or less Dennis's height, but muscular and olive-skinned, with short, thick black hair. His tie was loose, his shirtsleeves rolled, and sweat had gathered at his collar and formed a line down his spine. He was speaking to the small woman, who was standing on tiptoe, looking around. Moments later she elbowed into the crowd and was gone.

"Come back here!" he called out—not meaning to speak so loud, it just came out of him that way—and then he tried to follow her, but Dennis grabbed hold of his arm. "Relax, Keith. She'll be back."

But still he was jumpy. He'd never been to an opening before and didn't know what to do. He didn't even know the artist, who happened to be Susan's mom, which made it more important that he didn't make a wrong move. Also this was the first time he'd met Dennis and Natalie and he found them hard to talk to. Dennis knew nothing about sports, and what do you say to a doctor after you tell her about your aches and pains? All they wanted to know from him was how long he'd been seeing Susan, and when he said six weeks they didn't ask another thing.

Then Natalie said, "Over there," and he saw Susan waving at them and followed Dennis and his wife to a smaller, darker space that was hotter than the one they were in.

"This is my mother," Susan said, and Keith smiled hello at a round-faced woman who was twice the width of her daughter. Susan took after her father, he guessed (though later he would see that she hardly resembled either one). Mrs. Rifkin hugged her daughter, then Dennis and Natalie. She probably would've hugged him too if he let her, but he stepped quickly out of reach because he didn't like to be touched by anyone but his lover.

Barbara Rifkin stood in the archway between the rooms, one arm around her daughter, one around her daughter-in-law, while she and her son exchanged looks. Her eyes were practically throbbing, and her pleasure ran through him in waves. He had no desire to be in her shoes, to have personal objects on view to strangers—to be so *visible*—but he breathed in her feelings like second-hand smoke.

Barbara's arm was heavy, but Natalie didn't squirm away. There was something almost magical about her mother-in-law tonight, and standing in the circle of her arm some of it rubbed off. Although she'd seen her first patient at 7:45 A.M., took fifteen minutes for lunch and then did her hospital rounds; although her feet were swollen again and had to be shoehorned into her pumps and her back was stiff and crackling with pain, she felt happy under the weight of Barbara's all-embracing arm.

But not as happy as Susan—oh, no one was as happy as that! Not even her mother, who was dizzy with the success of her show, counting the red dots on the wall that showed which pieces had been sold, scooping her children into her arms and squeezing the breath right out of them. No one, no one quite as thrilled, because she was in love again. Susan loved Keith and he loved her. As soon as she got the chance she would show off the necklace he gave her for her birthday, a gold heart on a gold chain. *This is it!* she wanted to shout to everyone in the gallery. *The real thing. This is love.*

But then, unexpectedly, her arms tightened on their backs and Barbara made a sound in her throat. Susan and Natalie followed her gaze to where a man stood beside a window in the main room. People passed in front of him and they caught only glimpses of a guy in a blazer with his arms folded, pulling his ear. "It's Elliot," said Barbara, and Susan and Natalie thought, Of course.

It wasn't clear at first whether Elliot had come alone. He was speaking to someone with red hair, his head tipped close to hers in a way that signaled intimacy, but minutes later the woman was part of a group on the other side of the room. She looked familiar to Susan, who had seen her father's girlfriend once, if only in the background, when she surprised him with a visit and he hadn't even asked her in but took her to a doughnut shop. Either he was ashamed or protective of his new life, but in any case she was upset, and later Susan accidentally spilled coffee on his lap.

"Who told him?" Barbara said, and Susan answered, "I did. I thought he should know about your show." Her mother took a step back, but Susan said she was going to say hello and strode into the room.

Soon after, she came back with her father's arm hooked in hers. She introduced him to Keith, who was scowling at a hill of dishes, "*Untitled* (soup bowls)" that looked like a sinkful of dirty plates, which wasn't his idea of art. He shook Mr. Rifkin's hand, even sweatier than his own, and glanced at his face, which was scrunched up. It looked like the guy was in pain and Keith felt sorry for him: here was someone even more miserable than he was.

Susan was on her toes again, scanning the small room. She spied her mother in a corner, smiling at a short-haired blonde in tight leather pants. Susan yanked her father's arm and drew him toward them. "The unity of opposing patterns," the woman was explaining, "like motion and stillness. . . ." Dennis stood beside her, nibbling something golden on the end of a toothpick.

Elliot dropped his daughter's arm. He turned and circled the alcove, considering the plates and bowls. When he glanced back at the main room he saw someone familiar—Christ! the guy with the ponytail—just leaving the gallery.

All at once he was burning. Elliot unbuttoned his blazer, opened his collar, scratched his neck. Then he took a steadying breath and walked up to Barbara. When they were an arm's length apart she pulled Dennis between them. Dennis blinked his eyes behind his grease-smeared lenses, then introduced the blonde as his mother's friend Rita, who was having a show in Ottawa.

"Congratulations," Elliot said, looking directly at his wife.

"Next month," said Rita. "It opens on the fourteenth."

"That's our anniversary," Elliot said to Barbara.

Rita raised her eyebrows and backed away. Dennis dropped his toothpick and kicked it with the tip of his shoe. "I'm surprised to see you."

"Your mother's first show. I thought I should be here."

Dennis looped an arm around his mother's waist. She felt as hard to his touch as one of her fired bowls.

"I thought we could go for a drink later or something to eat," said Elliot. "When you're ready. After the show."

Dennis drew his mother, stiff and silent, against his hip. "All of us?"

"You, me, Barb, Susan, Susan's friend—and Natalie?" He turned his head. "Where is she?"

"The six of us?"

"If Barb agrees."

The men looked at Barbara, who was staring at one of her pieces on a shelf by her elbow, something she had called simply, "*Bowl Series, #1*," a wheel-thrown stoneware vessel, slightly flared and misshapen, blue-white and imprinted with barely visible brush strokes. What she saw in the lone dish was sturdiness and fragility, beauty and imperfection, emptiness and fullness—the unity of opposing patterns. What she said was, "Why not?"

They got to a restaurant late and had the whole place to themselves. Barbara chose a table near the window and sat at the head, flanked by Keith and Dennis. Elliot sat at the other end, the black window at his back reflecting him in silhouette so that he seemed blurred at the edges or double-exposed. Susan had her hand on his arm, as if to keep him fixed in his chair, while Natalie, on his right side, opened a cloth napkin and cleaned her husband's glasses.

The waiter bent his head toward Keith, then Elliot, and minutes later wine appeared and a green bottle of champagne. They raised their glasses to Barbara as Dennis made a windy speech about her focus, dedication, imagination and energy, the gratification of art and her wonderful achievement. Natalie started clapping before he was quite through, whereupon Dennis emptied his glass and everyone else did the same. Then Keith and Susan locked heads, laughing and whispering, and Dennis used his cellphone to call home and talk to the sitter. Elliot spoke to Natalie, although his head (and the head in the window) angled toward Barbara.

Who felt as if she were having an out-of-body experience, hovering close to the ceiling, surveying the scene. Dear Dennis, poor Dennis, trying hard to fill the role of good husband, good son as he questioned the babysitter and nodded gravely at his wife; and worn-out Natalie, dying to kick off her tight shoes, fall into bed and get some sleep before it was time to wake up and drag herself through another day. Then there was Susan, wildly in love—in love with her father, in love with Keith—planted between them like a flower blooming extravagantly in a glut of compost, moisture and light. If only she could love a little less intensely, Barbara thought, maybe she could hold on to her skittish-looking boyfriend and not scare off her father.

Who frightened so easily. By sudden tightness in his chest or an unexplained headache; by what might happen tomorrow or a change in routine. By a self-reliant wife when he needed attachment or a woman craving intimacy when Elliot wanted distance. She understood all that as she watched him from overhead. Like the image of his body and its shadow in the window, he was light and dark, clear and vague, solid and insubstantial. Much like Barbara's *Bowl Series*. Much like Barbara herself. She thought, at that instant, that someday they might be friends. Someday she might forgive him many things.

Then she grew suddenly dense and funneled down from the ceiling to inhabit her body again. No one seemed to have noticed that she'd floated off and come back, or that she was smiling, her eyes wet. Returned to her body and the bosom of her family, weighted with love.

Barbara's stomach gurgled, reminding her she hadn't eaten all night. She raised her hand to call the waiter and ask for a menu. A big bowl of hot-and-sour soup, she decided, and no sooner did she speak than everyone (except Keith) ordered the same thing.

Soon after, the waiter brought Keith's burger and yellow fries, a soup tureen and white bowls. Elliot stood up slowly, his reflection wavering in the glass, and ladled soup into the bowls. His hand was shaky, his cheeks puffed, as if he were holding his breath as he passed the bowls to Natalie, who sent them round the table. Everyone waited silently, watching the steaming bowls.

As they lowered their heads and drank soup, Elliot peered at each of them, then dipped his spoon in his bowl and sighed. Here he was, two years, two months and a handful of days later, dining with his family again as if he'd never been away. Not since the house was split had they all been together like this. He bent his head so the steam from the soup mixed with his sudden tears and no one would know how sentimental an old fool like him could be.

No one spoke till Barbara said, "It's good, isn't it? Good soup," and then the chatter began again, everybody speaking at once: "Mine's good, is yours good?" "Oh yes, very good." "Delicious, good." "Good?" "Good." "Just right." "Wonderful." "Really, this is so good."

And Barbara watched her daughter and son, their heads bobbing over their bowls, Susan's hair parted at the back and falling forward to expose her thin, arched neck and Dennis's pink and doughy one; necks as smooth and fragile as when they were babies. Seeing in their postures a reluctant acceptance of all that had come to pass, Elliot living with someone else and Barbara an artist: their parents living their own lives. But also, in the tilt of their heads, in the droop of their arms as they lifted their spoons, was sadness and regret—and maybe even wisdom—because their childish notion of selfless, predictable parents was gone. If Dad could take a lover and Mom stop baking pies, anything was possible, the future was uncertain. Love was unreliable. And this, Barbara knew, though they raised their glasses and wished her well, was a torment for her children.

And Elliot—what to make of him? Did he come alone tonight out of delicacy, embarrassment or family solidarity? Why was he here at all? Why go out with them after? Maybe the two lovebirds were squabbling in their love nest and so he was running home to his flock, humble and remorseful.

But surely there was no going back now for any of them. They were all different in small ways that mattered enormously. Barbara leaned back in her chair. Look at all she'd set in motion just by wanting to live alone.

Then Elliot put his spoon down and sat up straight. Behind him his reflection shrank, so that he lost his silhouette and became distinct. He cleared his throat for attention. Keith drummed his fork on the table, Natalie glanced at her watch and yawned, Dennis rolled his head in circles; but Susan turned to Elliot and Barbara crossed her arms and stared.

"I want to say," Elliot looked down at his soup bowl, "how good it is to be here, with all of you . . . right here." His voice fell to a whisper: "Around the table like this."

Dennis paused, Susan gulped, Natalie clamped her lips together and even Keith became still, feeling the weight of the moment. Only Barbara stayed as she was, cross-armed and waiting.

"I promise you," he went on, glancing at each of them in turn, but then dropped his eyes again and shook his head.

Susan put her hand on his arm—"Say it, Dad, tell us"—and Elliot smiled, his ears red.

"I'm happy tonight," he told them. "I can't remember the last time I felt this good."

Dennis and Natalie left first, and later the remaining four stopped for a minute on the street outside the restaurant. A gentle, clear spring night, the air smelling country-fresh even though they were downtown. His wife and daughter glowing in the beam of a streetlight. Like two angels, Elliot thought.

Susan opened her collar to show them a necklace, pulling it straight out from her throat. "A present from K-Keith," she said, and Elliot nearly groaned to see the trembling of her fingers and to hear her stumble over his name. How would she survive if he left? Clearly it was dangerous to be so helpless . . . and clearly it couldn't be helped, he knew only too well.

He told them he needed a ride, he hadn't brought his car tonight (Maryellen's car, that is, since Barb had the Buick), and Susan offered to take him home. Keith loved to drive, she said, and wouldn't mind one bit, but Barbara interrupted with, "I'll do it, it's on my way." Whereupon the young people said goodbye and hurried off.

When they reached the car and got in, he breathed in deeply. The Buick smelled familiar, a mix of vinyl, gas and food, and something of Barb—a sweet, leafy fragrance, as if she'd been out in the woods. She started the car and drove west. In the shadowy interior, blinking pale and dark as they passed under streetlights, her skirt seemed to move over her lap like a stream. Elliot folded his arms and tucked his hands in his armpits to keep from inadvertently running his fingers over her thigh.

"So how've you been?" Barb said.

"Not bad. Keeping busy."

"Still doing Tai Chi?"

"When I can."

"And your saxophone?"

"I don't play much anymore. Maryellen doesn't like—" He stopped short, cursing himself. He hadn't meant to bring up his other life.

She accelerated suddenly, then braked for a yellow light. Elliot jerked forward and his seat belt dug into his chest. "You should've gone through it," he said.

"Who's driving, me or you?"

He adjusted his belt. "Sorry I spoke. Old habit."

She made a sharp left turn, drove south a short way, then sped onto the Lake Shore. Elliot thought again of the night he drove back from Susan's and almost skidded into a post, his life frozen, about to end—and how it didn't matter. But here, tonight, this second, everything mattered a great deal.

"I really liked the show," he said carefully. "I'm glad I went."

"I'm glad too . . . though at first I was nervous. Then I thought I wanted you to see my work after all, to know what I do all day."

"But you didn't even invite me!"

"I'd never call you at *her* place."

"You could've sent a postcard."

She didn't reply.

He stared out the side window, gazing at pillars flashing by and electronic billboards. CHANGE YOUR LIFE . . . . Giant letters rolled across a moving screen, the rest of the message lost as the car shot by, but he took the words as a warning.

"I want to move out of there," he said, surprising himself as much as her because he hadn't known till right then he was going to say that. "I want to come home."

Barb took the next exit and drove the rest of the way along residential side streets, past softly lit homes, square lawns and budding trees, their branches blurred and cottony in the quiet dark. Her silence made him nervous.

"Aren't you going to say something? What do you think of my idea?"

She turned onto a street that he recognized as Maryellen's and pulled over near her house. "Is this the number?" Barb asked. "Or maybe that one over there. Susan told me where you live but I can't quite remember. Anyway, you're close enough."

He unbuckled his seat belt but stayed where he was. They were parked in a driveway, in the shadow of a lowrise. Barb looked ghostly and he feared she would vanish before his eyes. "Do you want me to come back?"

"It's up to you." Her voice was so low and weary, Elliot strained to hear her. "It's your decision, not mine."

"I won't live in the house again if you don't want me to."

"You didn't ask my permission to leave, so why do you need it now?"

"I want you to want this too."

She turned away and dropped her shoulder against the door. "I was part of a big show tonight. I finally feel like a potter, like I'm finally going somewhere—and now you want to turn back the clock and ruin everything."

"I wouldn't interfere with your life. We'd just be living under the same roof again like we used to."

"You move out, move in, bring visitors to the house.... All that affects me, it turns my life inside out. I've got peace and quiet now. Why should I welcome you back?"

He said, "We could have rules. Anything you wanted."

Barb said, "Just go. I can't talk about it now. I wasn't expecting any of this." She straightened up and smoothed her skirt along the rippled length of her thighs, while in the semi-darkness Elliot touched the edge of her dress fallen between their seats.

He knew then he would come back, with or without her blessing.

He decided not to push his luck and climbed out of the Buick. At least she hadn't said no. Barb drove away with a lurch, but he didn't reach for his house key or cross the road to the front door—Maryellen's front door. Instead he walked north for a few blocks and veered left, onto his old street.

The Buick was parked out front, close to the house. Turning onto the walkway, he looked up and saw that his apartment was dark. Maybe Ivan was out somewhere or maybe he'd gone to bed, with or without a partner. Tomorrow morning, first thing, Elliot would phone him and tell him he'd have to move. He couldn't stand to be away another day.

The hallway was also dark (Barb had probably turned

off the light on her way in), but the window on the ground floor shone reddish gold like the long, drawn curtains. Elliot stopped on a patch of lawn between the porch and the sheltering spruce, not sure what to do next. Call to her like Romeo or throw stones at the window? Warble a love song? What he did was something he hadn't done in too long, the 108 movements of Tai Chi Chuan.

He did it facing her window, to a crowd of tittering insects and under a tent of stars. He did the form flawlessly, twenty minutes altogether from Raise Hands to the last Single Whip and conclusion. He moved with poise and energy, balanced on the new shoots slippery under the soles of his shoes, smelling grass and trees and the tang of the night air. Waving his arms, swinging his hips and pivoting from corner to corner in his fluid dance. A happy dance. A dance of love. Just as he reached the end he thought he saw the curtain move. He thought he saw her peering out, a band of light above her head.

Then he turned and went home to give Maryellen the news. No doubt she'd be upset, even though he didn't love her. even though she was clearly unhappy in their relationship. No doubt she'd beg him to stay, swear they could work things out, bring him a cup of tea.

He'd leave as soon as possible, because it was better that way. He never meant to hurt her and was sorry to have let her down. But some things couldn't be helped.

Maryellen cried and cried. They were sitting in her big kitchen, all the lights turned on against the dark. Her nose was running, red-tipped; her eyes were puffy and pink and the soft flesh under her chin was swollen and shaking.

"We never . . . had a chance," she said, her speech broken by her sobs. "You never . . . got over your wife. You never did . . . love me."

Elliot said nothing: it was too late to lie now. He got up quietly and switched off the kitchen lights, the one overhead, the one by the sink, a couple over the counters. He thought he was being kind.

But Maryellen jumped up and turned each of them back on. "I want you to see . . . what you did. I want you to remember."

So he sat there and watched her in the unsparing, bitter light. The least he could do, though his insides were squeezed so small it was hard to breathe. He looked up, looked down: up for as long as he could stand seeing her distorted face, down for relief. The long table between them was bare. No teacups in their saucers; no plates of late-night snacks, yogurt and berries or crackers and cheese. The polished table reflected the dull globe of his head.

The next time he looked up she had stopped crying, wiped her face, and was merely sniffling. A teardrop pooled in the groove of her upper lip.

"Do you want a glass of water?" he said.

She shook her head. She spread her hands on the table and her fingers were as still as roots. She didn't plead with him to stay, promise they would work things out, ask for another chance, but sat there unmoving, like a portrait of a noblewoman, somber with forbearance. Elliot stared at Maryellen and rose a little in his seat, drawn to her in that instant as never before.

She got up. "I'm going to bed," she told him. "You can sleep on the couch. Get your things in the morning and go."

As he watched her leave the glaring room, he felt a tug, felt a snap, and suddenly she was out of range, out of his life. A few seconds and it was over. Just like that.

He flicked off the kitchen lights and entered the living room. He piled pillows on the couch, linked his fingers under his head and lay down. From behind curtains and window shades, from under the rug and out of corners, night oozed into the room and covered him, as slick as oil. He twisted, straightened, curled up, breathless, clammy, wide awake, hour after tedious hour . . . and couldn't help but think about the harm he had done.

16

Zoo Story

Dennis took the van so they could all go in one car. Natalie was on his right, calling out directions, while Keith and Susan sat behind, Raymond wedged between them in his booster seat, whining. In the rear seats Mattie and Stevie were playing an alphabet game, reading out road signs and shouting letters in sequence. It was Sunday morning, ten o'clock, they'd been on the road less than an hour, and already he had a headache.

Susan was talking about the time she got lost in the zoo. "It was near the polar bears," she said. "I got bored and wandered off, then couldn't find my way back. So I sat down on the nearest bench and finally a passerby took me to the Family Centre."

"Where Mom and I were waiting."

"She came in later and yelled that I was old enough to know not to run away."

"She never even raised her voice."

"What if she did?" said Natalie. "It's perfectly understandable, because she was so scared. You're a mother yourself now, you know the things that can happen."

"If it isn't one thing, it's another," Dennis sighed. He turned off the highway and onto the zoo road. "Kids, parents—it never stops."

"You're talking about Mom and Dad," Susan said, "aren't you? You think she's upset because he came home."

"I wasn't talking about them."

"I think she wanted him back in the house. I think it's the first step in getting them together."

"Give up already," Natalie said.

"How can she forgive him for what he did?" said Dennis.

"When you love someone," Susan began, but Raymond interrupted. "I have to pee!" he cried out, plucking at his seat belt and jiggling his legs.

Natalie reached back and squeezed his ankle. "We're almost there."

Dennis drove to the closest lot and parked in the first available spot. Susan helped Raymond out and he peed against a rear tire while Stevie and Mattie said, "Oooh, gross!" in one breath. When everyone else was out of the van Dennis got the stroller and opened it for Raymond, but he wouldn't get in. "I'm no baby." He crossed his arms.

"Yes you are, yes you are." Stevie ran around him. "Can't even hold your pee till you get to a bathroom!" Whereupon Raymond started crying and pain shot through Dennis's forehead, strong enough to make him wince.

Natalie took the child's hand and they set off for the entrance. "We know you're old enough to walk, but we'll take the stroller just in case you get tired later on." Keith and Susan walked behind them, Stevie and Mattie raced ahead, and Dennis, pushing the empty stroller, came last.

There were lineups at the admission gates and then, once they got inside, lineups at the washrooms, lineups at the snack bar. Finally they set out for the Australasia Pavilion, Raymond walking partway, then hoisted onto Dennis's back while Natalie pushed the stroller. Inside, the glass-roofed building was crowded and hot. They glimpsed a bat, a kangaroo, hairy-nosed wombats and crowned pigeons strutting about like big blue chickens. Raymond, now at Dennis's side, pulled him by his pant leg from one display to the next, so that all the exhibits ran together into a blurry landscape of people, creatures and tropical plants.

On the long, twisting road to the Americas exhibits, Raymond tired out at last and climbed into his stroller. Dennis took charge of educating Mattie and Stevie in the Americas Pavilion, correctly identifying a red-crested cardinal, two-toed sloth and a great-horned owl, but the children suddenly dashed ahead and when he found them again they were staring at an exhibition of huge, hairy spiders and Brazilian giant cockroaches. Stevie elbowed Mattie and they ran off to another wing, leaving Dennis behind to read interesting facts on insects.

Susan and Natalie (and Raymond in the stroller with his thumb in his mouth and eyes half-closed) caught up to him moments later but went right past him, speaking about his parents' anniversary party next month. Keith followed in their wake. When he saw Dennis he slowed down and the men walked on together.

Dennis struggled for something to say. He took a long time cleaning his glasses with the hem of his shirt. At last he came up with, "Been here before?"

"Not since I was sixteen. I took a girl once on a date and all I remember is we necked on the monorail."

Dennis paused to watch an otter swimming nervously back and forth in a small glass-enclosed pool. Keith tapped the glass and said, "Makes me think of Susan, the way she's always on the go and never stops moving."

Dennis started walking again and Keith fell into step at his side. "How did you meet her anyway? At the magazine?"

"No, the club."

"Country club?"

"Fitness club—New You. I'm one of the instructors."

Dennis was relieved to find the others just ahead of them, waiting by the exit. He hated making small talk, especially with a man like Keith—a fitness instructor, for godssake. Couldn't his sister do better than that?

On the way to the Africa Pavilion they regrouped: Keith and Susan in the lead, Mattie and Stevie circling them, with Dennis and Natalie trailing behind and Raymond asleep in his stroller. As soon as they were out of range, Dennis said to Natalie, "That man, Susan's boyfriend—he's a fitness instructor, of all things."

"Don't be a snob," his wife replied. "He seems very nice."

"He seems like an airhead."

"It's none of our business. Besides, they're only dating."

"Susan thinks she's in love with him. What if they have a baby?"

"I'm sure it'll be adorable. Keith's a really cute guy, in case you haven't noticed."

Dennis pushed the stroller with force. "As cute as Richard Blotsky?"

Natalie had to quicken her pace to keep up. "Dr. Richard Blotsky is a friend and colleague who happens to be an attractive man. What the hell's wrong with that?"

"Only that you wouldn't look at anyone else the whole night."

"What night are you talking about?"

"New Year's Eve. The Gordons?"

"That was months ago. Is that still bothering you?"

"I'm not bothered," Dennis said, shoving the stroller up a hill. "I only brought it up because of our conversation about Keith."

Natalie was breathing fast. "You're jealous," she said. "Of both of them."

"Certainly not."

"And a liar. Or maybe just completely out of touch with your feelings."

They were too close to the others now for Dennis to respond, which was just as well in any case because she'd left him speechless. He knew his feelings, all right: he wanted to grab Blotsky by his long, tanned, sinewy neck and squeeze until his dewy eyes popped from their sockets. But how could he tell her that? Better to be accused of deceit and repression than of homicidal tendencies.

Susan announced it was time for lunch and led the way to McDonald's, though Natalie had packed several peanut butter sandwiches and wanted to have a picnic instead. But Susan and Keith wanted burgers, and the kids insisted on pizza.

When they got to the restaurant the outdoor tables were full. Children swirled from side to side on molded plastic swivel chairs and the noise level was painful. Natalie pressed her face to a glass window and looked inside. Even the less desirable tables indoors were taken, and the lines at the food counter were dismally long. "I can't do this," she told Dennis. "I'm not going in." Dennis agreed to stay with his wife. He wasn't hungry anyway. In fact, his headache had gotten worse and he was feeling queasy. As soon as he saw a fountain he would swallow a couple of Tylenol.

Keith and Susan were already lined up at the entrance, Mattie and Stevie at their heels. "What about Stevie?" Dennis said. "Should we leave him with them?"

"This was supposed to be a family outing," Natalie said. "I brought drinks and sandwiches. Why can't he spend a little time with his parents and see something more impressive than a Big Mac?"

Dennis pushed his glasses up his nose and went to fetch his son. But Stevie wasn't budging. "We want to show you monkeys and elephants," Dennis said. "You like elephants, don't you? You said they were your favorites."

"I'll see them later," Stevie said.

"There may not be time later."

"I can see them on TV."

"Then we'll have a picnic and watch the gorillas outside."

"I don't want a picnic, I want pepperoni pizza!"

"We'll look after him," Susan said. "Meet us back here when you're through."

Dennis's forehead kicked with pain. The sensible thing to do, of course, was to leave Stevie where he was, but Dennis wasn't feeling very sensible at the moment. He grabbed his son by his small wrist, yanked him out of line and pulled him aside to a drinking fountain. Still holding him by the wrist, he rummaged in his pants pocket, worked the cap off the Tylenol, tipped some capsules out of the bottle and popped two of them into his mouth. He drank water and gulped them down.

"You're mean to me," Stevie said.

"I am not."

"You are so. We always do what *you* want."

"Your mother wants you to come, too. This is her favorite animal house and she can't wait to show it to you."

When they reached the baby and Natalie, she glanced at them with slotted eyes, then pushed Raymond up a small hill toward Africa, with Dennis and Stevie dragging behind. They entered the pavilion on the lower floor and stopped to watch blind naked mole rats in their glass cages, pink, hairless wrinkled things with thin tails and curved teeth. "They look like mice," Stevie said, but Dennis thought they were hominoid, the way they tunneled, sightless and ceaseless, in an underground maze.

The main level was softly lit and smelled sharply of hay, flesh, sweat and dung. They went to the lowland gorillas' cage, edging through the crowd until they were close to the glass. One gorilla climbed a rope, another swung from a thick net, while a huge silverback leaned against the glass, eating bark from a branch. "That's Charles," Natalie said to Stevie. "He's the leader."

"Why's he so fat? Does he exercise?"

"Not much."

"A male gorilla can weigh up to six hundred and forty pounds," Dennis interrupted. "But Charles is four hundred and thirty."

"That's about two times your Daddy's weight," said Natalie, and Stevie turned away from the cage to stare at his father.

"Are you telling me I'm overweight?" Dennis's forehead clenched in pain: the Tylenol wasn't working.

"I was only giving Stevie a means of comparison."

Dennis tried to laugh, but the sound he made was more of a bark. "Too bad I'm not as cute and slim as Dr. Blotsky."

Natalie shot him a dark look. "Yes," she said, "it's too bad."

A baby gorilla settled into his mother's arms to nurse, and the crowd clucked approval. Dennis said in Natalie's ear, "You want to sleep with him, don't you?"

She jerked the stroller away from the glass, wheeled it across the flagstones and stopped by the mandrills. "Stevie, look at this," she called.

Stevie liked their bony cheeks, red snouts and white beards. He liked how one mandrill monkey tirelessly scratched another's back, and how they sat in branches or chased each other around the pen. "They can be vicious," his father said. "Cruel as people."

"For godssake!" his mother replied.

Then Natalie pushed ahead and Dennis hurried to catch up. Not a word was spoken as they strode past fish tanks, crocodiles, tortoises and various birds. All the while Dennis's head was exploding in white dots. Up a ramp, down again, and when she paused to catch her breath beside a pen of warthogs, Dennis said, "I know you do. Why won't you admit it?"

Natalie looked at him coldly. "Maybe I don't *want* to sleep with Richard, maybe I already have." Then she pushed the stroller through an exit door and outside.

He found her by a rail fence, gazing at dusty elephants with trunks snuffling across the ground. He stood behind her, unseen, and squeezed his eyes shut a moment, trying to hold back pain. Then he walked up to her and said quietly in her ear, "You don't really mean that. I can't believe you'd do that."

She snapped around to face him, her head and shoulders thrown back. "And what would you do if I said I did?"

"It's not true. You know it's not."

She brought her face close to his. "I fucked him. Many times. Those nights I came home late and you thought I'd been working? I was in bed with Richard. I was fucking Richard Blotsky."

She grabbed the stroller and wheeled it quickly back inside the pavilion, Dennis trotting after her. "You're just trying to get to me. I don't believe a word of it."

"Get to you? Impossible. There's a prune in your chest where a heart should be."

She stopped by the gorillas again, patting her chest and breathing hard. Two gorillas wrestled each other in and out of headlocks; another built a straw nest. The baby gorilla was still nursing, fondling his mother's breast.

As Natalie watched, her mouth suddenly opened and her lips moved. Her hands rose up as she jerked her head from side to side and over her shoulder.

Dennis gripped her arm and said, "Tell me the truth. I have to know."

"Where's Stevie?"—wrenching her arm free. "Wasn't he with you?"

"Stevie? With me? What?" Dennis spun around in place. "But he was with you. I saw him with you."

"He's not here, I can't see him. Stevie? Stevie, answer me! My God, where is he? Where did he go? Don't just stand there, Dennis, find him!"

Dennis pushed through the crowd and worked his way to the mandrills, searching all around and even inside the big pen. Then he ran to Natalie waiting by the main entrance, frantically bouncing the stroller. "Last I saw him he was with you—you were showing him the monkeys—but he's not there now," he said.

"And then I took the stroller and he was behind me, walking with you."

"He wasn't with me."

"He should've been."

"He should've been with you—but your mind was on someone else!"

"Stop it, Dennis. Right now! Nothing happened with Blotsky."

"Nothing happened?"

"Find your son!"

A wail erupted from the stroller: Raymond was awake again. He always got up in a bad mood, asking for things he couldn't have. This time he wanted Coke. "There isn't any," Natalie said. She passed him a juice box, but he swung his arm and knocked it down, juice squirting over her sandal, dribbling between her toes. "You little brat!" She stamped her foot. "You no-good spoiled brat!" The child stared, whimpering, and Dennis spoke her name sharply. Raymond's face scrunched up and he started crying in earnest.

A groan at the base of his throat: Dennis wanted to cry too. He flattened his hands on either side of his throbbing head and pressed hard. No, no, he couldn't cry. This wasn't the time or place for that, he had to find his lost son and comfort his family. He had to be strong and sensible. He couldn't fall apart now.

"Mommy's sorry she said that, so don't cry, Raymie, please." Natalie squatted by the stroller and wiped the boy's face with her sleeve. "We have to look for Stevie first. He's lost and we have to find him. Mommy and Daddy are very upset, but you can help by looking around and telling us if you see him."

Raymond stopped sniveling and sat up in the stroller. "There's Stevie!" he called out, pointing at a boy who looked nothing like his brother. "There he is, there he is"—fingering another child. "I see him. Over there!"

Dennis's glasses slid down his nose and he smelled his own nervous sweat, sharper and fleshier than the stench of the animal house. "You wait here," he told his wife, "and I'll check the pavilion."

"We should try the Family Centre."

"He wouldn't know to go there."

"What about McDonald's? That's where he wanted to be all along."

"No, I think he's still here. Or maybe with the elephants. If he's not inside, he's out there."

"I'll look for him outside."

"I want you to stay put."

"I can't stand here doing nothing!"

"One place at a time," he said, "or everyone'll get lost. We have to be methodical."

"We have to find Stevie!"

He scooped her hand into his own and squeezed hard enough to feel her knuckles grinding together. "Do what I say and don't move. You hear me? I'll be right back."

"Stop it, Dennis. You're hurting me."

He let go of his wife's hand and went to search for Stevie.

Quickly he retraced his steps past fish and turtles and a blur of screaming monkeys; down to the lower level where blind naked mole rats were still burrowing mindlessly—but no Stevie anywhere. Calling his name again and again—*my God! my son! where is he?*—while other parents looked around and reached for the hands of their own kids. Then back up to the main floor, hurrying along the walk to the main door.

But Natalie and Raymond were gone. Gone! After he told her—! Panic made him stumble as he circled the pavilion and its outdoor exhibits, but his wife and child had disappeared. He even tried the Family Centre, but no one was there either, except for a thin-lipped attendant on the telephone. Not his sons, not his wife . . . only a wave of wretchedness that struck with the force of memory and threw him back to the day when his sister got lost at the zoo and he waited in this very room, feeling the same helplessness, the unexplainable anger.

The attendant put her hand over the mouthpiece—"Can I help you?"—but Dennis turned and ran out.

In the picnic area he collapsed on a park bench and dropped his head between his knees. That's when the tears came, running comically into his hair. He cried silently, unmoving, his mind wailing its lament: *Stevie, Raymond, Natalie.* . . . One by one he was losing them all.

A man sat down beside him, eating fries from a Styrofoam box. He sat unnecessarily close since the rest of the bench was free. The man poked Dennis's arm and told him to move over. Dennis slid to the end of the bench, but the man jabbed his arm again. "Get off," he said. "Get off the bench."

"Are you out of your mind? What is this?"

The man said, "I want the bench."

"I was here first."

"But it's my bench," the man said.

"What do you mean, *your* bench?"

"You have to sit somewhere else."

Dennis said, "I can't believe this."

"Believe what you want—but get lost."

"*Get lost?* Who the fuck do you think you are?"

The man punched his arm hard, almost shoving him off the end. "What're you going to do about it? Fight for a stupid bench?" The man pursed his lips in thought. "You don't look like a fighter to me, you look like a parsnip."

Dennis stood up and raised his fists. "I *will* fight," he said. "Get up!"

The man ate some more fries, then wiped his fingers on his shirt. "What if I have a dangerous weapon in my pocket? What if you never get to see your loved ones again—have you considered that?"

Dennis glanced at the man's pants and imagined he saw a slight bulge in one of his pockets. He thought of a play he saw once: a man in the park with a knife or gun.

The man slipped his hand in his pants and pulled something partly out, the handle of something. Dennis shuddered, stepped back. The man released his grip to drop a last fry into his mouth; then he threw the empty bag at Dennis's feet. He spread his arms across the bench. "Goodbye now."

Dennis backed away slowly, until he was out of range, then turned and ran. He headed for McDonald's, a terrible howling in his brain. When he got there he weaved through the plastic tables outdoors, flattened his nose against the glass and peered in. There, off to one side, Susan, Keith, Mattie, Stevie, Natalie and Raymond sat around two small tables pushed together. Natalie waved a hand at Stevie as if she were going to smack him, and everyone's expression was grim.

He pulled his face back from the glass. Part of him wanted to be inside, united with his family, but part of him wanted to run away, just like Stevie. He didn't want to stay where he was, but didn't belong in there either, among that unhappy group. He didn't fit in anywhere— not in the restaurant, not even on a park bench. Which is probably what his son felt, standing between his bickering parents in the monkey house. Wondering what he was doing there, if anyone gave him a second thought. Thinking that they wouldn't even notice if he took off.

The thing about the scene around the table was this: it looked complete. No one was standing, watching the door or searching for Dennis outside; no one waiting for him to arrive before they started talking. If he told them about the man on the bench, they'd shake their heads at his cowardice and quickly change the subject. No one was on Dennis's side, no one was missing him. And if he never showed up again, would they even care?

It was possible—probable—that Natalie only stayed with him because of the children. That she was having an affair, had already had one, or (if he could believe her that nothing happened yet) she was surely thinking about it. Watching as she scolded Stevie, he felt her edginess through the glass. Natalie was not content. He liked to think that theirs was a solid and mature marriage of like-minded people, but she would think otherwise: an uninspired union of the weary and overworked. What were the chances they'd still be together after the children were grown?

Not good. And he bumped his aching forehead against the glass.

Nevertheless, he went inside. Because of the children, he told himself. Because, only minutes ago, face to face with a lunatic, he thought for an instant he might never see them again. And now, more than anything, he wanted to kiss Stevie's cheek to make sure he was really there. To let him know he understood the impulse that had made him run, as well as the panic that made him go where he'd be found and kept him hunched down in his seat, pushing bits of pizza crust around a greasy box while his mother gave him dirty looks.

When Natalie saw Dennis she said, "He lied to Keith and Susan. He told them we knew he was here, we'd catch up to him later."

Dennis ruffled Stevie's hair, then sat in an opposite chair and reached over to touch his hand.

"He said you walked him to the door and waited till he sat down, and I believed him," Susan said. "I figured you didn't want to come in because of the stroller."

"I knew he was lying," Mattie said.

"Then why didn't you say something? You never speak up when you should."

Mattie peeled a coin of pepperoni from her pizza and sucked it noisily into her mouth. Stevie giggled, looked away, and Raymond threw a piece of soggy bun across the table. "Everyone's here," Mattie told her mom, "so now we can go home."

Keith played a plastic fork against the table. "Good idea."

Susan turned to face him. "We've hardly seen anything. It cost a fortune to get in, the least we can do is look around."

"I saw plenty already."

Raymond knocked his cup over and Coke streamed across the table. Natalie jumped up and grabbed a fistful of napkins, wiped up the black pool, yanked the boy out of his chair and plopped him back in the stroller. At once he began to cry. She gave him the rest of his hamburger bun and he squeezed it till it oozed out between his little fingers. She cleaned his hands as he pulled her hair and tried to stand up, then pushed him down and strapped him in. "I've had it too," she said as she swept hair away from her face, the strands sticky and speckled with crumbs.

Dennis walked around the table to help his wife with the stroller, but she steered it toward the front door. "I can manage," she told him, and of course she could, she always did. They had that much in common.

They filed out of the restaurant with Natalie leading, Susan trailing, the men and youngsters in between. They chose the most direct route back to the main gate, a steep, nearly empty hill that ran through a forest. Thick trees on either side, baneberry, violets, bleeding hearts and trilliums, but no one noticed the scenery. The stroller threatened to bolt away and Natalie had to lean back, grip the handle and move slowly, as if she were yanking the reins of a colt. Dennis had a dark vision of Raymond hurtling into the woods and rushed over to the stroller, clutching the handle with his wife. Mattie and Stevie threw twigs and skipped down the pavement, while Keith followed by himself, hands in his pockets, till Susan caught up to him and walked at his side.

Anyone watching would think what a pretty picture this would make: a spring day, treed lane, a shy young couple; two frolicking children and a little boy waving his arms while his doting parents, shoulder to shoulder, handled his stroller. Anyone watching would take heart. For who could deny the harmony of young people in the woods, ambling through sun and shade, like figures in a storybook, forever happy, carefree; forever blessed.

ᴵᴺCelebration

By five o'clock, Sunday, Dennis and Natalie's living room had been cleared of several items and the rest of the furniture shoved back, so that the center of the room was empty, except for a rug. Two tables were loaded with Saran-wrapped platters of food, and one held a coffee urn. There were floral arrangements on these tables, as well as on small occasional tables in the corners. Natalie rested on a sofa pushed against the west wall, a hand across her forehead. Her sister-in-law was on a matching love seat opposite, while Dora sat between them on a straight-backed chair.

"Coral or jade," Susan was saying. "That's what you give for a thirty-fifth."

"I thought it was emerald," Natalie said. "I bought them something emerald."

"Coral or jade. I looked it up."

"As if your mother pays attention to such things," said Natalie.

"I'm sure they'll love whatever they get," Dora interrupted. "Now what time will they be here?"

"Seven sharp," Susan said. "Everyone else is coming at six."

"Barbie's always late, of course. Don't expect them till seven-thirty."

"Dad'll be here on the dot."

Dora said, "You mean they're not arriving together?"

"We invited them separately," Susan said, "so they wouldn't suspect anything. We told them it was just for dinner—Dennis, Natalie, me and you—so it could be a big surprise. The best parties always are."

"We shout 'Surprise!' when Elliot comes and then again for Barbie?"

"No, no," Susan said. "Whoever gets here first has a drink with Natalie on the porch. She makes up something about the kids—they can't come in because Dennis is trying to get the kids to bed—and then, when they're both here, tells them it's okay to go in . . . and everyone comes downstairs yelling 'Surprise!'"

"Wouldn't it have been easier to tell them about the party?"

Natalie said, "I doubt they would've come if they knew what we were up to."

"I don't understand," Dora said. "They're living under one roof again and seem to be getting along, so why wouldn't they come to their anniversary party?"

"They're still in separate apartments."

"There are still certain tensions. . . ."

"Because of that woman, the redhead? It only lasted a few months. Anyway, as far as I'm concerned that was Barbie's fault. I warned her what would happen. Men can't live alone, no matter what they tell you."

"Mom likes living alone. She likes the peace and quiet."

Natalie said, "Who wouldn't."

From the kitchen came the sharp sound of dishes clinking, children squabbling. Natalie snapped her head around. "Dennis, how are you doing?" she called.

"Almost done!" he answered. "The kids are just finishing, then we're going upstairs."

"Could you bring us a bottle of wine first?"

In a few minutes he walked in with a corked bottle and three glasses on a tray. He was wearing a long, stained apron over a white dress shirt and khaki-colored trousers, his glasses crooked on his nose. He looked around, unsure of where to set the tray down, then finally put it on the floor close to his wife's feet.

"I can't find the corkscrew."

"I'll look," Natalie said. She got up and followed him into the kitchen.

Soon after, the children ran through the living room and upstairs, Dennis racing close behind. There was more noise from the kitchen—the banging of doors and slamming of drawers—then Natalie reappeared and sat on the edge of the sofa.

"I looked here, I looked there—I can't find it anywhere! Dennis will have to run out and buy another corkscrew."

"Nothing's open Sunday night."

"He'd better find something," Dora said. "Imagine if the guests arrive and you can't open the bottles."

Natalie threw her arms up and fell back on the sofa. "Let Susan deal with it. This whole thing was her idea."

Dora shook her head at Susan. "Why you'd want to celebrate their cockamamy marriage is beyond me."

Outside a small store with buckets of flowers and fruits and vegetables under an awning, Elliot was trying to decide which tulips to buy. He settled on a mixed bunch of purple, white and yellow ones, then went into the store to pay. And there by the counter was Barb, buying a bouquet of pink gladioli.

Elliot waved the tulips. "Hi there!" he said. "I was just getting flowers."

Barbara said, "So I see."

"You're buying flowers too."

The clerk behind the counter wrapped the gladioli. "I'm going to a dinner party," Barbara said.

"Me too." Elliot gave his bunch of tulips to the clerk. "Wait a minute, I'll walk with you."

He followed her outside. The evening was clear and mild; the sky yellow, blue and pink. The street was busy and noisy with traffic and pedestrians. "You look nice," he told her. "I've always liked you in that dress."

She was wearing a simple, short-sleeved, light blue cotton dress and a white sweater, unbuttoned. Barbara raised her bouquet, so that it covered part of her face.

Elliot sniffed his tulips. "Aahhh, fresh flowers," he said. "Since I moved back I've discovered how much I like them. They brighten a room, make it cheerful."

"You never took an interest before."

"I'm fixing up the apartment," he said. "I ordered a new coffee table—Ivan ruined the old one—and threw out an armchair Hammer clawed to smithereens."

"I saw you put it outside with the garbage. What a mess."

"I think that was Hammer's way of telling me he was pissed off for leaving him with Ivan."

After a pause Barbara asked, "What became of him anyway?"

"Ivan? He moved in with an old flame, Ramona."

"Think it'll work?"

"He says he wants to settle down, but you can't tell with Ivan. He's so impulsive."

"I wouldn't know," said Barbara.

As they neared the house Elliot said, "What time is your party?"

"Seven, seven-thirty."

"Mine too," he said, "which gives us at least an hour. Why don't we go for coffee?"

"Coffee? You and me?"

"We'll sit and talk."

"About what?"

"Just a nice friendly chat."

By six-thirty Dennis and Natalie's living room was filled with guests. Waving a corkscrew, Dennis entered from the kitchen with Jake and Ida Murray-Meyers. "You have to go upstairs," he said. "They'll be here soon."

"We'll shout 'Surprise!' when they walk in," Ida said. "I promise."

Jake stared at the drink in his hand. "What if they see us and turn and run?"

"Why would they do that? Didn't we invite them over—I can't remember how many times—even after they split up? Not that they ever showed."

Dennis said, "Can't you continue this upstairs? It's not going to be a surprise if everyone waits in the living room. They'll see you through the window."

Natalie rushed into the room and grabbed hold of Dennis's arm. "Raymond won't go to sleep," she said, "and Stevie had a fight with Mattie and locked himself in the bathroom. So now the guests are coming down here to use the toilet!"

Dennis gave her the corkscrew. "Here, open some more wine. I'll deal with the children."

"Where did you get that?"

"I found it in the boys' room. Look after the wine, okay? Then get everyone out of the room."

"But your parents are coming any second. I have to be outside!"

"I'll come down in a few minutes and wait on the porch. Just clear the living room."

Dennis picked his way among the guests on the staircase, finally reached the second floor and knocked on the bathroom door. "Stevie, can you hear me? Open the door."

"No way!"

"Stevie, tell me what's wrong."

"I hate Mattie, that's what! She thinks because she's bigger she can treat me like a baby."

"Only babies hide in the bathroom. Be a man and open up."

Stevie opened the door a crack and Dennis slipped in, closing it quietly behind him.

"Mattie hates me."

"No she doesn't."

"Mommy hates me too—because I wouldn't let her friends in here."

"Mommy loves you. So do I. We're just a little nervous because the house is full of people and we're waiting for your grandparents so we can surprise them. Would you like to surprise them too?"

"Mommy told me to stay in my room."

"You can join us later if you promise not to make trouble."

They left the bathroom, edged past people in the hallway and turned into the boys' room, where Raymond was sniveling in his bed. A lamp in the shape of a bear beamed a circle of yellow light. Stevie got a box of Lego and lay on the floor in front of the lamp, building an airplane, while Dennis sat on the bed, next to his younger son.

"So, Raymond, you're not tired? You want to stay up all night?"

"Stay here," said Raymond.

"I can't sit with you all night. Mommy needs me downstairs to help with the party. But Stevie's here, and you can even play with his Lego."

"No he can't!" Stevie said. "He loses all the pieces."

Raymond started whimpering and put his head on his father's lap. Dennis stroked the boy's hair and Stevie went back to his airplane, making loud whirring sounds. In the next room Susan and Mattie were arguing.

"I should've left you home," said Susan.

"Why didn't you?" Mattie said.

"If I knew you were going to act like this—"

"What about how *you* act? I heard you on the phone with Keith. I heard what you called him. I bet he never sees you again!"

Their voices dropped to a burble behind the wall. Raymond slid out of bed and sat on the floor with his brother. When he reached for a Lego piece, Stevie shoved him away.

"So I guess you won't be coming downstairs later," Dennis said.

Stevie got up, went to a closet and came back with a toy train. "He can play with this thing. I don't like it anymore."

Raymond moved the train around in circles. "You can go now."

Downstairs, the kitchen and living room were crowded with guests. Natalie was nowhere in sight. Dennis opened the front door and stepped out onto the porch. Looking around, he saw no one and sat down on a porch swing.

Behind him the party roared, but here, looking out at his lawn, his neatly clipped hedge and the street beyond, he could almost pretend that things were running smoothly. For the moment he almost felt calm.

Barbara and Elliot walked into a greasy spoon with rickety stools up front, a cook flipping burgers and a chesty, copper-haired waitress dragging on a cigarette. They chose a rear table for four, laying their flowers on separate chairs. The waitress stubbed her cigarette and came to take their order.

"Coffee, please," said Barbara.

"Same for me, Gracie."

"You want I don't bring the toast?"

"Not today."

"You not hungry?"

"Just coffee for now, thanks."

When the waitress left, Barbara said, "Sounds like she knows you."

"I've been here before."

Music was playing loudly from a nearby speaker; then they heard a traffic report. After that, Gracie arrived with their coffees. Elliot's cup had a spoon in it, to draw the heat. She stirred his coffee and blew on it before setting the cups down.

"Now it's cold, how you like it."

"Thanks, Gracie," Elliot said.

"You want more?"

"No, that's fine."

Gracie winked and hurried off.

"She was flirting with you," Barbara said.

"She flirts with all the regulars."

"A regular, is it? I guess there are things I don't know about you anymore." She poured milk in her coffee, lifted her cup and drank quickly. From overhead, a radio announcer gave a news update.

"By the way," Elliot said, "I got an estimate for the roof. And I want someone to have a look at the porch and balcony, they're falling apart."

"I can't afford home improvements right now."

"I'll pay for it this time. It's my house too and I want to see it in good shape."

"Was *her* house in good shape?"

"You mean . . . ? Well, yes, it was."

"So why come back to a dump like ours?"

"I wanted my own place again." He dabbed a finger in his cup to make sure his coffee was cold. Then he looked at her over the cup. "Also, I missed you."

She turned her cup in its saucer. "I just hope you don't think now that you're living here—"

"Now that I'm here I see how much I like having my own space."

She said, "Then you're *not* thinking of doing any renovations inside?"

"Inside?"

"Oh, like . . . taking down the apartment doors."

"To make it one house again?"

"Would you like that?"

"Would you?" he said.

She moved her cup to one side. "No."

"Me neither."

"Really? You surprise me."

"It's a question of privacy. . . ."

She clapped her hands against her chest. "You don't know how relieved I am to hear that."

A country-western love song was playing on the radio. Someone at another table tapped his foot and hummed along. Elliot listened, sipping coffee, then put his cup down. "Today's our anniversary. Did you remember?"

"Yes, I did."

"We were just kids when we married. We've been through a lot."

"Grew up."

"Made mistakes."

"Argued."

"And here we are, still together. Living in our own way."

Barbara put her elbows on the table and leaned forward. "People are going to talk. They won't understand the way we live."

"Let them. Who cares?"

"Susan and Dennis don't like it. They'll keep trying to turn back the clock."

"They'll get used to it in time."

"Oh—the time! What time is it?"

Elliot checked his watch and frowned. "Almost seven-thirty."

"I have to go."

"Why don't you phone and say you'll be late?"

"I promised them I'd be on time. Natalie's cooking dinner tonight. . . ."

"You're going to Dennis and Natalie's? That's where I'm going too."

"You are? But I don't get it. Why didn't they tell us?"

"Maybe they meant it to be a surprise."

"For us?"

"Our anniversary."

"An anniversary party—of course!" Barbara stood up, grabbing her flowers. "Let's go, let's go! We're missing our own party."

"I'll call them," Elliot said, "and say we're running a bit late."

At seven-thirty the wall phone in Dennis and Natalie's kitchen rang and Jake Murray-Meyers, none too steady on his feet and clutching a drink in one hand, stumbled to answer it.

"What? I can't hear you. Speak up. Who is this?" Jake put a finger in his free ear. "Elroy? Elton? Well just who do you think you are!"

He hung up the phone and it rang again immediately. He picked it up. "You again! You'll have to speak louder, there's a party going on and I can't hear a word you said.

What was that? Denise who? Nobody here by that name."

Jake banged the receiver down. The phone rang a third time and another guest reached for it, but Jake interrupted. "No, leave it! Don't answer. It's just some nut pretending he's Elton John."

Natalie entered the room, breathless. "Where's Dennis? Is Dennis here?"

Jake patted her shoulder. "No one here by that name."

She ran into the living room, chock-full with people. A CD was playing loudly, platters of food had been unwrapped and several guests were nibbling cold cuts and carrot sticks. Natalie elbowed across the room and found Dora talking to a couple of men.

"Have you met Joshua?" Dora said. "And this is Ivan, Elliot's friend."

Natalie ignored them. "People shouldn't be eating yet. Can't you keep them away from the food?"

"Everyone's hungry—so am I. Let's get the party rolling."

"That's not how we planned it." Natalie swung her head around. "Where's Susan? She can help."

"Upstairs, the last I saw her."

"What's she doing upstairs?"

"Crying, I think."

"Crying *now*? Don't tell me, I don't want to know." Natalie squeezed her head in her hands, then said she was going outside to wait for her in-laws. "In case they happen to show up."

On the front porch she saw Dennis and stopped short. "There you are. Swinging!"

"I told you I'd be on the porch."

"The guests have taken over the house. They've even started eating the food! There won't be a thing left for your parents—*if* they ever get here."

"They'll get here," Dennis said.

"What if they found out there's a party going on and decided to stay away?"

"I'm sure one of them would've called."

"What if something happened to them?"

"To both of them? Unlikely."

"We should phone their apartments."

"They're probably on their way by now. Forget about it," Dennis said, "and try to relax."

The swing creaked loudly as she sat down beside him. But when he raised his arm to hug her, Natalie pulled away.

"Don't touch me."

"Why not?"

"I don't want to be touched right now."

"You never want to be touched anymore."

Just then the screen door opened and slapped shut. Stevie and Raymond, holding hands, walked up to their parents.

"Now what?" said Natalie.

"Raymond can't sleep because it's too noisy," Stevie said. "And I want to know when Grandma and Grandpa are getting here so we can surprise them."

"We're still waiting," Dennis said.

"We want to wait too."

"Come on over." He tapped the swing. "But don't bother your mother. You can sit on my lap." Dennis scooped his younger son onto his left knee and Stevie climbed the other. "There you go, that's it. We'll all wait together."

Natalie hopped off the swing. "I've waited long enough. I'm going to call them."

Barbara's bedroom was lit reddish gold by a small lamp. Long curtains were drawn across a large window facing the street; the window open a crack so that the drapes shuddered with a breeze and the room smelled of grass and pine. Barbara and Elliot were lying naked on her bed.

She was stretched out on her back while he was propped on an elbow, trailing his fingers over her breasts.

"How did we wind up here?"

"I think it was your blue dress."

"We should've gone straight to the party."

"You had to get your car keys. . . ."

"I never should've let you in."

He kissed the hollow of her throat. "High time we did this."

"The *wrong* time, Elliot. It's so late."

"It's only eight."

"Natalie's probably frantic."

Now he was licking her ear. "I'll be frantic if we stop."

She turned her face to him and smiled. "I think it was the way you looked at me over your coffee."

"They'll just start without us," he said. "Anyway, I left a message that we'd be late."

"You left a message?" Barbara said. "Why didn't you talk to them?"

"I tried reaching Dennis, but all I got was a dumb drunk."

"A drunk? Who could that be?"

"Anyone, from the sound of it. They're having a real to-do over there."

"You mean it's not a small dinner for me, you and the children?"

"From what I heard over the phone, they're having a big bash."

"Now I *really* feel bad. We ought to be there, Elliot."

"A few more minutes won't hurt. We'll make it a quickie this time."

His hand moved across her belly, then around in circles, and Barbara sighed, "That's nice."

"While we're on the subject"—his hand stopped moving—"there's something I want to ask you."

"About what?"

"That young man. The one with the ponytail."

"You want to ask about him *now*?"

"It just came to mind, so. . . . Is he—was he—special to you?"

"We're not lovers, okay? Not that you have the right—"

"I know I don't have the right"—he dipped his hand between her legs—"but it's still good to hear that."

She lay back and closed her eyes. Suddenly the phone in the bedroom rang sharply and they both jumped.

"Don't answer it. Let it ring."

"What if it's Dennis or Natalie?"

"I'm sure they got my message by now and know we'll be late. If you don't answer, they'll just think you're on your way."

The phone stopped ringing. A moment later they heard jingling from upstairs.

"Now they're trying my number, only to find I'm not in. Which means they think we're both on our way."

"Except we're not."

"Not yet." His fingers moved between her legs. "Feel good?"

"I did miss you, Elliot."

"You missed me . . . or missed this?"

"I missed you—and that, too."

The bedroom phone rang again.

"Damn it! Why don't they give up?"

"I bet they know we're still here. I bet they know just what we're doing."

The bedroom phone stopped, but the one upstairs started again.

"They'll never forgive us, Elliot. They must've been planning the party for months."

"Of course they'll forgive us. They want us to be happy, right?"

"Well, I suppose so."

"And nothing makes me happier. . . ." He rolled on top of her, his face just above hers. "And you?" he said. "What makes you happy?"

"You do."